PAYBACK

A Delta Force Unleashed Thriller

By
J. Robert Kennedy

James Acton Thrillers

The Protocol
Brass Monkey
Broken Dove
The Templar's Relic
Flags of Sin
The Arab Fall
The Circle of Eight
The Venice Code
Pompeii's Ghosts
Amazon Burning
The Riddle

Special Agent Dylan Kane Thrillers

Rogue Operator
Containment Failure
Cold Warriors
Death to America

Delta Force Unleashed Thrillers

Payback

Detective Shakespeare Mysteries

Depraved Difference
Tick Tock
The Redeemer

Zander Varga, Vampire Detective

The Turned

PAYBACK

A Delta Force Unleashed Thriller

J. ROBERT KENNEDY

CreateSpace

ISBN-10: 1507722400

ISBN-13: 978-1507722404

First Edition

10 9 8 7 6 5 4 3 2 1

For the nearly 500 healthcare workers who have died fighting Ebola.

PAYBACK

A Delta Force Unleashed Thriller

"People are still dying horrible deaths in an outbreak that has already killed thousands. We can't let our guard down and allow this to become double failure, a response that was slow to begin with and is ill-adapted in the end. It is extremely disappointing that states with biological-disaster response capacities have chosen not to utilize them. How is it that the international community has left the response to Ebola—now a transnational threat—to doctors, nurses and charity workers?"

Dr. Joanne Liu, Médecins Sans Frontières
January 13th, 2015

PREFACE

Joeblow, Liberia is a town so small it doesn't even appear on most maps. Yet if you were to Google it today, you would find hundreds of hits, for it is now a town that should never be forgotten.

A town where just recently, the last mother died.

Since the Ebola outbreak began in late 2013, early 2014, every single mother in the small town has died, it tradition that the women of the village take care of the sick, and without the proper knowledge or equipment, these caregivers inevitably contracted the virus themselves, again being cared for by the surviving women.

I wonder who took care of the last mother.

This book deals with difficult topics, with much of the imagery taken from actual accounts, photos and reports of the outbreak. It was difficult at times to write, and I am sure will be difficult at times to read.

But this virus cannot be ignored.

And discussing it must not be avoided simply because it makes us uncomfortable.

Howard University Hospital, Washington, D.C.

"I'm afraid it's bad news."

Command Sergeant Major Burt "Big Dog" Dawson felt his chest tighten at the words. To say he was surprised would be a lie. He had known all along what the answer would be, but until it was confirmed, they had all been in a holding pattern, waiting, wondering, helpless. He could hear the feet shuffling in the room, no one sitting, no one talking, everyone waiting, hoping for the best, fully expecting the worst.

And now that their worst fears were confirmed, it made no difference.

They were still helpless.

Their friend was still dying.

Dawson had known him for years—many years—and had never seen fear on his face until today. And he thought nothing less of him, none of them did. If he were to die today from what had happened, he would die a hero. History would decide whether or not their overall mission had been a success, but history could never question that this man had done the right thing, had put the life of others before his own, despite the fact he had a family, a son.

He tore his eyes away from his friend, a friend who felt a million miles away on the other side of the isolation chamber's glass walls as he felt the tiny hand in his squeeze harder. He looked down at the little boy whose father lay so close yet so far away.

And the grip on his chest ratcheted another notch tighter as he saw the fear on his Godson's face. He looked at his friend's wife, Shirley, a woman he had also known for years, a woman he respected immensely, who had never questioned her husband's career choice, his constantly being called away at the last minute, the nature of the job not only preventing him from telling her to where, but making it necessary for them both to lie to their family and friends.

For no one could know they were Delta Force. Officially 1st Special Forces Operational Detachment-Delta, they were America's elite Special Forces, created in 1977 by Colonel Charles Beckwith as an answer to the growing threat of terrorism around the world. After an ignominious beginning in the deserts of Iran during the Iran Hostage Crisis—known as Operation Eagle Claw—they had served with honor and distinction, successfully carrying out hundreds of missions over the ensuing decades.

Their failures were few.

And despite his friend now lying in a hospital bed, dying, there was no way he was going to let anyone think his friend had failed, even if he himself had. Dawson blamed himself for what had happened. He had been too slow, their enemy far better prepared, far better connected than they had anticipated.

They had been betrayed.

And he should have anticipated it.

He exchanged glances with the rest of the team, all their faces impassive, their concern revealed only by their eyes and their silence. Shirley tried to speak but the words got caught in her throat. She turned to Dawson, her eyes beseeching him to take over.

"What's the word, Doc?"

The doctor's face was grim with a hint of fear, this the man who had taken care of his friend since the moment he had arrived.

And he, along with several others on Bravo Team, had all been exposed.

"The testing confirms Mr. Belme has Ebola."

Shirley gasped out a cry and nearly collapsed, two of his men catching her and helping her into a chair. Bryson began to cry, more because his mother was crying rather than an understanding of what was really going on. He hugged Dawson's leg, hard. Dawson patted him on the head as he battled to control his own emotions.

"What's the prognosis? I've heard the fatality rate is up to ninety-percent."

"With the massive dose he received, and the method in which it was delivered—I hesitate to guess."

Dawson looked at his friend through the glass. He was asleep and hadn't heard the verdict. He'd at least have a few more minutes of peace before the horror of his new reality would set in.

And Dawson swore he'd kill the man responsible.

The man responsible for infecting the best friend he had ever had.

Master Sergeant Mike "Red" Belme.

Across from the Norfolk Waterside Marriott Convention Center
Norfolk, Virginia
Four days earlier

"Let me take the shot, BD."

Command Sergeant Major Burt "Big Dog" Dawson shook his head, peering through his binoculars at the scene across the street. He was prone on a rooftop across from the Norfolk Waterside Marriott Convention Center with three of his men and a sniper team from his unit. Sergeant Carl "Niner" Sung, the best sniper he had ever known, had made the request. A request Dawson so desperately wanted to approve.

"Negative. Kill him, the rest of the hostages die."

"But I'd feel *so* good putting an extra hole in this bastard's head."

"You'll get your chance before the day's out."

They had been training at The Unit just a few hours ago when word had come down the pipe that the Secretary of Defense had been taken hostage along with another twenty-two guests at a conference. Security had been tight but light, relying more on the small size of the conference, its rather contained location, and the fact no one knew he was going to be there.

But somebody had known.

And leaked it.

Their best guess was eight hostiles, the security team forced to stand down the moment a waiter serving drinks placed a weapon against the Secretary's head.

It was a no win situation. If the detail of eight were made up of his own men, he would have taken the shot knowing full well that his team would eliminate anyone else that popped up.

But that was what they trained for, day in and day out, and on far too many occasions actually put into practice. They were all Delta Force operators, part of Bravo Team, led by him, though command structure in Delta was quite loose. They were all Non-Commissioned Officers, NCO's, sergeants, the grunts of the trade. Officers might run the wars, but a soldier in the trench didn't run to his Lieutenant for advice when his ass was under fire, he ran to his sergeant. Sergeants were the true leaders of men on the battlefield, experienced, well trained, and used to the trenches where the men they led suffered, not the command tents the officers usually found themselves in.

His men were Delta Force, the most highly trained group of soldiers in the world, and the only military unit in the entire US Armed Forces that could legally operate on American soil, the President having the sole authority to suspend Posse Comitatus if he saw fit.

Which was why they were legally present here today beyond just an advisory capacity. Local SWAT had been pulled back, and were none too pleased at first, but Dawson had assuaged their commander's ruffled feathers fairly easily.

"If this turns into a Charlie-Foxtrot and the Secretary of Defense gets killed, do you want us to take the blame, or you?"

The man hadn't replied, but Dawson could tell he was processing the words.

"If we screw up, we take the blame. If we succeed, we were never here, you take the credit. Either way, it's win-win for you."

The man pursed his lips then sighed. "You're Delta, aren't you?"

Dawson shook his head with a slight smile. "Never heard of them. Some kind of airline or something?"

The man had laughed, the ice broken. "I'm a former Ranger. So are some of my men. If Delta—or *whoever*—wants to take over, we'd be honored to back them up."

With the majority of the Delta Force being made up of former US Army Rangers, support had been quickly garnered and local SWAT was now securing the perimeter, keeping the cameras out of sight. With today's 24/7 live news coverage, one of the last things they needed were the terrorists inside watching a live feed of his assault on their building.

Which was why Control back at Fort Bragg was monitoring every news feed whether over the air, satellite, cable or Internet, for any possible leaks. Cutting cable and power meant nothing nowadays. With cellphones and satphones there was pretty much no way you could guarantee your hostiles' communications had been terminated.

So the press was kept back.

The shot rang out, a crack that echoed between the buildings, and yet another hostage crumpled to the ground, the terrorist saying nothing, merely turning on his heel and walking back inside, his back to the police, a final insult to law and order in this great country, knowing they wouldn't dare touch him.

"Bravo Zero-One, Bravo Zero-Two. We're in position, ready to breach, over."

It's about damned time.

He didn't blame his second-in-command, Master Sergeant Mike "Red" Belme. Maps of the sewage system had been late to arrive, but as soon as they had, it had only taken fifteen minutes for Red's team to get into position. Red was his best friend. Dawson had been best man at his wedding and was Godfather to Red's young son, Bryson. He trusted Red with his life, as he did every single man on his team. They had been through hell and back over the years, and he'd die for any one of them.

But let's try to avoid that today.

"Acknowledged. Control, Bravo Zero-One. We're ready to execute. Advise of any flags on the play, over."

"Bravo Zero-One, Control, you're cleared for entry, over."

"Roger that, Control. Bravo Team, Bravo Zero-One. Eliminating rooftop targets in three, two, one, execute!"

Two muffled but still loud shots could be heard, Niner's M24A2 Sniper Weapon System firing a shot at incredible velocity across the street to the target rooftop. Before the report even registered the target was down, a moment later the second target dropped, taken out by another sniper team on the opposite side of the building.

"Control, Bravo Zero-One. Any sign of activity, over?"

"Negative, Bravo Zero-One, you're still clear, over."

Two down, six to go. Or more.

He rose, the sun low in the horizon behind them, at just the perfect angle to blind anyone who might be looking out the window of their target building. But according to Control they were clear. Sergeant's Will "Spock" Lightman, Trip "Mickey" McDonald and Eugene "Jagger" Thomas stepped up beside him. "Ready?" he asked, already knowing the answer. These guys were the definition of born ready.

Spock cocked an eyebrow. "Aren't we always?"

"Then let's do it."

He raised his grappling gun, took aim at the roof below them and fired, the hook sailing through the air dragging a coil of rope sitting at his feet. Three more fired beside him, the lines arcing gracefully and silently through the air, embedding with a thud into the concrete below, small puffs of pulverized concrete dust indicating the impact points.

They quickly tightened off all four lines and Dawson hooked his harness to the rope and stepped to the edge, the others doing the same. "Bravo Team, Bravo Zero-One, proceeding to target rooftop, over."

He stepped off, leaning back in the harness and slid down the steep incline. This was always the exciting moment for him, his heart skipping a few beats as he eyeballed the hook at the other end, wondering if it would pull out. If it came loose before he was too far, he could brake then swing backward, hard into the building he had just come from, and depending upon physics, he would probably survive with a few broken bones, perhaps just some bruises.

But once past the point where the rope was longer than the drop to the ground, he was hitting pavement no matter what he did.

And those broken bones might never mend properly.

Which would mean he'd be out of The Unit.

I'd rather be dead.

He wasn't sure if he actually meant it. There were enough men in Delta that had been injured seriously enough to never be able to return to duty, at least not Operator status. Some were able to go back into combat in the regular forces or command a desk, but Delta needed all of its personnel at 100%.

99% didn't cut it.

He passed the point of no return, not that there was any possibility of return, gaining speed as he did so. He had his hand ready to pull his Glock 22 from its holster on his hip just in case he had to cut loose and shoot out a window in the hopes of sailing through it rather than being yanked back and onto the pavement.

He cleared the edge of the roof, a slight sigh of relief escaping as he braked, rapidly killing his speed as his feet hit the roof, running to a stop.

He unhooked himself and quickly checked the two bodies confirming the kills as the others regained their footing.

"Bravo Team, Bravo Zero-One. We're on the rooftop. Bravo Zero-Two, execute breach, over."

"Bravo Zero-One, Bravo Zero-Two. Proceeding with breach, over."

Dawson motioned for Spock and Jagger to secure the door leading to the stairwell when a cellphone began to ring. Dawson spun toward the hostile Niner had taken out and saw a cellphone flashing in the man's hand.

"Control, Bravo Zero-One. One of the hostiles has a cellphone ringing up here. We're about to be made, over."

"This is Control Actual," came Colonel Thomas Clancy's voice over the comm. "Proceed at your discretion, over."

"Roger that, Control Actual, proceeding, over."

Now let's just hope they assume we're jamming their signal.

"What a wonderful stink we've discovered."

Master Sergeant Mike "Red" Belme smiled at Sergeant Leon "Atlas" James as he tried breathing through his mouth, which while masking some of the smell threatened to overwhelm him with the taste. He wasn't sure which was worst.

He swallowed.

Taste.

He switched back to his nose.

"Not much longer," he said. "According to the map we've got a hundred feet to go then we're directly under the parking structure."

In the loosely organized Bravo Team, he was considered second-in-command merely based on seniority, and the fact someone had to be. All of the men were essentially equals with their own area of highly specialized expertise. Their unit was top secret, their missions highly classified, and with them usually being undercover quite often, they were allowed to sport civilian haircuts and beards, privileges reserved for the Special Forces community.

Which was why he kept his hair completely shaved, his scalp kept clean with the blade of his prized Bowie knife. The guys always laughed at him when he would break it out in the field to take off a little stubble, but it was the sharpest blade he had, and its length meant fewer strokes.

It was just more practical than a shaving kit.

And cooler.

His son Bryson loved watching him perform the ritual, it necessary because his namesake red hair was far too noticeable and far too out of place in most of the locales he found himself in.

Shaved heads however were far more common, and often went unnoticed with a traditional keffiyeh covering his scalp.

"There it is," said Atlas, the ridiculously muscled man's deep voice echoing through the sewers they were now in. Red looked up and saw the access hatch above, highlighted by Atlas' flashlight.

Red motioned and Sergeant Zack "Wings" Hauser rushed forward and unfolded a ladder, Sergeant Danny "Casey" Martin jumping up the steps, lighting a Broco cutting torch as he did so.

"Bravo Leader, Bravo Zero-Two. We're in position, ready to breach, over."

Dawson's voice acknowledged and the all clear was given by Control. Moments later the order they were waiting for came through.

"Bravo Team, Bravo Zero-One. We're on the rooftop. Bravo Zero-Two, execute, over."

He smiled, motioning for Casey to proceed. "Bravo Zero-One, Bravo Zero-Two. Proceeding with breach, over."

Within moments Casey was cutting through the metal cover that would give them access to the conference center's parking structure. As they waited updates came in over the comms and by the time Casey was through, Dawson and his team were safely on the roof, the two lookouts eliminated.

"I'm through." Casey tossed the torch down to Wings then punched up with the heel of his hand, the metal hatch lifting up then hitting something. "Shit!" hissed Casey as he pushed the hatch, it again hitting something. He shoved his head up and peered through the several inches of opening. "There's a goddamned car parked here!"

"What?" Red stepped forward, looking up at the hatch then the map on his tablet computer. "This isn't a parking spot!"

"Well, somebody's parked here."

"Cut the hatch off, see if we can squeeze under," said Red as he activated his comm. "Bravo Zero-One, Bravo Zero-Two. We've got a problem here. There's a car parked over the hatch. Give us a moment to see if we can still make entry, over."

"Roger that Bravo Zero-Two. We're entering the stairwell now, over."

The torch was relit and Casey made quick work of the hinges, now exposed with the hatch open a few inches. Within a minute he was handing the torch then the hatch down. He stepped up.

"No way we're fitting under this," he said. "But it's on a bit of an incline. If I can cut the brake cables it might roll out of the way."

"Do it."

Casey pulled a set of cutters and went to work, the snap of lines being cut indicating excruciating progress, this a delay he hadn't counted on.

It would just mean a little more hustle on their part assuming Casey succeeded.

"Shit."

"What?"

"Transmission's engaged. I'll need to cut through the driveshaft. Hand me the torch." He reached down then stopped. "Wait a minute. Hammer."

Atlas handed it to him. Tapping then the sound of something metal hitting the concrete was followed by a laugh. "Thar she goes!" said Casey as he stepped down. "The driveshaft was almost rusted through. That thing's a deathtrap."

Red looked up and smiled as the undercarriage slowly began to move, gaining speed, emergency lighting suddenly revealed as the way cleared.

"Go! Go! Go!" he hissed, motioning for the others to climb the ladder as Casey pushed himself through the opening. "Bravo Zero-One, Bravo Zero-Two, we're through, over."

"Roger that, report when in position, over."

Red stepped up the ladder and raised his hands, Mickey and Wings hauling him up. There was a smashing sound, not too loud, to his left. He looked to see the car, a Jaguar XK-8 convertible, pressed against the far wall at the bottom of the incline, the front end a little crunched, but nothing too severe. He looked around. "What the hell was that doing parked in the middle of the lane?"

Casey shrugged. "It's a Jag. Probably broke down right here."

"Where's the owner?" asked Wings as they headed for the stairwell, sweeping the entire area for hostiles.

They reached the door, Atlas checking the window. "Looks clear."

Red activated the comm, about to notify Dawson when a noise behind them had them all spinning. He raised his MP5 submachine gun as something in the shadows rushed toward them.

"Halt and identify yourself or we *will* kill you."

Shoes skidded on dirty concrete, the sound suggesting the smooth soles of dress shoes. Wings activated the tactical light on his weapon, aiming it at the new arrival.

A business suit filled with a terrified civilian was revealed.

"Hands up!"

Hands, trembling, shot up.

"Identify yourself."

"Brimah Macaulay."

Unusual name. "What are you doing here?"

"Hiding in my car. I heard gunfire just after I parked and have been down here ever since."

Red kept his weapon trained on the man, his skin a dark black just like all of the hostiles. He just couldn't take the chance. He was about to have Atlas frisk the man when a shot rang out and Wings dropped. Red spun toward where he thought the shot came from as he dropped to a knee, the hard surfaces of the parking garage creating an echo chamber. Mickey fired, three rounds, toward the left. Red adjusted his aim, spotting the shooter coming down the ramp doubled over, at least one of Mickey's rounds having found its target. Red squeezed the trigger, taking the man down as Atlas rushed toward the new arrival, weapon raised.

Something moved to their right. Red hit the ground, rolling once as he took aim at their civilian. Macaulay was reaching behind his back for something and just as Red got a bead on the man the grip of a Beretta was revealed.

He fired twice, both shots hitting the man in the center of his chest, his eyes bursting wide in shock as the wounds quickly stained his shirt. Red scanned the rest of the garage for other targets but found none.

Wings moaned.

Red didn't look, instead continuing to cover their position as he activated the comm. "Bravo Zero-One, Bravo Zero-Two. Shots fired, I repeat, shots fired. Two hostiles down, Bravo One-Two has taken a hit, standby, over." He watched Atlas give the thumbs up as he disarmed the corpse. "You okay?"

Wings moaned again. "Yeah, took one in the vest." Red stole a quick glance and saw Wings push himself to his knees as he examined his body armor, wiggling the round free. He stuffed it in his pocket. "That one had my name on it."

"You good?"

"Yeah." He stood, sucking in a deep breath as he stretched out his chest. "Ribs are tender, not broken."

"Good. Sort yourself out." He pointed to Macaulay. "Get the body out of sight, check for intel."

Casey quickly patted the man down, shaking his head. "Nada. Just a couple of mags and a cellphone."

"Okay, take the cellphone and the weapon."

Mickey nodded, shoving the weapon in a loop on his utility belt then dragged the body in behind a parked car, a bloody streak revealing the hiding spot should anyone really be looking. Atlas tossed his own man into the back of a pickup truck as if it were a sack of potatoes.

I'd love to see him arm wrestle Stallone.

One of Red's favorite movies when he was a kid was Over the Top. He didn't know why, it wasn't that great a movie. But something about arm wrestling just appealed to him and he had exercised his right arm like a madman, challenging everyone he could, even mimicking the turn of the ball cap, a switch that transformed him from ordinary, skinny teenager, to full blown, musclebound action hero.

He rarely won.

It wasn't until his late teens that he had his growth spurt, put on six inches in height and forty pounds of body weight and decided the Army was the life for him.

He had thought he was strong until he met Atlas.

The man redefined the word.

Atlas jogged back to their position, smacking Wings on the chest with the back of his hand. Wings winced, knocked back a step. "You good?"

Wings frowned. "I was until you hit me, Thor."

Atlas grinned. "Sorry, sometimes I forget I shouldn't bring the hammer down so hard."

"Ha ha." Wings shrugged his shoulders up and down a few times then back and forth, loosening himself up. "I'm good, let's get back in the game."

Red smiled, activating his comm, the relief he felt that his man was unharmed hidden from the others.

I'm not losing anyone on my watch.

Dawson rushed down the stairs as quietly as their soft soled boots would take them. So far they hadn't encountered any resistance, but Red's report had him concerned and his jaw was clenched tight as he held his tongue, waiting for Red to report further, his 'standby' request suggesting the situation wasn't completely locked down.

They hadn't heard the shots, which he hoped meant the hostiles hadn't either, but they had to be expecting them since they had lost contact with their lookouts on the roof.

Which meant time was of the essence.

And delays in the parking garage could cost lives.

"Bravo Zero-One, Bravo Zero-Two. Two hostiles eliminated, Bravo One-Two tenderized but operational. We're in position, over."

Dawson exchanged grins with Spock who was just behind him as they continued their descent, coming to a stop at the door leading into the foyer. "Roger that, Bravo Zero-Two, we're in position. Control, Bravo Zero-One. All teams in position. Status, over?"

"Bravo Zero-One, Control. Windows all clear. Heat signatures above ground show nobody outside of the ballroom except for your team. We have no intel on the parking garage except for what Bravo Zero-Two reported, over."

"Roger that, Control. Bravo Zero-Two, proceed in three, two, one, execute!"

Spock yanked the door open and Dawson stepped through, immediately scanning left to right as Jagger covered right to left. "Clear!" he whispered, Jagger doing the same, the four of them breaking left and right, out of sight of the double-doors to the conference room just ahead. Dawson crossed the marble floor quickly, coming to rest at the far wall where the entrance to the room stood, Spock beside him, Jagger and Mickey on the opposite side.

They slowly made their way to the door, hugging the wall, and when in position he activated his comm. "Bravo Zero-Two, we're in position, over."

"Bravo Zero-Two in position, over."

Dawson pulled a scope from one of the pockets on his vest and extended the telescoping stalk, activating the camera on the other end. The transmission was picked up by the tablet Spock was now holding, the video beamed back to Control. Dawson glanced between the screen and the end of the camera, making sure he didn't tap the glass in the door.

"I'm seeing six hostiles," reported Spock. "Two in front of this door, two at the front of the room with the Secretary, two walking among the hostages." He paused. "Shit!"

"What is it?" asked Dawson, looking at the screen.

"They've got half the hostages on their feet."

Dawson cursed. "Okay, did everyone copy that? Four hotel-tangoes in the clear, two among the hostages. Bravo Zero-Two, your team take the two by our door and the two on the stage—you should have clean shots from your entry point. We'll take the two in the crowd. Watch for additional hostiles pretending to be civilians. When in doubt, wing them. We'll sort out the lawsuits later. Acknowledged?"

The confirmations came through the comm and Dawson took one final look at the screen as Jagger and Spock crouched down, gripping the handles of both doors. "Teams One and Two, proceed in three, two, one, execute!"

He did an additional three count then nodded, Wings and Spock pulling open the doors as he and Jagger advanced. Across the room he could already see Red's team entering, the two hostiles by his door down, the two on the stage collapsing as he watched. He got a bead on the first hostile on the left, spinning toward the stage in shock. "Federal authorities, everyone on the ground!"

Screams erupted as those standing among the hostage takers realized it was do or die time, most not reacting fast enough. He squeezed his trigger, taking out the first hostile as he heard Jagger's weapon fire beside him. He scanned the crowd, not for weapons, but for faces. The civilians would be panicked, the enemy not necessarily. They'd be more likely to remain standing for just a moment longer, looking for where the threat was coming from, whereas the civilians wouldn't care.

They'd just hit the deck once their brains and bodies realized they should.

Someone made eye contact.

He fired, nailing the man in the shoulder. He spun around then dropped to the floor as both teams advanced, Dawson motioning for Spock and Wings to secure the Secretary. Another shot was fired, this time by Red's team, another person among the hostages dropping with a cry. The mix of men and women were crying out in panic, some screaming, others simply confused.

The sexes were equal today, the screams and cries of panic a mix of low and high pitches.

"Everyone on the ground, face down, hands on your heads, now!" he shouted, the same order being repeated by Red from the other side. "I want to see hands clasped behind your heads or you *will* be shot!"

The orders were quickly obeyed as he reached the man he had shot, pushing him over onto his back with his boot. A gun was raised toward him.

Dawson put two shots in his chest, the question of whether or not the man was innocent settled for eternity. He scanned the crowd, now all on the floor as his eight man team trained their weapons on them. Jagger stepped on the hand of the man he shot then reached down and yanked his jacket up.

Beretta.

"Control, Bravo Zero-One. Hostages secure, seven hostiles dead, one wounded. Have SWAT secure the foyer, we're going to start sending the hostages out one at a time, over."

"Roger that Bravo Zero-One, SWAT moving into position now."

Dawson pointed at Red's team. "Begin searching them, one at a time. When they're confirmed clean, send them out the doors for processing."

"Yes, Sergeant Major."

Jagger hauled the wounded hostile to his feet, the man yelping in pain.

"Cuff him, search him, then hand him over. We're out of here in five."

Jagger nodded, binding the man's wrists with a zip tie. Tight.

Dawson walked over to the Secretary of Defense. "Are you okay, Mr. Secretary?"

He nodded, then motioned toward a body nearby, a black man who looked like he had been dead for some time. "They were after him, not me."

Dawson's eyes narrowed. "Are you sure? Who is he?"

"Vice President Okeke of Sierra Leone. He was here for a security meeting to discuss our Ebola response in West Africa."

"What makes you think they were after him?"

"They shot him first then secured the room. It was as if he had to die and they couldn't risk not succeeding."

Dawson frowned. "What about their demands? They wanted quite a bit of money to let you go."

The Secretary of Defense shook his head. "Smoke screen. At least that's my opinion."

"Mr. Secretary!"

He looked toward the door where several suits were rushing in, clearly a Secret Service detail and some aides.

"That's my ride, I guess." The Secretary extended a hand. "I have a feeling I know who you are. Thank your men for me. You have my eternal gratitude."

Dawson shook the man's hand, pleased the person responsible for managing his line of work for the Executive Branch had a solid, dry handshake. "Thank you, sir. I'll pass it on."

The Secretary left immediately with his escort as the room filled with G-Men. Dawson activated his comm. "Bravo Team, Bravo Zero-One. Stand down, repeat, stand down, we leave in two, out."

Dawson watched as the last of the hostages left, nothing but law enforcement and bodies remaining.

And wondered why the Vice President of some small, poor Ebola ravaged country would be worth so many lives.

Murray Town Barracks, Freetown, Sierra Leone

Major Adofo Koroma sucked in a deep breath then nodded to his driver. The transport truck, signed out by him that morning from the motor pool, lurched forward. He had to admit he had butterflies. Not from fear but anticipation, fear drummed out of his psyche months ago after watching his wife and son waste away and die from Ebola, turned away from the only treatment center hundreds of miles from his village.

We're full, sorry.

The cities were being paid attention to while those in the north, traditionally not supporters of the government here in Freetown, were being ignored.

Silence us all through death.

He had been a loyal soldier, and still was in a way. He loved his country, believed things were getting better, but more for those who were in the cities. The rural areas were left to their own devices to solve their problems. He understood that the Ebola treatment centers had to be placed where they were most needed, but to completely abandon the rural areas was inexcusable.

They had to at least provide them with supplies, some aid workers to at least provide advice.

But his village had been abandoned, even the local government representatives leaving to stay at a military base to avoid the virus and the questions.

And now his daughter was sick.

Five years old.

Already devastated by the death of her mother and brother, she was too young to understand what was going on and it tore at his heart. Enough so that he was here today, committing what in most people's eyes would be treason.

Unless they had been placed in an impossible situation like he had, and had the resources he did at his disposal.

And that was men.

Loyal men.

Men that were willing to die for their cause.

And eleven already had.

One thing about living in a poor country with traditionally large families was that it was almost guaranteed you had relatives in the United States. Over the past twenty years many from his village and the surrounding area had given up and emigrated, most to America. Almost anyone who had managed to get an education was gone. It was a brain drain that the great Western democracies refused to acknowledge. They sought out those with skills they needed, and took them from the poor countries that needed their expertise even more.

It should be a crime against humanity to take a doctor from a third world country.

The only advantage of losing the youngest and brightest from their poor communities was they sent money home. That hard currency gave their poor relatives, unlucky enough to not have the skills that the West desired, a chance to buy the essentials of life.

But nothing could buy the care needed when Ebola struck.

Treatment centers couldn't be bribed, not with Western doctors controlling the intake process, and there just wasn't enough room even if they could.

The situation was desperate, especially in his village where nearly a quarter of the population was either sick or caring for someone who was.

His wife and son were among the first to die.

And it was all so unnecessary.

The West had the money and the expertise to solve this. But because it was Africa, because they were black, and because they didn't have oil, the reaction had been slow. Sure there were now British and Canadian troops along with dozens of aid organizations setting up new facilities in his country, but it had taken six months to get a reaction.

Thousands had died, tens of thousands more would still die.

All because it hadn't been an interesting enough story for the news stations to cover.

And someone had to pay.

It was a decision he hadn't come to lightly and today was the second part of his plan, the first part carried out last night in Washington by his brother and several others from his village and the surrounding area who now lived in the United States.

Vice President Okeke was now dead.

And so were his brother and friends.

But they died for a purpose, a purpose no one in America knew.

But when his plan was complete, it was a purpose no one in America would ever forget.

Then maybe they'll pay attention.

They rounded the corner, the vehicle bouncing over a large pothole, jarring his entire body painfully. He pointed ahead. "There it is."

His driver nodded, the dockyards just ahead.

Dockyards loaded with medical supplies from a slowly awakening America.

Hastings Ebola Treatment Center, Freetown, Sierra Leone

Dr. Sarah Henderson shoved her knuckles into the small of her back and kneaded the sore, aching muscles. She had only been here three weeks and had planned on an eight week tour, but the physical toll was already making its presence felt.

But it was nothing compared to the mental one.

She had seen death in her line of work, too much death. As a volunteer for Médecins Sans Frontières, or Doctors Without Borders, she often found herself in war zones. She tried to give two months out of every year to the organization founded in 1971 by a small group of French doctors who had worked together during the Nigerian Civil War, it now a widely recognized and respected organization she was proud to contribute toward both monetarily and with her time.

But this was something different, something she had never dealt with before.

Ebola.

Every day in the treatment center where she was volunteering dozens died, dozens more were brought in to fill the freed up beds, and even more were refused at the door, there simply not enough room.

Which meant those infected were sent home to die, and worse, to infect their loved ones.

It was heartbreaking.

Entire families were being wiped out, quite often because one of them made the uninformed mistake of helping an infected neighbor take a family member to a treatment center, exposing themselves to the deadly disease.

Fear was the enemy, fear was one of the greatest causes of the spread.

If only anyone who thought they or a loved one might be infected told the authorities, and quarantined themselves, they might actually break the back of the pandemic, but there was little hope of that. People were terrified of what their neighbors might do to them if they revealed one of their own was sick, so they kept them hidden away, but without proper protocols, they too were almost guaranteed to become infected.

Thousands were dead, thousands more were dying, and if things continued unchecked, the Centers for Disease Control was predicting over a million cases within months.

And if it hit those numbers, there was no hope in saving these people.

She feared the solution, should it reach those proportions, would be for the Western nations to completely pull out then isolate the countries so the population would simply die off, the disease's incredible mortality rate its own greatest enemy.

But for now she was here, on the frontlines, doing her duty as a doctor, fulfilling the Hippocratic Oath she had so proudly taken just ten years ago. She was trying to stem the tide against overwhelming odds, working sixteen hour days to save those brought in early, to comfort those who were too far gone. She cried herself to sleep the first week, but now she was becoming numb to it all.

And it scared her.

Would this experience change her so much that she no longer was affected by the death of her patients? She was an Emergency Room surgeon in Los Angeles which meant she was constantly faced with death from gunshot wounds to stabbings. But back home there was always somebody to blame.

Here there was no one.

It was a disease.

And the only real way to save someone was to throw everything modern medicine could offer at each individual patient.

Which was simply too expensive.

The individual cases in the United States that had been treated—and not all successfully—cost over one million dollars each on average. An insane figure that would overwhelm even the richest of countries should it face tens of thousands of victims like these poor African countries were dealing with.

And yet she did her small part.

She knew in the grand scheme of things it made little difference, her efforts merely a finger in the dyke. But tens of thousands of fingers *could* make a difference, especially with the right equipment and facilities.

They didn't need modern hospitals, they needed beds, manpower, and isolation equipment. They needed locals to properly dispose of the bodies, to provide the nursing efforts, to properly transport the sick to the quarantine centers.

Which meant they needed to be trained, and paid well for the risks they were taking.

Money was beginning to pour in, but money was of little value without manpower and supplies. Experimental vaccines and treatments were fantastic, but if there were only a few thousand samples in existence, what good was it?

She bent over, touching her toes, not an easy task in her personal protective equipment. She felt the tension slowly ease from her muscles, knowing that soon the pain would be back, and worse.

"Are you okay, Dr. Henderson?"

She turned her head, still bent over, and looked up at Doctor Tanya Danko, her voice muffled from her suit. She smiled as she straightened up. "I'll live."

Tanya looked at the long line of beds, all full.

"I'm afraid few of them will."

Tanya was a short-timer. She was due to leave in two days, returning to her native Ukraine only to probably deal with more carnage.

But at least there they had someone to blame.

Russia.

And that was what she hated so much about this disease. There was no perpetrator, no weapon with a human at the end of it.

And it didn't choose its victims because they were from some ethnic group, some political leaning.

It didn't care whether or not you were a doctor or a dock worker, a mother or a child, black or white.

It just killed.

Sarah stood for a moment, watching the nurses administering to the patients, shaking her head. "I'm afraid you're right."

"If only we could get more people who've been cured to donate their blood, we might be able to stop this."

Sarah nodded. Tanya was right, though it would be a slow process. It was at the moment the most effective treatment. Take the blood from those who survived, and give it to those who were sick. The transfusions would transfer the antibodies built up in the healthy survivor into that of the infected, and quite often cure them.

Which meant *their* blood could then be used.

But each survivor could only donate so much blood, and it took time for those cured to recover enough to actually provide the blood.

Eventually the treatment would win out as a critical mass of people survived.

But how many tens if not hundreds of thousands would die first?

"There's just too many," she said, her shoulders slumping. "We've got two hundred patients here and only four getting transfusions."

Tanya motioned toward the four who were nearest them. "Those four will hopefully survive, and provide blood for four more. The four who provided blood for these four will also provide more. Those eight will then provide blood and so on." Tanya placed a gloved hand on Sarah's shoulder. "Don't lose hope yet, Sarah, you've only been here a few weeks."

Sarah shook her head. "I don't know how you've kept your optimism through all this. Eight weeks!"

"I was like you when I first arrived. Overwhelmed. Completely. I lost track of how many tears I shed. It's the children dying that I think get you the most. If I could, I'd stay here until it was over, but I have a family back home and I miss them."

Sarah sucked in a deep breath then sighed, her eyes filling with tears as she pictured her husband, Steve, and their little boy, Tommy. Tommy was twelve, old enough to claim to understand why she had gone, but she wasn't convinced he really understood. He hadn't cried at the airport, but his lip had trembled and his eyes had watered.

But he hadn't sobbed.

Steve told her after she had cleared customs and given them a final wave before heading to her gate, that Tommy had cried the entire way home from the airport. Only a trip through the McDonald's drive thru had settled him down.

And then only for a few minutes.

A tear rolled down her cheek.

"I miss my family too."

"Don't you start crying otherwise I will too, and there's no blowing our noses in these infernal outfits."

Sarah laughed, sniffed hard and rapidly blinked her eyes clear. "You're right. Don't we make a good pair? Better not let the men see us or they're going to think we're the weaker sex."

"Bah!" cried Tanya, batting her hand. "I saw Jacques heaving this morning. They're not tougher than us."

Sarah chuckled. "Couldn't have happened to a nicer guy."

Tanya punched her gently on the shoulder. "Sarah!"

Sarah shrugged. "Sorry, but that guy's an asshole. There isn't anything with a heartbeat and a vagina around here that he hasn't hit on."

Tanya snorted, bending over slightly as she stifled a laugh. "He hit on you too?"

"I think wedding bands just attract the pig."

"Too true, too true."

Sarah looked at the clock on the nearby wall. "Looks like our shift is over. Dinner?"

"Absolutely, I'm famished. I wonder what's on the menu tonight."

"Nothing good, I'm sure."

"They try."

"I know, I know. But I'd kill to have grilled chicken on a bed of fettuccini just oozing with a creamy alfredo sauce."

"Oh woman, you're torturing me."

"And myself. At least you're leaving soon."

"I can't wait to have some home cooked meals, even if I'm the one who has to cook them."

They stepped through the first door of the isolation chamber, one of the local staff beginning to hose her down with a soapy spray. "Steve does most of the cooking at our home."

"Lucky girl."

"Yeah, he's way better at it than me. I do toast and coffee well, but that's about it."

"My mother raised me to cook. I love it. With my job though it does make it hectic sometimes."

The man with the spray motioned Sarah forward, turning the chemical shower on Tanya. She stepped through another set of doors and a local began to remove her gear, a checklist being read by a second, a third watching Sarah closely to make sure she didn't touch herself, all of the actions very deliberate, very carefully done.

This was where you'd get infected.

If you were properly covered, the chances of becoming infected were very low. But touch something contaminated with your glove, then touch your face with that glove when your headgear had been removed and you could be infected.

And become another statistic.

She stepped out of her booties and into the next chamber where she was decontaminated once again, her light clothes tossed into a basket leaving her in nothing but her panties and bra. A thorough shower and she was dressing when Tanya appeared wrapped in a towel.

Tanya tossed the towel aside, her European lack of concern over nudity still something Sarah was getting used to. "Just give me a minute and I'll join you for dinner."

Sarah looked away, hoping it wasn't too obvious. "Okay, I'm going to go to my room first and see if I can get in a quick call home."

"Okay, enjoy!"

Sarah stepped outside, the stifling heat of the afternoon now just starting to give way to what she hoped would be a cooler evening. The Doctor's Lounge was air conditioned, but not much else was. Her room had an oscillating fan and little in the way of creature comforts.

But she wasn't here to be comfortable.

She walked down a hallway of the repurposed police training school, opening the door to one of the classrooms. Inside she shared the room with four others, temporary walls having been put inside providing some modicum of privacy and not much of that, their acoustic shielding properties little to none.

But it didn't matter. At the end of a hard day's work she was usually so exhausted there was little difficulty getting to sleep.

Even when one of her bunkmates was "entertaining a guest".

There was little to do here in the form of entertainment. Many of the doctors were young, attractive, with no husbands or wives back home.

Which meant sex was quite often the chosen pastime.

She knew she felt the urge from time to time, but she loved her husband and it wouldn't even occur to her to cheat on him, despite the fact he would never know.

I'd know.

And that was more than enough reason to keep her libido locked up.

She opened her door and screamed, grabbing at her chest in shock as her mind reeled for a moment at the sight of a strange man lying on her cot.

"Jacques, what the hell are you doing here?"

"Why, waiting for you, mon chéri," he said in that thick French accent of his, an accent she had to admit was as sexy to her ears as the language of romance had been described to her.

Especially in her heightened state of arousal brought on by weeks of forced celibacy.

She snapped her fingers, jerking a thumb over her shoulder at the door. "Out. Now."

Jacques swung his legs off the cot and rose, standing only inches from her, his body heat radiating out toward her, a furnace of passion that made her tingle where she shouldn't, not as a married woman. "I assure you my intentions are quite honorable."

"I find that hard to believe."

Jacques' hand slapped against his chest, over his heart, his jaw dropping. "Mademoiselle, I am 'urt. You of all people I would 'ave thought above believing the 'urtful gossip surrounding me. It is a reputation I assure you is quite underserved."

She loved the way he didn't pronounce his H's. "I've heard you laying pipe to two different women this week in this very room—"

Jacques pointed to the floor with a sly grin. "*This* very room?"

"You know what I mean."

Jacques shrugged. "Who am I to say 'no' when a woman requires the comfort only I can provide."

The ego on this guy! Despite herself she found the physical attraction undeniable. And it disgusted her. "*Only* you?"

He shrugged again. "I am French. We are skilled in the art of the love making."

"Don't believe your own press." She jerked her thumb at the door again. "Now out."

Jacques smiled and sidestepped past her, stopping in the doorway. "Aren't you going to ask why I was waiting for you?"

She sighed, exasperated at his antics and her body's response to them. She kept her back to him. The last thing she needed was him seeing her flustered. "Fine, why were you waiting for me?"

"I was going to tell you that—" His voice cut off, a gurgling sound replacing it as he gasped for breath.

She shook her head as she turned around. "What are you playing it, Jac—"

She screamed, a bloodcurdling eruption cut off within moments as a gun was raised past Jacques and aimed directly at her. The look of shock and pain on Jacques' face was explained by the large blade shoved through his abdomen, the tip, several inches in length, twisting back and forth as the man it belonged to turned his wrist, scrambling the young doctor's insides while a hand held tightly over his mouth prevented him screaming from the agony he was clearly in.

She froze, bladder control momentarily forgotten.

She squeezed, stemming the flow, but enough had escaped that if she weren't so terrified, she might actually be embarrassed.

"You are Sarah Henderson?" asked the large black man with the gun, his partner pulling what appeared to be a machete out of Jacques' back.

She should have said no, but she wasn't thinking clearly, and she found her body almost irresistibly nodding as she trembled.

"The doctor?"

She nodded, it not yet occurring to her to ask why she was being asked for by name.

The man flicked the gun, motioning for her to move forward as Jacques was shoved to the side, still gasping for air, unable to speak. Their eyes met and she recognized the look immediately. It was a look she had seen hundreds of times since her arrival in this godforsaken country.

It was the look of someone who knew they were going to die.

"Let me help him."

The man with the machete reached forward and grabbed her by the shoulder, yanking her out the door. "He's dead already," said the man with the gun, looking down at Jacques' gurgling form, blood flowing freely from the wound.

And she knew he was right. Even with proper medical facilities he would be tough to save. Here? There was no way.

But she felt like she had to do something.

"Please, let me try."

The man with the gun growled. "Forget him." He switched the gun to his left hand then motioned with his right for the machete. The man tossed it to him. He swung, swiftly, his hand clearly practiced, and chopped halfway through Jacques' neck sending a spray of arterial blood across the room, some splashing across the thin white t-shirt she was wearing, some getting into her mouth.

She spat.

Pushing on Jacques' chest with his boot, he yanked the blade free, taking a moment to wipe it clean on her bed sheets. He tossed it back to her captor, he easily catching it with his hand then holding it against her throat.

Jacques took his last breath, a gasping rattle that had her eyes squeezing shut and looking away as all strength left her.

There was a double-knock on the door. "Sarah! It's me!"

Sarah watched in horror as Tanya pushed the classroom door open. She was about to shout a warning when a hand was clasped over her mouth, the grip viciously tight. She tried to will a warning toward her friend, her eyes wide, trying to make eye contact through the door, but it was too late. The man with the gun was already at the door, hauling the shocked Ukrainian inside, slamming the door shut as he pressed his gun against her forehead.

"Silence."

Tanya trembled out a nod as she finally made eye contact with Sarah then whimpered when she saw Jacques' blood staining her shirt. She gave a questioning look and Sarah motioned slightly toward her room, Jacques' body still visible through the door.

Tanya fainted.

"Is she a doctor?"

Sarah shook her head. "No."

"You lie."

"She's not a doctor."

"Then what is she?"

Sarah tried to think of something, a job that they couldn't possibly find important.

"Sh-she's a reporter."

"Then she's no good to us. Kill her."

"No wait! She's a doctor!"

The man glared at her for a moment. "Which is it? Reporter or doctor?"

"Doctor. I'm sorry, I lied."

The man with the gun motioned at Tanya's still unconscious figure. "Pick her up."

The man shoved his machete through a loop on his belt and hauled the poor woman off the floor, flipping her over his shoulder with ease.

"Wh-why are you doing this?"

"To send a message," replied the man as he poked his head through the open window.

"Wh-what do you mean? A message to whom?"

The man stepped through the window and onto the ground below. He looked back. "You stupid little girl. You know very well who the message is to." He reached in and grabbed her wrist, hauling her toward the window frame. She yelped and swung herself through, helping protect Tanya's head as she was roughly handed over.

Tanya began to come to as she was stood up on the grass. And that was when Sarah realized what was going on, what was truly happening. He had asked her name. They were here for her, not some random doctor. They wanted her specifically.

And there was only one reason for it.

Her father.

Vice President Philip Henderson's Office, The White House, Washington DC

"Mr. Vice President, I—"

Philip Henderson looked up from his laptop as his aide, Vincent Harper, entered the room. His eyes narrowed. Harper was usually a very confident man but the visage being presented now could only be described as one of fear.

But it wasn't fear.

He had seen fear. Fear was 9/11. Fear was Boston.

This was something different. It wasn't fear of some external threat.

He's afraid to tell you something.

"What is it, Vince?"

Harper stepped inside, closing the door behind him. Henderson caught a glimpse of his secretary.

And she looked terrified.

But again, it wasn't terror.

She's concerned for you.

His chest tightened. "What's happened?" he asked, rising, his thoughts immediately of his wife and daughter. "Has something happened to my family?" And as the words came out of his mouth he knew exactly what was going on. He collapsed back into his chair. "It's Sarah, isn't it?"

Harper nodded, handing him a file, opening it to the first page.

He didn't look. "What's happened? Is she—" He couldn't bring himself to say the word. He simply looked up at his old friend and colleague.

"We don't know, Mr. Vice President. All we know is that there was a murder at the compound she was at, in her room, and that she and another doctor are missing."

"Murder?" His hands gripped the arms of his chair tightly, his knuckles turning white with the strain. "Do they think—"

"No! God no, they don't think she did it. The man's head was practically chopped off—"

Henderson gasped and felt himself pale.

Harper lost a few shades as he realized what he had said. "Oh God, I'm sorry, sir, I didn't mean to say that, I mean, I'm sure she's okay, I mean—" Harper stopped, looking for a chair and dropping into the closest one, grabbing his hair. "I'm so sorry, sir. I just can't think straight."

Henderson's ears were pounding, blood rushing through his system as his heart slammed into his chest. He felt lightheaded.

Breathe!

He suddenly sucked in a breath, exhaling quickly as he let go of the one he had been unknowingly holding. The world began to come back into focus.

"Does her mother know?"

Harper shook his head. "Not yet. I figured you'd want to tell her yourself. I've ordered the car brought around and have confirmed Mrs. Henderson is home."

"How—"

"Security detail."

Henderson nodded, then breathed deeply. "Okay, give me the facts."

"All we have is the initial report from Doctors Without Borders. One of their doctors—the name is in the file, can't remember it—French I think—was found murdered in your daughter's room. They think a machete."

Henderson winced, causing Harper to stop. "Continue."

"There was an open window and they think your daughter and another doctor, a female from the Ukraine, were taken out the window by the assailants. There's no evidence they were hurt, and there's been no ransom demands, at least not yet."

"So they might not know who they have." It was wishful thinking. Of all the doctors to choose from, why his Sarah? He was certain they knew exactly who they had. And that might just save her life, at least for now.

"Possibly."

Harper sounded as doubtful as he felt.

"We both know they know who they've got. I'm guessing this Frenchman got in the way somehow."

"What about the other woman? Why not kill her?"

"You said she was a doctor?"

Harper nodded.

"Then maybe they've got multiple motivations." He chewed on his lip for a moment, his mind racing through the possibilities. If it were just his daughter, he would dismiss the possibility they were looking for a doctor. But to take two? He paused. "Any word of supplies being stolen at the same time?"

Harper's eyes narrowed. "Supplies?"

"You heard me."

"I don't know, not that I know of. That's more the CIA's department."

"Get them on it." He pushed himself up, straightening his tie. "I have to go tell my wife that her daughter is missing and I might be the cause of it."

Freetown, Sierra Leone

Dr. Sarah Henderson squeezed her eyes shut as the hood she had been wearing since their abduction was ripped off her head. She tentatively opened her eyes, blinking several times before finally focusing. She was sitting on a chair in what looked like a small warehouse, big enough to fit what appeared to be three transport trucks and a dozen men loading supplies into them.

Tanya was sitting beside her, eyes red, cheeks stained from tears, her bottom lip still trembling. The man who had held the gun during their abduction approached. He was wearing what appeared to be an army uniform. "I am Major Koroma and you are my guests."

Sarah's eyebrows popped up at this.

Guests?

The man had killed their colleague, assaulted them, kidnapped them, and he had the audacity to call them his guests? Apparently her expression was enough to convey her feelings on the matter.

"I see you don't believe me. That is understandable. You must understand that what happened was necessary."

"Killing Jacques was necessary?"

Koroma nodded. "A necessary *evil* as you Americans might say. His death will serve a greater purpose in the days to come."

"I fail to see any way in which his murder could benefit anyone."

Tanya whimpered, apparently terrified that Sarah was making it worse, and Sarah had to admit part of her was screaming at her to shut up, but she found she couldn't. She hadn't been raised that way. Her father had taught her from the beginning to speak up and to speak out, especially when an injustice was being committed.

And she could think of no greater injustice than murder.

Not to mention the fact there were now three less doctors at their treatment center. The impact would be dramatic, there only being ten of them to begin with. And that assumed they were the only two captives. For all she knew there could be others.

Major Koroma smiled. "That is because your view is shortsighted and based upon a lack of information."

For the first time Sarah noticed how well the major spoke English. Though English was the official language of Sierra Leone, it was not what was most commonly spoken. Amazingly, the lingua franca of Sierra Leone was descendent from Nova Scotian settlers, forced south from their homes centuries ago. Creole was the resulting language that had developed among these settlers, slaves and Caribbean natives, and after slavery had been abolished in the United States and many slaves were repatriated to West Africa, the Krio language resulted. A mix of many languages, it was spoken by 97% of the population of Sierra Leone, resulting in a heavily accented English when spoken by most locals.

But this man sounded American.

"Why don't you enlighten us?" she said, trying to keep the disdain in her voice to a minimum.

"In good time. Unfortunately we are on a tight schedule and must leave at once." He motioned to one of his men, also in uniform, and the ropes binding their hands were cut. Sarah gingerly rubbed her wrists, finding no cuts, only minor abrasions, her struggles minimal after Jacques' beheading.

"What will happen to us?" she asked as Koroma motioned for them to stand.

"You will come with me in the lead vehicle. She will go with the lieutenant." He nodded toward the man who had cut the bindings. "You will show your identification at any checkpoints we encounter and tell them that you are doctors transporting supplies to the Ebola treatment center in Port Loko."

"Port Loko? That's awfully far."

"We're not going there, you're just telling them that's where we're going."

"Then where *are* we going?"

"That's none of your concern." He pointed at her chest. "But make no mistake, should you try anything, either of you, you will both die horribly slow deaths."

Tanya yelped, slapping her hands over her mouth and Sarah felt her own knees weaken slightly. This was real. It was serious.

And she needed to shut up before she got them both killed.

"Do you understand?" asked Koroma, stepping closer.

She nodded.

"Good." He pointed to the nearest truck. "Get in." He pointed at the second truck, looking at Tanya. "You, over there."

Tanya shook her head rapidly. The lieutenant stepped forward, grabbed her by the arm and dragged her toward the open door, Tanya struggling the entire way. He stopped and punched her in the stomach, Tanya doubling over, gasping in pain.

"Hey, that isn't necessary!" cried Sarah as she rushed toward her friend. Major Koroma caught her by the arm before she could reach her, his grip viselike. "She's just scared. Let her travel with me."

"No."

"Please. If she's with me, she'll be okay."

"No, that is not the plan. In fact…" Koroma let go of her arm and pulled his weapon from its holster. He walked over to Tanya, still doubled over in pain, placing it against the top of her head. "She was never part of the plan."

The weapon cocked.

"No!"

CIA Headquarters, Langley, Virginia

Senior Analyst Chris Leroux nodded at the others gathered in his boss' office. He recognized them all as heads of various groups like his own team of eight. The best of the best were here. Not agents, not spies, but analysts. He and the others were the people that gathered the intel that agents like his friend Dylan Kane acted upon.

And judging by the look on his boss' face, they were about to get very busy.

National Clandestine Service Chief Leif Morrison looked up from a file on his desk, nodding at Leroux. "I'll be brief," he said, Leroux not knowing him to be anything but. "Several hours ago the Vice President's daughter was kidnapped in Sierra Leone along with another doctor, a Ukrainian national. A third doctor, a French national, was murdered we believe during the kidnapping. She was volunteering at an Ebola clinic as part of Doctors Without Borders." He closed the file. "And that's all we know."

"No ransom demand?" asked one.

"Not yet."

"Do they know who they have?" asked Leroux, it to him the most pertinent question. If they knew, then this was politically motivated. If they didn't, then it could simply have been a random snatch and grab.

A much more dangerous situation.

"We're not sure, but the fact it was her of all people suggests they did."

"But we have no proof."

"Not yet."

Leroux pursed his lips. "They took the two female doctors, but not the male doctor."

"Correct."

"Perhaps because they felt they would be easier to control."

"But that assumes she wasn't the target," said Donovan Eppes, another section head that Leroux respected immensely. He was also about fifteen years Leroux's senior, gatherings like this always reminding him of just how young he was. Now late twenties, Morrison had taken him under his wing and taken advantage of his ability to take often disparate information and find links between them that no one else seemed to make.

It was a gift. And a curse.

He had no desire to supervise staff but he had been given one despite his protests.

He was moving up the ladder, kicking and screaming the entire way.

His girlfriend, Sherrie White, an agent with the CIA, and way out of his league, was supportive, understanding his shy ways but trying to convince him that the additional resources would allow him to help more people.

While true, he was finding too much of his time was now admin work.

And no help to anyone except the HR department.

"Not necessarily," said Leroux to Eppes. "If they were just after her, then why take the other doctor? They obviously didn't have a problem killing. Why not just kill her and leave with the one hostage. That would be much easier to deal with."

"What are you thinking?" It was Morrison that asked the question the entire room had on their minds, everyone well aware of Leroux's talents.

He shifted in his chair as all eyes were now on him. "Well, umm, if it were up to me, I'd be, well, looking to see what else happened in the area around the same time."

"Such as?"

"Well, they just kidnapped two doctors. Did they also take supplies? Was anyone else kidnapped? Killed?"

Morrison leaned back in his chair, steepling his fingers. "You're suggesting they took them as doctors, not hostages."

Leroux shrugged. "Just a thought. It's the Ukrainian. Was she sharing a room with Doctor—what's her name?"

"Sarah Henderson. She kept her maiden name when she married."

"Probably not wise in hindsight," observed Eppes.

"Why not?" asked Cindy Fowler. "A woman can't keep her name?"

Eppes groaned. "Oh for Christ's sake, Cindy, not everything's a women's rights issue. All I meant was that if she had her husband's name, they might not have made the connection with her famous father."

"And if *she* were a *he*?"

"What of it? Then *he'd* be in the exact same damned boat as *she* is. Why don't we stick to reality rather than your conspiratorial fantasy? *She* is a *she*, with the same last name as her *father*, the *Vice President*."

"I'll stick to reality, as long as you stick to the relevant facts. The fact that she kept her maiden name isn't relevant."

"Oh, blow it out your ass."

"Enough!" snapped Morrison, the exchange too familiar among the group. Eppes and Fowler hated each other. They had dated about ten years ago and the breakup had been bitter, apparently wedding plans involved. Leroux didn't know much of the story, and he didn't want to know. The personal lives of his colleagues was no concern of his.

And right now it was just interfering with the real issue.

Morrison motioned toward Leroux. "You were saying, Chris?"

"Were they sharing the room?"

"No, I don't think so, but we'll have to have that confirmed. Our intel is very sketchy at the moment."

"Well, if we assume no, then she was a target of opportunity most likely. They could have killed her right then and there, making their resolve even clearer to the Vice President. But the fact they didn't suggests they saw a use for her too."

"Her skills as a doctor," said Eppes, his head bobbing slowly as his red cheeks slowly returned to their normal pasty pale white. "So if you kidnap a couple of doctors…"

"You probably want them to treat somebody, which means they need equipment, supplies."

Morrison pointed at him. "Your team is on that."

Leroux nodded.

"Are there going to be boots on the ground?" asked Fowler.

Morrison nodded. "I think you can count on it."

Belme Residence, West Luzon Drive, Fort Bragg

"Uncle Dog, can you fix my train set?"

Command Sergeant Major Burt "Big Dog" Dawson looked over at young Bryson Belme as he tugged on his t-shirt. Dawson was the young boy's Godfather, a responsibility he took very seriously. The little guy had been in his life coming up on nine years now and he had to admit he was quite fond of the kid.

"Leave your uncle alone, Bryson, Daddy will fix it later."

Dawson put his beer down on the patio table and winked at Bryson's mom Shirley. "You know Red, he'll just break it."

Master Sergeant Mike "Red" Belme flipped him the bird from the barbeque.

"Mike! Not in front of Bryson!"

Red made a face at Bryson who giggled. "Sorry, hon."

Dawson followed Bryson into the house and down the hall to his room. It was a simple, humble home, provided by the military for a reasonable rent. A lot of the guys had them, especially the married ones. He lived on-post as well though he spent little time there now, his girlfriend Maggie having a nice place in town and the perks of staying over outweighing his Xbox One.

A quick fix of the accidentally knocked apart tracks and Bryson was up and running after a hug of thanks. Dawson returned to the patio to find steaks coming off the grill.

"Success?"

"Reading Railroad is running again."

Red slapped a steak on Dawson's plate as he sat down. "How many times do I have to tell you, '*reeding*', not '*redding*'?"

"And how many times do I have to tell you *you're* wrong?"

Shirley turned toward the open patio door. "Bryson, supper!"

Tiny feet pounding on parquet could be heard before the little bundle of energy burst through the door. He climbed into his chair and grabbed the hamburger his father ladled onto the plate.

"Give me your plate, BD, I'll fix you up with some salad."

Dawson handed his plate to Shirley who spooned a large helping of homemade potato salad then a three bean affair that he never would have thought he'd like but actually did, he never a bean person. It was fairly standard fare here, steak and cold salads a regular occurrence at the Belme household.

And he had an open invite.

Red was his best friend. Best he had ever had. They were as close as any two men could get without actually sleeping together and with their bond forged under fire, they were tight. He couldn't imagine life without his friend or the family that had taken him in. He had a sister that wasn't too far away. She was married with a daughter, and he adored his niece Tammy, but saw them far too infrequently. He was making more of an effort though ever since his job had dragged them into his secret world when he and his team had been targeted by a madman. He still hadn't completely forgiven himself for their kidnapping. It wasn't his fault, and his sister continually told him that, but he still felt responsible.

It had been a bad day, and he counted himself lucky. Their good friend Stucco and his family hadn't been so lucky, murdered while he and the rest of the team stood powerless to save them.

It had changed them all.

They had lost men before in combat, but those were missions. In the field you knew you could die. But at home, on base? With your family?

Never.

Their identities were protected, their jobs classified, their deployments secret.

But that day, someone had figured out who they were.

And it had made them all that much more cautious.

"It's too bad Maggie couldn't join us today," said Shirley as he cut into his steak. Blood flowed freely.

Yum!

"Rare enough for you?" asked Red as he cut into his own.

Dawson dropped his ear to within an inch of the steak. "Bryson, do you hear that?"

"What?" asked the boy between chews.

"Don't talk with your mouth full," scolded Shirley.

"Sorry, Mommy," replied Bryson, repeating the offense.

Shirley shook her head.

Bryson swallowed and leaned toward Dawson's steak. "I don't hear anything."

"I swear I heard a 'moo'."

Bryson stood in his chair, leaning over the table, getting his ear as close as he could. "I don't hear it."

Red bent over, his head under the table. "Moooo."

"I heard it!" Bryson's face brightened as he leaned in closer. Then he frowned. "You can't eat that, Uncle Dog. It's alive!"

Red laughed, mooing as he sat back up.

"Daddy!"

Bryson looked pissed and Dawson tousled his hair as he sat back in his seat. "Don't worry, Bryson, we'll get him back later."

"So where's Maggie?"

"Visiting her sister," said Dawson as he dabbed his steak in a bit of horseradish, finally getting his first bite. *Oh God yeah!* He pointed at the rib eye with his fork. "Fanfriggintastic."

"Not bad if I do say so myself," replied Red, taking a sip of beer.

"Hey, don't act as if you raised, slaughtered and aged the thing." Dawson winked at Bryson, eliciting a giggle.

"Hey, I'll have you know if it weren't for my barbecuing skills you'd be eating a slab of charcoal right now."

"Hey, I thought we agreed we wouldn't talk about that ever again!" cried Shirley, mock horror on her face.

Dawson laughed. "The one time you cooked the steaks—"

"Cooked? I did a quick recon for the flamethrower. Ow!" Red reached down and massaged where Shirley had kicked him. He looked at Dawson. "BD, I think I'm injured. I'll have to sit out the next op."

"Suck it up, princess."

His phone vibrated in his pocket. He pulled it out and frowned.

Everyone became silent, even Bryson stopping in mid-chew, he far too familiar with their lives constantly being interrupted with the job.

"Hello?"

"Mr. White, you're needed at the flower shop."

"Twenty minutes."

He pocketed the phone and attacked his steak. "I've got five minutes to stuff this in me."

"I can pack it up for you if you'd like," offered Shirley.

"What, and fail the challenge in front of me?" mumbled Dawson through chews, his hand covering his mouth.

Bryson pointed. "Hey! He talked with his mouth full."

Dawson turned and opened his half full mouth at Bryson. He laughed.

"BD, you're just encouraging him!" admonished Shirley.

"Sorry," he mumbled, winking at Bryson.

"What do you think it is?" asked Red as he took his time with his own steak.

Dawson shrugged as he swallowed. "Probably an op."

"Do you think Mike will have to go?" asked Shirley, reaching out and squeezing her husband's hand.

"Depends on the op. If it's just a four man team, I've got Niner, Jimmy and Atlas on deck." Dawson stuffed another piece of steak in his mouth then reached for his beer. "Oops, better not."

Red was in mid sip. "Shit, yeah."

"I'll get you two some water," said Shirley, heading for the kitchen.

"This is why I'm a firm supporter of the space program," said Red as he shoveled some potato salad into his face.

"Me too. The day we meet the damned Ferengi and get the recipe for synthehol, the world will be a better place."

"Amen to that," said Red, smiling at his wife as he took the glass of ice water she was handing him.

"What's syntheball?" Bryson didn't look at them as he asked the question, he instead holding his finger above his head, a piece of processed cheese on the tip of it.

"All the reward, none of the punishment," replied Dawson as he finished the last bite of his steak.

"What's that mean?"

"Your dad will explain it to you when you're twenty-one," said Shirley.

"If you're anything like your dad, it'll be a lot sooner than that." This time Dawson got kicked after a smiled glare from Shirley.

Bryson shrugged, sucking the cheese off his finger.

Dawson wiped his mouth with the paper napkin and rose, waving off Red who began to stand. "If it's nothing, I'll be back."

"It's never nothing."

"True dat."

"Who are you, Niner?"

Dawson laughed at the mention of their Korean American comrade. Sergeant Carl "Niner" Sung was the life of any party and the quickest wit he had ever met. He was also one hell of a sniper.

"If you tell him I said that I'll deny it to my grave." He bowed slightly to Shirley. "Thank you, as always, for a delicious dinner."

"You're always welcome, BD. I just wish you didn't have to rush off."

He shrugged, eyeing the salad still on his plate. "You know—"

Shirley leapt to her feet. "I'll get you a container and a fork."

He grinned at Red. "I'll eat it at the stop lights."

"There's no lights between here and The Unit."

"Stop signs?"

"Main gate, maybe. Just don't eat it in front of the Colonel. You know what happened last time."

"Yeah, how could I forget!" The last time he had arrived chowing down on some of Shirley's cooking from a Tupperware container the Colonel had made him phone Red and bring him some.

Shirley had only been too happy to prepare a plate.

They all respected the Colonel, and he them. Colonel Thomas Clancy was a soldier's soldier who understood combat and the risks that came with it. And he always had their backs. Even when they were on an op where if caught their government would deny they knew anything about them, Clancy would be working the back channels to free them.

He strongly believed in the 'no man left behind' doctrine.

Shirley appeared with a Tupperware container and quickly filled it with salad and made a jab at what remained of her husband's steak.

He blocked her fork with his knife. "Hey, I've killed for less."

"He has," agreed Dawson, laughing. He took the container and fork, thanking her. He looked at Bryson. "See ya later, little man."

Bryson stood on his chair and saluted. Dawson snapped him a quick salute and headed for his car parked in front of the Belme residence. Just the sight of his prized 1964½ Mustang convertible in original poppy red, handed down to him by his father, brought a smile to his face. He jumped in, revved the engine and hit the gas, the tires giving a pleasant chirp as he glanced at the salad on the passenger seat.

And already his spine was tingling with excitement in anticipation of heading out once again.

I love my job!

Leaving Freetown, Sierra Leone

"Your friend better not give us away," said Major Koroma as the driver geared down for the approaching checkpoint. It was dark now, the area lit by harsh lights, their glare bathing the entire area in a clinical blue-tinged white, several flashlights now playing across their windshield as the guards approached.

Tanya whimpered and Sarah squeezed her hand. "Put your head on my shoulder, pretend to be asleep." Tanya's head quickly dropped onto her shoulder, her entire body still trembling. Sarah had pleaded with Koroma not to kill her, convincing him that if he needed doctors, Tanya was one of the best.

He had spared her life.

Which had confirmed one thing to her.

If she had been taken because of *who* she was, she had also been taken because of *what* she was. The fact this argument had saved Tanya, and they were riding in the front of a three vehicle convoy loaded with medical supplies in an Ebola stricken country, meant there was more than one motive at play.

She was certain a ransom demand of some sort would be forthcoming, she fully expecting to have to read some prepared statement condemning her father and the American way of life while pleading for money for some bullshit cause. She was pretty sure Koroma had called the driver Muhammad, and this being a majority Muslim country, she wouldn't be surprised if these were Islamic terrorists, beheading Jacques certainly a dead giveaway. During her briefing before coming here she had been told of the growing problem of Muslims burning Christian churches and murdering those they considered infidels. They never expected a problem in Freetown, most people living peacefully, especially with the shared misery of this epidemic. The biggest danger now was from communities turning on their neighbors that were infected or suspected to be infected.

Which was why every single patient who was either confirmed not to be infected, or cured, was given a certificate proving they had been tested free of the virus.

As the truck came to a stop, two police officers walked up to the passenger side window, obviously knowing the man in charge never drove. They demanded something in Krio, a language Sarah found curiously frustrating because she spoke English and French fluently, could pick out at least a quarter of the words, but was usually left baffled as to what was actually being said. Major Koroma, sitting at the passenger side window, responded then jerked a thumb at her.

"Explain your business," said one of the policemen when she leaned over, Tanya's head sliding down her arm.

She should've used the driver's shoulder.

"We're doctors from Médecins Sans Frontières. We're transporting supplies to the Port Loko Ebola Treatment Center."

The man took a step back. "You infected?"

She smiled, as disarming a smile as she could manage under the circumstances. "Absolutely not, none of us are. We're merely delivering supplies."

The man's partner frowned. "What's wrong with her then?" he asked, motioning toward Tanya with his chin. "She sick?"

Sarah shook her head. "No, just dead tired. We worked all day today in protective gear. It can reach forty-six degrees Celsius in there."

The man's head bobbed in agreement. "Yes, it's true, my brother, he works at a clinic. He said it is extremely hot." He stepped back and waved them through. "Good luck, doctors."

"Thank you," replied Sarah as the driver put the truck in gear and pulled away. No one said anything until they had placed a good quarter mile between them and the checkpoint. Koroma watched in the side view mirror then turned to the driver.

"We're clear."

Tanya gasped, suddenly bolting upright, Sarah having forgot for a moment that she had been faking sleep. Tanya leaned toward her and whispered in her ear. "I think I peed my pants."

Sarah took Tanya's hand in hers and squeezed. "It's okay, I did earlier." She reached over with her other hand and gently pushed Tanya's head onto her shoulder. "Get some sleep, you're safe for now."

"There will be several more checkpoints before we reach our destination," said Koroma, holstering the weapon she just noticed he had been hiding in his lap. "We'll reach the village in the morning."

Sarah leapt on the revelation. "Village? What village?"

Koroma frowned. "No place you've ever heard of, I assure you. No place my government has ever heard of apparently either."

"Is there an outbreak there? Is that what the supplies are for? Why you've taken us?"

"*You've* been taken because of who you are, Dr. Henderson. The fact you're a doctor and your friend is just means you'll survive longer."

"So you intend to kill us."

"Yes."

Tanya whimpered.

Sarah's chest tightened and she felt her bladder threaten to give way again.

"Why?"

"Once you've served your purpose, we'll have no need for you."

"Why not let us go? Why kill us?" She was trembling now along with Tanya, each feeding on the other's fear.

"Enough questions."

"You know who I am, that means you know who my father is. He's a very powerful man. If it's money you want, you'll have it."

Koroma laughed. "Money? You think that's what this is about?" He shook his head. "Silly Americans. You think the entire world revolves around your almighty dollar. This has nothing to do with money."

"Then what does it have to do with?"

Koroma pulled out his gun and placed it on the dash. "Enough questions."

Sarah closed her eyes but there would be no sleep for her. Her mind was racing with what Koroma had said. She had been kidnapped because of her father, and the fact she was a doctor. It sounded like they might be put to use treating Ebola patients in Koroma's village, but she was stunned at the revelation it had nothing to do with money.

Yet not at all surprised they were going to die.

Daddy, help us!

1st Special Forces Operational Detachment - Delta HQ, Fort Bragg, North Carolina
A.k.a. "The Unit"

Dawson had managed to chow down half the salad in line at the main gate and was shoveling the last few spoonsful into his mouth as he hurried toward the Colonel's office. It was too much food, Shirley having put way too much in the container, but he didn't mind. God only knew when he'd see a decent meal again if he was sent on an op.

He nodded hellos to various personnel, The Unit a tightknit community of operators and support staff. They numbered nearly a thousand, his Bravo Team merely a dozen men, all Non-Commissioned Officers who had gone through some of the most intensive training known to man.

And their support staff was the best of the best, all experts in their own rights, and all people he trusted and knew he and his men could rely on.

Including the Colonel.

He walked into the Colonel's outer office and placed the container and fork on Maggie's desk, the woman he hadn't yet acknowledged he loved, but had a sneaking suspicion he might just actually, away at her sister's. She had been gone three days and he had to admit he missed her. It was different on an op. He might be gone days or weeks, but that was part of the job. It was different when she was away. He realized it was a double standard, but part of him felt she should, or would, always be there when he was home.

Now maybe you know how the better-halves feel.

He doubted that. They had only been dating a few months. People like Red and Shirley had been married coming up on ten years.

Ten years!

He couldn't imagine that.

He grinned in the mirror Maggie kept on her desk, confirming he was free from parsley surprises, then knocked on the Colonel's door. It was a Sunday and there was no secretary, if that's what they were called anymore. He had never actually asked Maggie what her job title was, but he was pretty sure calling her a 'secretary' was some sort of faux pas. He'd have to remember to ask her when she got back, just in case he was ever asked what she did.

She works for the Colonel.

That had been his response the one time he had been asked. It was his sister when she had detected a different tone in his voice a couple of weeks after he began seeing Maggie—or more accurately, Maggie had begun seeing him. She had been the one to chase him, and he had tried to ignore it for as long as he could but had finally given in, she simply too gorgeous and too nice to disregard forever.

It wasn't until his sister had said he sounded happier that he had realized he was. He had always dismissed the idea of a long term relationship, his job too dangerous. He respected the men that did get married and start families, but he had been to far too many funerals where the grieving widow was handed the folded flag to ever want to risk doing that to someone.

And it had left an empty hole inside him that he hadn't realized was there.

Until Maggie.

Shit, you've got it bad!

He knocked again.

"Enter!"

He opened the door and stepped inside, closing it behind him. "Good afternoon, Colonel."

"It's Sunday and I'm here. There's nothing goddamned good about that if you ask my wife."

Dawson chuckled, taking a seat, the Colonel not one for formalities when alone. If the brass was in town, or some honcho from Washington, he'd go through the motions, but here, in The Unit, with his men? Never.

Clancy shoved an unlit cigar in his mouth, chomping on the head.

"I thought you quit."

Clancy looked down at the stogie. "I have."

"Uh huh."

"Hey, as far as my wife is concerned, I've quit. And as far as I'm concerned, unless there's smoke coming out of the end of it, I'm not lying."

Dawson raised his hands in defeat. "Hey, I'll never come between a man and his wife. Or cigar."

Clancy grunted, pulling the cigar from his mouth, staring at it. "When the hell did these things ever become bad for you?"

"Probably around the time the war on cigarettes was pretty much won."

Clancy nodded, stamping the unlit cigar out in his clean ashtray. He shook his head as he caught himself. "Now they want to tax candy bars and potato chips." He glanced back at the cigar. "Perhaps dying early from lung cancer isn't such a bad thing."

"When they start taxing fun, I'm moving to Cuba."

"You mean sex. And if they start taxing that, I'm joining you."

"Bringing the missus?"

"As long as you're bringing Maggie."

Dawson smiled then shrugged. "You never know."

"Hmmm. You better not lose me a perfectly good secretary."

Secretary!

"She's a big girl."

"Yes she is, with a heart of gold. And the best damned assistant I've managed to find. Don't eff this up!"

Assistant?

"It's only been a few months, sir, I think we're getting a little ahead of ourselves."

"Riight. That's what I said to my buddies when I started dating Cheryl. Thirty years later and I still don't know what the hell happened."

"Shotgun wedding?"

"Nope. But if her pappy was still around, there'd be shotguns involved if I ever tried to divorce her."

"Let's hope they don't bring in the tax then."

Clancy chuckled, grabbing the cigar and shoving it back in his mouth. He jabbed a finger at a folder on his desk, pushing it toward Dawson. "Vice President's daughter is missing in Sierra Leone. She's a doctor, volunteering for two months with Doctors Without Borders at an Ebola treatment center. A male doctor, French national, was found beheaded in her quarters. She's missing along with a female Ukrainian national, also a doctor. This is from the top. They want you in Sierra Leone like yesterday. Find her, get her out of the country, and they don't care what you have to do to get it done."

"Team?"

"Four man, your choice."

"I'll take Niner, Jimmy and Atlas."

"Good choices."

"Cover?"

"You're Diplomatic Services. You'll be permitted side arms and that's about it. But if the need should arise, you can get supplied from the USS Simpson. Details are in the file."

"When do we leave?"

"In six hours."

"Any leads?"

"Nothing yet, but hopefully the CIA will have something for you by the time you get there."

"Do we have a motive? Any ransom demands yet?"

Clancy shook his head. "Not a peep, but it just happened earlier today. They might be still securing them."

"So no idea who's behind it."

"Negative, but there is an Islamist problem in the area."

"Church burnings if I'm not mistaken?"

Clancy nodded. "Now that their civil war is over, it's given them a chance to remember that the country is over twenty percent Christian. That just doesn't sit well with some people."

"Too many people."

"Too true, but it's not our job to judge, that's God's."

"And it's our job to arrange the meeting?"

Clancy laughed. "You know, I talked to Stormin' Norman about that. He never said it. Loved it, but never said it."

"Too bad, it fit him."

"Fifty years ago they would have blamed Patton." Clancy suddenly became serious, looking straight at Dawson. "Listen, we don't know who took her or why. All I do know is that Ebola is running rampant there. You need to be damned careful, all of you. The last thing I need is one of you becoming infected. The paperwork will kill me."

"If the paperwork doesn't, Maggie will."

Clancy leaned back in his chair. "She's the first one who's managed to get her claws into you without having her heart broken in sixty mikes. How are you feeling going out on ops knowing that she's back here, waiting for you?"

Dawson shrugged. It was something he had been asking himself, and to be perfectly frank, he felt it hadn't impacted his ability to do his job at all. He still took the necessary risks, still did whatever it took with the same regard for his own life as he had been trained for. Just because he was sent by his country on dangerous missions didn't mean it expected him to die for it. It spent millions of dollars training people like him to do just the opposite. Dying for your country was a necessary risk, but never an expectation, not in today's battlefield. Casualties would happen, but everything would be done to avoid them. Gone were the days of throwing infantry at fortified positions in the hopes that eventually someone would break through.

Could a war like that happen again?

With the way Russia kept doing moronic things, he sometimes wondered. There were only three countries he could think of where mass casualties might arise should there be a conflict. Russia, China and North Korea. They were about the only countries with standing armies that could be a genuine challenge, but none had anything America would want, so any altercation would involve fighting them on soil foreign to both sides.

Poland, Taiwan, South Korea.

He shifted in his seat, realizing Clancy was waiting for an answer. "I can't say it's really affected me. I just focus on the job as always. During the downtime I think about her, but it's no different than it is for the rest of the guys who have wives or girlfriends back home."

"No, but you've always been a loner."

Dawson nodded. "True. But I've always had family, my men, The Unit." He paused, his eyes narrowing. "Why, you worried about me?"

Clancy chuckled. "Not at all, Sergeant Major, not at all. The day I start to worry about you is the day you're out of The Unit."

Dawson smiled. "Trust me, sir, you'll have my resignation first."

"Of that I have no doubt." He pointed at the door with his cigar. "Now go, and be careful. Leave the viruses where you found them."

Dawson rose giving the Colonel a slight bow then left the room, glancing at Maggie's empty chair.

And wondering what it was going to be like going into a true hot zone for the first time with someone back home he cared about.

CIA Headquarters, Langley, Virginia

Chris Leroux combed through thousands of hits to the search requests he had input, his eyes occasionally glazing over forcing him to sit back and blink a few times. It wasn't that he was tired, it was just staring at the screen all day.

And it had been *all* day.

His entire team was working overtime, half now, half for the night shift, trying to find some bit of intel that might lead to the Vice President's daughter but so far there had been nothing. But he knew it was just a matter of time. MYSTIC had been activated, the National Security Agency system capable of recording every single phone conversation in an entire country. Currently, unbeknownst to the Sierra Leonean government, their entire country was being eavesdropped on. And as the computers sifted through the phone calls, converting them into text where possible, flagging calls with certain keywords, satellites and listening stations around the globe were pushing reams of data into Echelon, another system much older than MYSTIC that recorded every single phone call, among other methods of communication, made from outside the United States.

The data was there, or it would be. Someone would mention something, and someone would eventually catch it.

The key was catching it in time.

And recognizing it for what it was.

There was a rap on his door.

"Enter!"

He still felt a thrill of imitating one of his heroes, Captain Jean Luc Picard. Yes, he was a geek, and proud of it. Well, maybe not *proud* of it, since he had led a pretty sheltered, lonely life because of it. But he loved his Star Trek, Star Wars, Stargate, Battlestar and pretty much anything else with 'star' in it, and he wasn't going to change.

The door opened and he smiled as his girlfriend, Sherrie White, entered carrying a bucket of the Colonel's finest. "I brought you some dinner since I knew you'd be working late," she said as she stepped inside, closing the door behind her. She gave him a peck then placed the bucket and a large KFC bag on his desk, removing her jacket and hanging it on the coatrack in the corner.

He took a moment to appreciate her fantastic curves while she was looking away.

She caught him.

"See something you like?"

He looked away quickly, his eyes shifting to the large brown bag of food, the KFC logo emblazoned on the side, grease stains already permeating through the paper, the aroma causing his empty stomach to growl in appreciation.

If women wanted men to pay more attention to them, perfume should smell like fried chicken, not flowers.

"You're thinking about the fried chicken perfume again, aren't you?"

He felt his cheeks flush. "You know me too well." He stood, opening the bag. "I should patent it like Dylan says. We'd be rich."

"Bah, being rich is too complicated. I like our lives the way they are."

He looked inside. "Christ, how much did you get?"

"You said half your team was here, so I got enough for everyone."

"Maybe I better get on that patent," he said as he removed two large boxes of French fries. "This must have cost a fortune."

"It wasn't too bad. Besides, my raise just came in."

"A whopping one percent like mine?"

"Yup. But I still get to shoot guns and blow things up, so my meagre salary to keep our nation safe is still acceptable."

"When I agreed to let you move in I figured you'd be making James Bond type money. I had no idea your salary would be half mine."

She shrugged. "If you're marrying me for my money, you're wasting your time."

Marrying!?!

She looked at him, a smile on her face. "Did I scare you with that word?"

He shook his head a little too quickly. "No, I mean, um, no."

She laughed. "Don't worry, honey, I'm not Beyoncé. You don't have to put a ring on it to get some of this." She slapped her ass. "But it wouldn't hurt," she said with a wink, opening his office door. "Chris bought KFC!" she called, immediately eliciting excited, hungry outbursts. His office was quickly filled with the four people who were working the classified search engines with him.

"Thanks, boss!" said one of his senior analysts, Marc Therrien, as he took the paper plate Sherrie handed him. Chicken, fries and potato salad were dished out and everyone stood around, eating and making idle chitchat, Sherrie, far more outgoing than Leroux, having everyone in stitches with a tale from her training at Quantico. Like Leroux, most of his staff were more the introverted type, but Sherrie simply had a way of putting people at ease.

One of the many reasons he was desperately in love with her.

Perhaps marriage isn't such a bad idea?

The thought terrified him. And excited him. He never would have imagined he'd even have the option of getting married, he a loser in his own mind, his friends all online besides Dylan Kane, a CIA Special Agent who had taken him under his wing when they were kids at the same high school.

And because of Kane's job, he almost never saw him.

Sherrie falling for him while on assignment was the best thing that had ever happened to him, and he was terrified every day that she might change her mind. But it had been almost two years now and they were still going strong.

Maybe it's the fact we're both potential targets of The Assembly.

He dismissed the thought. The Assembly, a secret organization he had accidentally uncovered that claimed to have been around for centuries if not longer, manipulating world events to their liking, was his top secret side project that Director Morrison had assigned him to. Since the organization had shown no qualms about killing, he was under 24 hour guard.

His only truly private time was in the confines of his apartment, though it was swept before he entered by his detail.

He hadn't left a sink full of dishes since it started.

"What's that?" asked Therrien, pointing to Leroux's screen. It was flashing with a priority hit result from one of his searches. He sat down, putting his plate aside and opened up the details.

And smiled.

"This could be it," he said, the entire room gathering around the monitor. "A large amount of medical supplies were stolen just hours before the kidnapping. Looks like they posed as soldiers and the dockworkers just loaded the supplies into the back of their transport trucks."

"Could have actually been soldiers for all we know," said Therrien.

"True." Leroux quickly entered another search and pointed at the result. "But real soldiers don't need to steal their own transport trucks. Three were reported stolen an hour after the supplies were picked up." He printed off the details then turned to the room, the food forgotten. "Okay, here's what I want. Check for any hits thirty minutes on either side of the two thefts in the same geographic area. We might get lucky if someone used a cellphone or radio to initiate the theft or to notify someone of their success. Start pulling satellite imagery, CCTV footage, everything. We need to find those trucks." He stood up, shaking the pages. "I'm going to see the Chief. We might just have our first real lead."

The room emptied save Sherrie. He smiled at her sheepishly. "Sorry, hon, but dinner's going to have to wait."

She stepped over and gave him a kiss that threatened to awaken something tucked away at the moment. "I love it when you get all boss-like."

His cheeks burned as he searched for something to say. "So what are you going to do?" he finally asked as she stepped out of the office, he following.

"Head home, watch some Netflix." She smacked him on the ass. "Now go save the world." She winked and slinked off, putting a wiggle on for his benefit.

I'm the luckiest man alive.

Sung Residence, Mango, Florida

"Aww, Umma!"

Sergeant Carl "Niner" Sung feigned mock exasperation at his mother. She wagged a wooden spoon at him. "Set the table. That's your job."

"But I don't live here anymore, Umma. I'm a grown man!"

"Nonsense. You'll always be my little boy. Now go!" She ended the conversation with a jab of the spoon, pointing toward the dining room. Niner stood up from the kitchen table, his shoulders slumped in defeat, then stomped from the room, winking at his dad who merely shook his head then the newspaper he was reading.

"Don't provoke your mother. I'm the one who has to live with her after you leave tomorrow."

Niner switched to tip-toes, his nephew giggling and pointing. "Uncle Carl funny!"

Sergeant Jerry "Jimmy Olson" Hudson shook his head. "I have to work with that." He rose, following his buddy to the cabinet where the family kept their dinnerware.

Niner smacked his ass, making a kissing sound. "If you don't like it, you can always ask for reassignment."

"Then who'd keep you out of trouble."

"I never get in trouble."

Jimmy laughed. "With that mouth? It's a wonder you have your original teeth!"

"I'll have you know this mouth has saved both our lives on more than one occasion."

"Right, like the night you chose your new nickname."

"Hey, it's not my fault those rednecks decided to get into an intellectual debate unarmed."

"Is that what you're calling it now? An intellectual debate?"

"What's an interlectial rebate?"

Jimmy turned to Niner's nephew, apparently unsure of what to say.

"Now whose mouth is getting us in trouble?" Niner grabbed a stack of plates and handed them to his friend before turning to his nephew. "It's where stupid people open their mouths, and smart people like your Uncle Carl shove their foot down it."

"Carl!"

Niner cringed at his mother's shout. "Sorry, Umma!"

Jimmy grinned.

The night in question had started off as a celebration, the twelve man Bravo Team heading out to a bar for some brewskies, but instead encountering a group of "intellectuals", one of whom took a disliking to Niner's Korean American heritage, hurling some fairly lame racial epithets at him including slant-eyed.

Niner had responded with a string of gems, including Nine Iron.

Embarrassed, the man had taken a swing at a Delta Force operator.

Further reinforcing the notion he was an idiot.

Niner had dropped him with one punch, the man's friends joining in, triggering a melee that the regulars at the bar still spoke of to this day.

And Niner had insisted his new nickname be Nine Iron. Dawson had wisely shortened it to Niner over time.

Niner liked the story of how he got his nickname, it rare that you got to choose your own, but no one was going to turn him down.

Jimmy on the other hand…

Someone had found out that Jimmy was the editor of his high school newspaper. Jimmy Olson had been the result. Dawson's Big Dog had been something from basic training, matching his initials. He knew Dawson hated it, but that was part of the charm.

You never knew what you would end up being called, and quite often, you didn't like it.

So when an opportunity to pick his own had come along, he had jumped at it.

Some weren't bad. Red had been given his nickname because of his red hair and wasn't the only one named because of a physical trait. Mickey's ears, Jagger's lips, Spock's eyebrow and Atlas' physique had all earned them monikers that he wasn't sure they were happy with at first. Now they were just names, none of them really thought about their meaning anymore.

His was the only one he knew of though that had been earned after punches were thrown at him. None had landed, but they had been thrown.

He finished setting the table with Jimmy, Jimmy having visited the Sung household enough times for them to have a routine that worked. They were done within a few minutes.

"Dinner is in five minutes. Everyone wash up."

The heavy pounding of nieces' and nephews' feet filled the air as a lineup quickly formed at the single bathroom of the modest bungalow. His family wasn't rich by any means and was barely middle class anymore. They had been forced to downsize when their mortgage had come up for renewal during the crisis at a value higher than the house was worth. His father had been forced to do what millions of other Americans had done.

He declared bankruptcy.

They walked away from everything they had built and rented this house. His father had been lucky to keep his job as an accountant and they were one year away from having the blemish removed from their credit history, at which point they hoped to buy another home.

It was something his father never discussed, but his mother did on rare occasions, never when her husband was within earshot.

He was ashamed.

In Korean culture, as in any, losing one's home for any reason was one of the supreme embarrassments. In fact their relatives back in Korea had no idea why the change in address had occurred.

It simply wasn't discussed.

Niner had felt terrible when he heard the news. He had offered to help but his father had refused to even hear his pleas to save the family home he and his siblings had been raised in. Always practical, his father had said the house wasn't worth the amount of the mortgage, the bank refused to refinance for the full amount until housing prices recovered, so rather than try to borrow the difference, which would wipe them out financially regardless, it was actually better to wipe the slate clean. He wasn't too concerned with the ramifications on their credit history since millions upon millions of Americans would have the same blemish on their records. If banks didn't want to issue credit to this massive minority of the population for seven years, then that was their loss.

Things hadn't worked out the way his father had planned, that much was clear since they were still renting. His mother had told him once that his father was saving for as large a down payment as he could, wanting to take on as small a mortgage as possible so they couldn't get burned again. They were in their early fifties and he didn't want to be saddled with a large mortgage for the rest of their lives.

It made sense, but the fond memories he had growing up in the family home were all that were left. He'd never see it again, never see the room he had spent more than half his life in, never sit in the backyard he used to play in, never drive the streets he had learned to drive on.

When he had heard the news he had let himself cry for a few minutes, a mix of self-pity and the shared pain and embarrassment he knew his mother and father must be going through.

They had moved during the night.

One day they were waving to the neighbors good morning, the next day they were gone, the shame too great to face people they had formed relationships with for decades.

The Sungs had simply disappeared into the night.

It had been hard on the family, hard on the marriage, but his parents were traditionalists—divorce was never in the cards. They had weathered the tough times and he was certain his father would have them back in a home they owned soon, in better shape than they had been before the crisis.

He had faith.

As he washed his hands in the sink he looked in the mirror and frowned at what he saw. He was tired. They had just come off the op yesterday, rushed to Florida after the debrief to salvage what remained of their weekend plans, leaving little time to rest.

And he never slept well here.

It just wasn't home.

They say home is where the heart is, but his heart was back where he had grown up. He loved his parents and loved seeing them, but this house wasn't his home. He envied some of the guys who had grown up military. They truly did understand the concept that home was the family, not some building you slept in. Bouncing around the country and sometimes the world with their father or mother, living in half a dozen different towns or cities growing up, they learned to make friends quickly and never become attached to the room they slept in—it may change the next day.

But Niner had grown up in only two homes—the first he was too young to remember, then the family home he had spent over fifteen years in before leaving to join the army.

Something that his father had been intensely proud of. He had wanted his son to become an accountant like him, but math had never been Niner's passion. He could do it, he just didn't like it. Whether it was some sort of rebellious reaction to the subject his father loved, or that he was simply more interested in physical work, he wasn't sure. All he knew was he had been drawn to the military, especially after 9/11. His country was hurting and he felt a duty to help it heal—by confronting those who would hurt it.

And the best way he could think of was to join the military and defend his country from those who would do it harm.

It hadn't taken him very long to set his eyes on Delta.

His phone vibrated in his pocket. He pulled it out and saw the call display. *Uh oh.* He swiped his finger. "Go for me."

"Need you back here ASAP."

"Got it. Jimmy?"

"Yup."

"Okay, he's here with me. It'll take us a bit. We're at my folk's place in Florida."

"Helo's waiting for you at MacDill."

Niner's eyebrows popped. *Must be important.* "Okay, on our way."

He hung up and stepped out of the bathroom, waving his phone at Jimmy. "That was BD. We've been called up."

"Any details?"

Niner shook his head. "Nope, but must be important. There's a whirly bird a waitin' for us."

It was Jimmy's turn to be surprised as he pulled out his own phone. "I'll check the news for any buzz."

"I'll break the news to Mom." He started to walk down the hall when Jimmy grabbed him by the arm. "What?"

Jimmy lowered his voice. "Ask her for some take-out."

Niner's eyes narrowed, a smile creeping up half his face. "Just cuz we're Korean doesn't mean we own a restaurant. Why don't you bring your dry cleaning next time?" Jimmy blanched causing Niner to laugh, smacking his friend on the shoulder. "Just kidding, buddy, you should see your face. Of course I'm asking for food. I don't want this trip to have been a complete waste." He jerked a thumb over his shoulder. "Grab our gear, I'll be a minute."

He continued down the hall to break the news.

News all too familiar in the Sung household.

Somewhere in Sierra Leone

"Wake up!"

Sarah Henderson felt a none-too-gentle jab in her side as she was startled awake. She opened her eyes and was momentarily disoriented, forgetting where she was, but as her eyes came into focus the terror of her new reality gripped her chest tight.

She had been abducted with her friend, forced to lie their way through checkpoints while on their way to their eventual death.

She couldn't imagine it getting any worse.

That was until she looked over at Tanya and saw the terrified expression on her face. Sarah looked down and saw the driver's hand caressing Tanya's leg.

She nearly vomited.

She felt her own mind beginning to shut down, to protect itself against what might be to come. Her arms wouldn't move and her chest was so tight she felt immobilized, as if a massive weight were pressing her into the back of the seat.

She closed her eyes, already unfocused as she imagined them both being gang raped for days or weeks on end until they both eventually died from the ordeal.

She could imagine nothing worse.

Except perhaps dying from Ebola.

Ebola.

The thought hooked her, her downward spiral halting for just a brief moment as her mind focused on the line that had been tossed it by her subconscious.

Ebola.

Death from it was horrendous, painful, lonely. But it could be fought with some success. And so could this situation. They couldn't win against these men if they were determined to physically harm them, but Major Koroma had implied their expertise as doctors was partially why they were here.

You can't repeatedly rape your doctors and expect them to save your people.

Reality rushed back as a modicum of hope resurfaced. She turned to Koroma and pointed at the driver's hand. "Are you going to allow that? I thought you were supposed to be an honorable man?"

Koroma leaned forward and looked, snapping some curt words at the driver whose hand immediately darted away.

"Thank you," she said, wrapping her arm around Tanya's shoulders, pulling her tight against her as the poor woman sobbed.

She's going to be of no use.

She was already mentally broken and Sarah feared if her friend didn't snap out of it soon she might not be able to serve any useful purpose beyond being a piece of meat for the letches they could find themselves surrounded by.

"We're going to be okay," she whispered in her friend's ear. "You need to think of your family. You need to be strong for them if we're going to survive this. Just keep thinking of them, okay?"

There was no response, but she did feel Tanya's chest heave as a deep breath was sucked in and held.

At least it was something.

The truck came to a stop, it now pitch black, artificial lights few, flaming barrels and torches more common, the stars brilliant in the night sky, the new moon nowhere to be seen. Major Koroma climbed down then held out his hand for her. She decided it was best to take it. If she could establish some sort of connection with this man—a non-sexual connection ideally—he might take pity on them. Her goal was survival, and if that meant sleeping with the man, she might just do it, though the very thought disgusted and enraged her.

If I were a man this wouldn't be happening.

She took a breath, helping Tanya down.

If I were a man I'd be dead already.

She shouldn't have to use her sexuality to save her life, but at this moment she could only think of three things she had to offer. Her father's money, her skills as a doctor, and her body.

She hoped the first two would suffice but Koroma had certainly indicated they wouldn't.

She jumped as they were suddenly surrounded by a group of men, handshakes exchanged as the other two trucks pulled up. Flashlights played around the group and the sounds of a sleepy village beginning to stir, lights and lanterns being lit around them suggesting many more might be about to join them.

Which was never good in an Ebola plagued country.

Crowds meant death.

And these people didn't seem to understand that.

She turned to Koroma. "If you have an Ebola problem here, I suggest nobody shake hands or touch, and you minimize the size of the crowd."

A floodlight flicked on and Koroma's face was suddenly visible, a frown creasing it, his eyes suggesting concern. He nodded. "Keep everyone in their homes. I need three crews to unload the supplies, everyone else home. I don't want to risk spreading the disease."

A hush descended upon those gathered as they seemed to recognize the foolishness of what they had done. Shouts erupted and the sounds of doors slamming shut could be heard up and down the street they were on as three crews were hastily chosen, the unloading beginning within moments.

"Follow me."

Koroma led them toward the only building that seemed to have some lighting. A dilapidated sign in front indicated it was a community center, but someone had spray painted the word 'Ebola' over 'Community'. A skull and crossbones had been tacked underneath it.

A sense of foreboding swept over her as she felt a shiver race up her spine. She was in regular clothes, no protective gear, and they were about to enter what might be a building loaded with Ebola patients.

She grabbed Koroma's arm. "Wait."

He turned. "What?"

"Are there infected people in there?"

"Yes."

"We're not properly dressed. We need personal protective gear."

"My people have never been provided them by your governments, so why should *you* get them?"

She paused, thinking of a suitable response to counter his political argument. She smiled. On the inside. "The longer we stay free of infection, the longer we'll be able to help your people. If we get exposed, we could be useless within days and no help to anyone. Let us treat your people properly and we may be able to save many of them."

This argument seemed to at least give Koroma pause.

"What do you suggest?"

She pointed at the stack of supplies quickly forming. "Don't bring any of that inside." She stepped toward the pile and spotted what she was looking for. "You have the proper gear here. We'll need to inventory everything we have, but first we need to see what's happening inside. Let us suit up and do an assessment, then I'll be able to tell you everything we need to do."

Koroma looked at her for a moment, saying nothing. It began to make her nervous. He finally spoke. "You realize cooperating won't save your lives."

A pit formed in her stomach, but she fought it off. This was the early minutes. If she could prove their worth, their chances of survival would increase. And the longer they stayed alive, the more likely they'd be rescued.

For she had no doubt her father would stop at nothing to rescue her.

But she couldn't tell Koroma that.

"I'm not doing it to save our lives. I'm doing it because I'm a doctor, and I took an oath."

Abbotts Park Apartments, Fayetteville, North Carolina

"Baby, if you keep feeding me like this, I might just have to marry you."

"Don't you be making promises you're not going to keep, Leon."

Sergeant Leon "Atlas" James smiled as he tucked into another slice of lasagna. His girlfriend was going to culinary school and this week was Italian food.

And he was loving it.

In fact he couldn't think of a type of food he didn't like and he had tried pretty much everything in his travels. He had met Vanessa six months ago at the grocery store. He was picking up a couple of hundred hamburgers and buns for a Unit barbecue, she was picking up the ingredients for her first cooking assignment.

They had both arrived at the cashier at the same time.

He had let beauty go first.

And a conversation had resulted.

Hamburgers were a little late that day.

He held up his beer as she sat down. She lifted her glass of chianti and they clinked. "To the cook!"

She smiled, took a sip and cut off her own first bite with the edge of her fork. Chewing, she swallowed and shook her head. "Not enough Italian seasoning."

"Bah, it's perfect."

"Of course you're going to say that. You just want sex later."

"Baby, you know you can't resist me, so telling you the truth is risk free."

"Mighty full of ourselves, aren't we?"

He swallowed another bite. "I have it on good authority that I cure whatever ails you."

She smacked his shoulder, giggling. "You're terrible."

"My mama says I'm perfect just the way I am."

"I've met your mama. That woman spoils you like nobody's business."

Atlas bit into a piece of garlic bread. "Right now, baby, you're spoilin' me."

"Don't compare me to your mama. I don't need that kind of pressure."

Atlas laughed, crumbs erupting from his mouth as his hand darted up to try and deal with the aftermath of the accident. "Don't make me laugh when my mouth is full."

"You shouldn't talk with it full then."

He reached over and squeezed her leg, lowering his voice. "You're beautiful, baby."

She put her fork down and placed her hand on top of his. "I know," she said with a wink. "And I also know this needs more Italian seasoning." She jumped up and grabbed a pencil, making a note on the page containing the recipe.

Atlas' phone vibrated in his pocket, the distinct pattern indicating work.

Shit.

He had been looking forward to a quiet night in with his girlfriend, yesterday's plans already screwed up by the hostage taking in Norfolk. He fished it out of his pocket and answered.

"Hello?"

"Sorry, buddy, but we've been called up." It was Dawson delivering the news.

"Understood."

"Not again!" cried Vanessa.

"You at Vanessa's?"

"Yup."

"How much time do you need?"

"How much time do I have?"

"You're a machine, my friend. Niner and Jimmy are coming in from Florida, so you've got a couple of hours."

"Vanessa thanks you."

"I'm sure she does. See you at The Unit."

The call ended and Atlas returned his phone to his pocket, looking at Vanessa.

"So?" she asked, sitting back down.

"I'm needed at The Unit."

Her shoulders slumped. "Sometimes I hate your job." She shook her head. "Can't they logisticate or whatever the hell it is you do without you?"

Atlas laughed. "Logistics. I help coordinate the delivery of supplies to our troops across the world. I guess there's an op or something that they need stuff organized for, and us Sergeants do the grunt work while the officers sit at home with their wives, sipping their fine wines, eating their store bought lasagnas that aren't anywhere near as good as the one prepared by my incredibly talented girlfriend."

She melted.

All was forgiven.

"How much time do you have?"

"Two hours."

"Then eat up, big boy, you're going to need all the energy you can get."

He grinned, shoveling the food into his mouth, determined to give his girlfriend a great time, her status of *not* being his wife meaning she couldn't know the truth about what he really did for a living.

Which meant their entire relationship was built around a lie.

And he hated that.

Somewhere in Sierra Leone

Sarah Henderson stepped through the door, Tanya behind her, Major Koroma following them both. Sarah and Tanya both were in full personal protective gear but the Major was only wearing a facemask, refusing to don the proper equipment.

Fool. I hope you die.

As a doctor she found her thoughts repugnant, but this man was repugnant. He was a criminal and deserved to die. Her father had raised her to respect the law and she had always felt it was better to be tough on criminals rather than hug them to goodness. She was a firm believer that the smaller crimes like vandalism and theft should be punished far more harshly to nip the behavior at an early age. She had been known to express her feelings that vandals should be shot because these people served no purpose in society. At least thieves were stealing to profit, but vandals were merely out to destroy.

She didn't really believe they should be shot, but vandalism angered her so much she felt a good baseball bat to the knees was definitely in order.

And the mentality of thieves she simply couldn't fathom. To think you were entitled to someone else's hard earned belongings was unthinkable to her. A few years ago when she and her husband had moved to a new home they had to transport the propane tank for the barbecue themselves, but the car was simply too full.

She left it on the doorstep.

They came back an hour later and it was gone.

Who would have the brass to walk up to someone's doorstep and steal a propane tank?

And what had really floored her was that it was a residential street with almost no traffic. She was convinced it had been a neighbor walking by that spotted it and felt they were entitled to it. They would have had to take it and carry it down the street for all to see.

And this was an upper middle income area.

If only I had my baseball bat and caught them!

Men like Major Koroma definitely deserved the death penalty. She tacitly supported it but had reservations. Far too many innocent people had been put to death over the years, even more luckily found innocent before it was too late. If the proof was irrefutable, then sure, murderers should meet their maker's fallen angel, but what was irrefutable? DNA evidence could be planted, even faked now, video evidence could be edited or faked, witnesses could be mistaken or lie.

Better to let them rot in prison for the rest of their lives just to be sure.

She secretly prayed some American Special Forces sniper would put a new hole in Major Koroma's head for what he had done to Jacques.

And for what he had promised to do to them.

Koroma opened a door and flicked a switch on the wall, the room suddenly bathed in a bright, sickly white light. She blinked a few times, shielding her eyes with her gloved hand, allowing her eyes to adjust.

Then she gasped.

It was a large, rectangular room, a stage at the head of it, clearly what used to be some sort of community hall. There were a few beds but most of the victims were lying on the floors, some on blankets, others on the cold concrete. Few had pillows or any type of creature comforts. The air was thick, as if the windows hadn't been open in weeks, and the stench was unbelievable.

Their suits protected them from accidental exposure to fluids, but they breathed the same air as the patients, these stolen suits having no air filters.

She wasn't worried about contracting the disease this way, but more from desperate people tearing at her suit.

Hands reached out as the patients began to wake, realizing that help might have finally arrived as the two doctors advanced slowly into the room. Some started to sit up, others trying to stand, their desperation clear.

"Keep them where they are, Major, otherwise we'll have to leave."

Koroma pulled out his side arm and yelled something. The patients hesitated, a few resuming their advance, almost like zombies.

He fired a shot into the floor.

A few screams, more weak cries, followed by whimpers.

And those who had been advancing returned to where they had been lying, many in pools of their own blood, sweat, urine and feces.

"This is unbelievable," said Tanya, almost sounding like her old self. "These poor people. How can you let them live like this?"

Koroma turned on her. "Do you think we do this by choice? We have no alternatives. The government won't provide us with supplies and they are too sick to bring to the treatment centers. Those that aren't, we try to bring there but they are always full." He pointed at those around them. "These are my friends and family. I grew up with them all. I serve my country with honor and distinction, yet my country turns its back on my home. And you"—he spun, pointing his finger at Tanya then Sarah—"are also responsible. Your countries do almost nothing to help us. You spend hundreds of billions to make war yet balk at spending millions to save possibly hundreds of thousands of lives."

"We're trying now," replied Sarah. "And people like us were here long before this became an epidemic."

"You are the exceptions. And unfortunately there are too few of you, too late."

Sarah knew there was no arguing with the man because he was right. The West had dropped the ball. Organizations like hers had begged Western governments for money but little to none had come until thousands were dead or dying. This could have been stopped early if the funding had been made available, but with nothing of strategic or economic interest in these countries, there was no perceived benefit.

Until it arrived on Western shores.

All it took was one infected man to lie to the authorities and the first case of Ebola arrived in America.

And America and the rest of the Western world woke up.

Albeit still too slowly.

All the stops were pulled out back home of course. Over a million dollars was spent on each of the Ebola patients back there to try and save them. Here in Sierra Leone it seemed like pennies.

She looked at Koroma through her mask and could sense his desperation. She wondered whether or not he had been a good man at one time and was now driven to desperate acts to save the ones he loved.

But she could never condone what had been done to Jacques.

"Let us help you, here, now. Maybe we can save some of these people, and perhaps stop it from spreading to others."

Koroma looked at her and nodded. "What do we need to do?"

Sarah put her hands on her hips, slowly turning.

"Is there another place where we can move these people?"

"No."

"What is the weather forecast for tomorrow?"

Koroma shrugged. "Sunny and warm."

"No rain?"

"No."

"Good. First we need to clean this place, top to bottom."

"How?"

"Do you have bleach or some other cleaning supplies?"

"We have bleach. And I know where to get more."

"Good. Water?"

"We have several good wells."

"Excellent. Get us as much bleach and water as you can. We'll need to move these people outside as soon as it's warm enough. Anybody who's strong enough to move themselves and help others, we'll use. Anyone else, we'll need to suit up some volunteers."

"Are you crazy? You want to let the infection out of here?"

"It's spread through bodily fluids, not the air." She pointed at the windows. "And that's another thing. We'll need all these windows opened. We need these people to get fresh air, especially at night so we can cool this room down." She looked at Koroma. "Can you get volunteers?"

He nodded. "My men are from this area. Some of their families are in here as well. They'll help."

"Good. Then let's get started."

Number One Observatory Circle, Washington, DC

Residence of the Vice President

"I don't care if you have to invade the goddamned country, I want my baby back home, now!"

Philip Henderson held his wife, tight, battling his own tears. The news about his daughter had been a shock, an emotional rollercoaster no parent was ever prepared for, and one no parent could understand unless they had been through something similar.

Fortunately most parents in America didn't go through something like this.

Unfortunately too many did.

They had been crying and talking and arguing for hours, interrupted constantly by phone calls with updates on the investigation's progress—or lack thereof, and they were both exhausted. He had immediately driven home to tell his wife the news while his aides arranged meetings with everyone that needed to be informed or pulled in to help. He had met the President who had pledged his full support, immediately authorizing deployment of a Delta Force team. With the assassination of the Sierra Leonean Vice President the day before, he—and his advisors—had a feeling the two events were related. What wasn't known was whether or not it was in retaliation for the death, or in conjunction with it.

Frustratingly, there had still been no communication with the kidnappers.

He kissed the top of his wife's head. "I promise I'll do everything I can to bring her home safe."

"This is all your fault," she sobbed, her words punctuated with her hyperventilating breaths. "You never should have gone into politics."

He shook his head, ignoring her angry, ridiculous words. He had been in politics for over forty years, before they had even met. And if anyone were to blame it was Sarah for going to Sierra Leone in the first place.

He mentally kicked himself for the thought.

He was proud of what she did, though he actively tried to convince her to go to safer places. Ironically he had thought Sierra Leone might actually be safer than some of the war zones she usually found herself in. Things were quiet there now that the civil war was over and Ebola had settled down the Muslim on Christian violence. It had never occurred to him that she might get kidnapped.

His wife pushed away, retreating to the far end of the couch. "What are you doing about it?" She grabbed a tissue and blew her nose.

"CIA, NSA, everyone's on it. And you didn't hear this from me, and you're not allowed to tell anyone—I mean *any*one—we're sending in Delta."

"What's that?"

He stopped himself from smiling. His wife was well-read and well educated, but she had a habit of avoiding stories on terrorism, which meant her exposure to the Special Operations world was limited.

"They're Special Forces. The best."

"Like those seal thingies I keep hearing about?"

"Navy SEALs, dear. Sea, Air and Land teams, and yes, like them."

"Only better?"

"You'll never hear me say that," he said with a smile.

She didn't appreciate the humor. "You joke at a time like this?"

He wiped the smile off his face. "Of course not." He took in a long breath, thinking of what to say that might help reassure her without pissing her off. "We're doing everything we can and will have boots on the ground by tomorrow. They'll find her, that's what they do."

His wife jumped to her feet and held out a hand, stopping him from rising. "No, I need to be alone. In the morning I want to be formally briefed on what's being done to bring back my daughter."

"But—"

"Just do it!" she screeched.

His mouth dropped open but he didn't dare say a word as she stormed off. Instead he waited for the bedroom door to slam shut then pulled out his phone, dialing his aide to arrange a briefing her security clearance—or lack thereof—would permit.

It would be a dog and pony show, but as long as she felt included, and it looked impressive enough, it might just reassure her enough that the job she blamed for getting her daughter into trouble, might just be the one that could save her.

And the hollow in his stomach was making it crystal clear that he too needed the same reassurance.

The Unit, Fort Bragg, North Carolina

"Sorry for ruining your weekend, boys."

Dawson stood at the front of the small briefing room, Niner, Jimmy and Atlas at the table. A flat screen had the Joint Special Operations Command logo spinning on it, each man with their own laptops in front of them with the classified files loaded.

"My mom has placed an old Korean curse on you," said Niner. "Either your first born will have a third leg or you're going to lose all your hair, I'm not sure which."

Jimmy snorted. "Ron Jeremy's dad must have been cursed by a Korean then."

Atlas spit his coffee at the door.

Dawson shook his head, chuckling as he swiped his thumb, killing the screensaver. "Okay, *gentlemen*, and I do use the term *very* loosely, here's the situation." He quickly gave them a briefing covering everything known to this point.

"How confident are we that she's alive?" asked Atlas, his voice reverberating through the room. Dawson swore there was a Jurassic Park ripple in his coffee.

"We're hoping she's been abducted, along with the Ukrainian national, not just because of who she is, but what she is. If they want a doctor, my guess is they're not going to kill her any time soon."

"Makes sense," agreed Niner. "And there's no chatter?"

"None, which is odd. They seem to have a complete communications lockdown on this. My guess is that it's a small, dedicated group and all messages are being delivered personally."

"No uptick?" asked Jimmy.

"Huge, but that started within minutes of their VP being assassinated."

"And the survivor from Norfolk?"

"I'm heading over to interrogate him in five mikes." He nodded toward Niner. "You'll come with me. Atlas, you and Jimmy put together an equipment list. Cross reference with the USS Simpson. Anything they don't have, bring it. We've been delayed until 0900 tomorrow so there's plenty of time to get it right then get some rack time."

"Why the delay?" asked Jimmy.

"We're hitching a ride with a forensic team and they couldn't get their shit together as fast as us."

Dawson snapped his laptop shut, signaling the end of the meeting. He rose and headed for the door, the others following.

"Do you think we'll get anything out of the prisoner?" asked Niner at his side.

Dawson shook his head.

"Not a peep."

Leroux & White Residence, Fairfax Towers, Falls Church, Virginia

Chris Leroux's four man security detail had already checked the route to his apartment, a routine that had long ago become tedious for him, but was still necessary due to the threat from The Assembly. The worst they had ever found was someone passed out in the stairwell, but as the lead agent had told him, that drunk could be someone merely pretending in the hopes of being ignored.

It was the only time he hadn't been allowed into his own home.

Tonight however was uneventful. Sherrie was already home and had texted him she was awake so a coded knock was used, the pattern changed based upon the day of the week then randomized every four weeks.

Sherrie opened the door, her lithe figure wrapped in a housecoat, revealing nothing but her smile.

"Hey, Baby!" she said, pulling him inside.

Leroux turned to the two men who had accompanied him, the other two covering the foyer. "Thanks guys, I'll see you tomorrow morning."

The lead agent gave a two fingered salute. "Have a good night."

Sherrie closed the door and pulled Leroux by the hand to the couch. She pushed him into the seat then crouched in front of him, grabbing his left shoe.

"What's all this?" he asked, not sure what was going on. She removed his shoe then moved to the other, this something she had never done before.

She shrugged. "I was watching an old movie, saw the wife do this for her husband when he came home." The other shoe was set aside. *Husband!*

She took his foot and pushed his leg up, resting his heel on her shoulder as she began to massage his feet.

He moaned as he closed his eyes and leaned his head back. "That feels amazing."

"Thought you might like it." She switched to his other foot, her thumbs kneading away the tension built up over a long day in dress shoes. She let go of his foot, gently placing it on the floor then pushed his legs apart, scooting forward, her head deliciously close to his lap.

"Just what kind of movie was this?" he asked as he opened his eyes and looked down at her, his heart rate picking up a few beats as something stirred below.

"Just an old Bogart flick." She lay her head on his crotch and it was everything he could do to not squirm in delight.

"Somebody's happy to see me."

"Uh, can you blame me?"

"I wasn't talking to you."

He laughed as she sat back up, removing her housecoat, revealing her completely naked body underneath.

Lift off.

"Something tells me you've been watching more than old movies."

She climbed up the couch and bit his lip, her breath hot on his face as he reached up to embrace her. She grabbed his arms and shoved them back against the couch. He struggled slightly, the thrill of the restricted movements only enjoyable if he didn't actually try too hard to win.

She pulled back, just a few inches, her hands clasped around his upper arms, pinning him in place. He leaned forward, just his neck, trying to reach her lips, but she pulled away just a little bit more.

"You want some of this," she whispered, staring into his eyes as she seductively licked her lips.

All he could do was nod, the ability to speak forgotten.

Suddenly his left arm was free as her hand darted down below, squeezing.

He moaned.

And his phone vibrated in his pocket, the familiar pattern of the office signaling an end to their fun.

She felt it too.

She fished the phone out of his pocket, frowning, but not letting go of the death grip she had on his most favorite body part. She handed him the phone.

"H-hello?"

"Hey boss, we got an ID on that face." It was Sonya Tong, one of his analysts, a girl he was pretty sure had a mini-crush on him.

"Who is he?"

"Major Adofo Koroma. He's in the Republic of Sierra Leone Armed Forces."

"Do we have anything else on him?"

"Nothing yet. We've requested info from the Sierra Leoneans so hopefully we'll have something in a few hours."

Leroux looked down as his fly was unzipped.

His mouth went dry.

"O-okay, run his name through everything we've got. And don't wait for the Sierra Leoneans—just hack their system. See if there's—oh my gawd!" He leaned back as Sherrie took him to a different world.

"Are you okay, boss?"

"Um, yeah. See if there's any connection to the suspects in Norfolk—ugh—and get back to me if you find any—oh gawd—thing else."

"Okay, boss. You sure you're okay?"

"Yeah."

He ended the call.

And rolled his eyes into the back of his head.

Providence Hospital, Washington, DC

"Let me guess, if you told me who you were, you'd have to kill me?"

Niner grinned as the FBI agent handed back their IDs. "We'd feel bad about it, I assure you."

The man shook his head, a slight smile appearing. He pointed to the elevators and began to walk. "I'm Agent-in-Charge McKinnon. We've got the prisoner under guard on the third floor."

"Has he said anything?" asked Dawson, noting the heightened security. There was no pretense of keeping it unobtrusive today, not with such a high profile terrorist event. Armed, uniformed police and FBI were at every entrance and patrolling the halls, IDs being randomly checked.

Tension was high.

With nobody claiming responsibility, but it not a lone wolf one-off, the assumption had to be they were part of a larger, coordinated group and that they might want their man back.

Or dead.

No risks were being taken, not with him possibly being the only person left alive in the country who might know where the Vice President's daughter was.

"He hasn't said a peep, not even the usual anti-Western kill-all-the-infidels-Allah-is-great garbage they usually spout. This guy's been completely silent."

The elevator doors opened and they boarded, an armed officer standing at the rear. He nodded at the new arrivals. McKinnon hit the button for the third floor as the guard stepped forward, waving off anyone else from boarding. The doors closed.

"Interesting," observed Dawson. "Even at the hostage taking their demands seemed secondary. Makes me wonder if this is Islamist related at all."

McKinnon shrugged. "Ninety-nine times out of a hundred it is, but there's always that one and this could be it." The bell chimed and the doors opened, more armed guards challenging them. They handed over their IDs. "If it isn't Islamists, I don't know how I feel about that. The last thing we need are more nutbars bringing their hate over here."

Dawson stepped aside as a male nurse boarded the elevator, snapping off a pair of latex gloves before pressing the button for the ground floor. Dawson followed McKinnon toward the room just as an alarm sounded and a Code Blue was announced over the speakers. Several medical personnel raced past causing them to hug the wall, two pushing what he assumed was a crash cart.

"Shit!" McKinnon bolted toward the door the team had just rushed into, Dawson and Niner following, the two guards on either side of the door looking confused. "What the hell's going on?"

Nobody inside the room answered, instead vital signs were being shouted out as a doctor prepared the paddles to shock what looked like their suspect. Dawson glanced at the monitor.

Flatlined.

"I thought he was stable!" said Niner, stepping back into the hallway.

"He was!" McKinnon was grabbing at his hair, walking around in a circle. Dawson grabbed him by the shoulder, pulling him gently out of the way of one of the medical personnel as they rushed from the room, yanking their gloves off and tossing them into a nearby garbage bin.

His mind flashed back to the nurse who had boarded the elevator. The man had taken his gloves off in the elevator, something that didn't make sense now that he thought of it. Any contamination could be spread by not disposing of them immediately after leaving a patient's room.

And where was he going to throw them out?

And if racial profiling was of any benefit today, the man had been black, just like their terrorists.

"It's the nurse," he said, looking back toward the elevators. "Where's the stairwell?"

McKinnon froze for a moment, then pointed to the far end of the hall. "End of the hall, left. What nurse?"

Dawson took off at a sprint. "Make a hole!" he shouted, shocked medical personnel jumping out of the way as he could hear Niner's footfalls right behind him. "The nurse who got on the elevator as we got off! Find him!" he shouted over his shoulder, McKinnon's jaw dropping for a moment before he grabbed his radio.

Dawson rounded the corner and spotted the door for the stairwell. Shoving at the bar, he threw the door open and took the stairs two at a time, grabbing the railing and swinging his legs over to the flight below. The elevator had been indicating it was going down, that much he was certain, he remembered the red light above it when they got off. The man wasn't in any hurry at the time, and would probably try not to draw any attention to himself, so a calm, steady pace was what Dawson was hoping for.

They burst through the ground floor doors and into a busy hallway, much to the surprise of the public in their way. Dawson pulled his ID as he approached two guards. "You two with us!" he ordered as he blew past them. He had learned long ago that simply acting as if you were in charge was enough for most soldiers and law enforcement to fall in line.

And these two did.

The four of them tore toward the elevators, Dawson keeping his eyes peeled the entire time.

"Anything on our suspect?" he asked over his shoulder.

"Negative," replied one of the officers.

Dawson rounded the corner and spotted the doors of the elevator he had taken earlier beginning to close.

"Hold that door!" he shouted, diving toward the elevator, skidding along the tile floor. His hand caught one side of the door just as it was about to close, halting his skid as they closed over his fingers.

He winced.

But the safety mechanism kicked in and the doors opened, Niner advancing with his weapon drawn as Dawson jumped to his feet, the other two officers, not sure what was going on still, pulling their own weapons.

Dawson looked inside, knowing full well their suspect wouldn't be there.

That wasn't why he had stopped it.

He looked at the officer riding the elevator. "Nurse, male, black, got on at the third floor just as we were getting off. Where'd he go?"

The man looked startled for a moment, then his eyes narrowed as he tried to remember. "He got off here. Went left."

Main doors.

Dawson bolted toward the main entrance, pointing at one of the officers. "Call it in, last spotted on the ground floor heading toward the main entrance. We need someone on the cameras, now!" He didn't bother making sure the officer was following his orders, he simply knew he would. The split second he would waste making sure the man actually grabbed his radio and relayed the correct information could mean the difference between stopping their man before he climbed in a getaway vehicle, or watching that same vehicle pull away, out of range.

"Make a hole!"

They shoved through the main doors, hitting the cold autumn air of Washington. It was nighttime but the area was well lit allowing Dawson to scan the area left to right. There were scores of people within sight. His eyes came to rest on a garbage bin, something light green catching his attention. He pointed. "Check that."

One of the officers grabbed the item and held it up.

Nurse's top.

"He's not wearing a jacket!" He ran down the steps and farther away from the building, his trained eye rapidly scanning and dismissing candidates, wrong color, wrong sex, wrong build.

Bingo!

He pointed. "There he is!"

He sprinted across the several lanes of traffic, a taxi almost taking him out, honking his horn and shouting at him. The screech of the tires and the blast of the horn were loud enough for the suspect to turn to see what was happening.

And realize that he was made.

The man sprinted for the parking lot, keys being fished from his pocket. Dawson took his eyes off the man and instead focused on the cars, watching for flashing lights, listening for the chirp of an alarm system disengaging.

Lights flashed to the left, the man obviously not remembering exactly where he had parked.

Dawson sprinted toward the car rather than the man, saving precious steps in the race, the sound of feet pounding behind him, orders being shouted over the radios by the officers, told him there was no way their suspect was getting away.

But they needed him alive.

Dawson drew his weapon.

"Halt!" he shouted, his weapon aimed directly at the man's chest.

The man continued to run, reaching his car, Dawson within fifty feet. The man yanked his passenger door open, a red flag raised as Dawson realized he was going for something in his glove compartment. There could be only one possibility.

"Gun!"

The man spun, the weapon gripped in his hand. Dawson resisted shooting him, wanting to take the man alive.

But he wasn't given the option.

The man raised the gun to his chin and looked directly at Dawson.

"For my people!"

He squeezed the trigger, the gun firing, tearing a hole through the top of his head. He collapsed to the pavement in a heap, a pool of his own blood quickly forming as Dawson arrived, kicking the gun aside.

Niner knelt down beside the man and checked for a pulse, a useless but necessary gesture. He shook his head.

"Goddammit!" Dawson kicked the tire of the man's car then stepped back.

Niner holstered his weapon, shaking his head. "It looks like we're going in blind."

Somewhere in Sierra Leone

Sarah was impressed. The spirit of these people, even the sick, was inspiring. When the sick and dying had been told of what was needed of them, those who could walk hadn't hesitated to help the others, especially once it was explained to them that if they could move themselves, it could help prevent the spread. She and Tanya had helped since they were suited up, but nobody else had been needed. Volunteers had set up blankets on the ground outside and the thirty-three people inside were moved out into the open.

Half a dozen volunteers in protective gear first swept up everything inside, the supply trucks used to take it a mile outside of town to be burned. Water hoses and pumps were then used to spray everything down, bleach mixed in with the drums of water to try and disinfect every surface. It took hours, but when it was done, it was unrecognizable.

"Now we can try to save some lives," she said to Tanya, her arm over her friend's shoulders. Focusing on the work had resulted in Tanya staging a remarkable recovery. They were both exhausted, but the day was young, it barely noon. The women of the village had set up tables in the street and food was being brought out for the volunteers, the entire community contributing, but avoiding contact, her warnings apparently being heeded.

She just hoped those preparing the food weren't infected, or living with someone who was. She had insisted Major Koroma personally confirm the households that were contributing food were free of obviously infected people, and he had obliged her, she getting a sense that the progress they were making was actually encouraging him that there might be hope.

"We need to set up a triage area," she said. "We'll put the dying at the far end of the room and make them as comfortable as possible. Those we think we can save we'll put at the center, and those we're not sure are infected we'll put at the front."

Koroma frowned. "Why put them together? Don't you risk spreading the disease?"

"No. You only enter through this door at the front of the room, and exit through the rear. Each section will be separated. We'll hang sheets to delineate the areas. In the first area we keep each person isolated from each other as best as possible so that if someone is infected, they don't spread it to others. Once we've confirmed they are infected, we move them to the next area and try to treat them. That section is only for people already infected, so we don't need to worry about spreading the disease from the first section to the second, nor do we need to worry about spreading from the second to third areas, since they're infected as well."

Tanya spoke up. "The key is to never move backward. Never move from the second area to the first. And to reinforce the habit, never move from the third to the second. Always only move forward, that way you never risk moving the infection back."

Koroma's head was bobbing as he seemed to grasp the concept. "It makes sense." He motioned toward the wall that had the infected patients on the other side of it, still resting in the sun. "And what of them? Are any well enough to be treated?"

Sarah nodded. "Yes. My initial assessment is nineteen of them might be able to be saved. You have to understand, the mortality rate is as high as ninety percent, but with proper care we've been able to bring that down to about fifty percent if they're reached in time. I'm afraid that we should be expecting closer to the ninety percent since we don't have any IV fluids to treat them."

"What's that?"

"Essentially water with some additives," replied Tanya. "It's to keep them hydrated, restore their electrolyte balance. We need to keep them comfortable, hydrated, and fed if they can keep anything down. We need to let their bodies fight the virus and hopefully win. If someone wins the battle, then we need to get them to fully recover so they can donate blood for the sick."

"Donate blood? What do you mean?"

Several men entered the room in shorts and t-shirts, the protective gear no longer necessary since it had been disinfected. They were carrying ropes and sheets. Sarah smiled and walked to about where she wanted the first line run. "Please run a line across here," she said, motioning with her arm. She walked toward the other end, stopping about thirty feet from the far wall. "And another line here. Don't hang them too high. The sheets need to reach the floor."

The men set to work as Tanya continued to explain to Koroma how the immune system worked and the concept of antibodies. "Those who've beaten the disease have the cure within their blood. We can take that blood and transfuse it into the sick. If we catch it in time, the antibodies will go to work and help fight off the illness. If we're lucky, those people get cured, and they too can become donors."

Koroma was shaking his head. "Amazing. I had no idea. We have several people who were sick and are now cured, but they have been shunned by the others in the village. Everyone assumed that these people could still make the others sick."

Sarah frowned. "Unfortunately that's what most people think, but it's like any virus. Once it has been beaten, the virus is gone, but the antibodies remain, just in case the virus were to return. About the only risk is that men can infect their partners for up to seven weeks after they have been cured."

Koroma's eyebrows jumped at this revelation, but he said nothing. They watched as the ropes were strung, the sheets thrown over the tops, their staged quarantine zones quickly taking form.

"What's next?" he asked.

"Everyone out there is sick, of that there's no doubt. We bring those we think we might be able to save in through the rear door and into the second area, then those we don't think we can save through the same door, into the third area. That will keep this area clean. It is essential that nobody who has been in those two areas come here. I suggest you post a guard."

Koroma nodded. "Done." He paused a moment. "You said it is spread through bodily fluids."

"Yes."

"How?"

"Blood, mucus coming into contact with open wounds or mucus membranes like the nose or mouth, usually from coughing, sneezing or bleeding onto someone or onto a surface that is later touched by someone."

"Blood. So if an infected person's blood were to get into a healthy person's blood, they would become infected."

"There's a very good chance. It's highly contagious."

"And how would you get this blood into another person's blood?"

"It doesn't really need to work that way. They could swallow it, for example. The infected people begin to bleed heavily as their cells break down. If they sneeze for instance, it can send a mist of blood that someone else could breathe in. Quite often it's spread because someone touches an infected person's blood when they're trying to get them to a hospital. They then rub their eyes, their mouth, or have an open cut." Tanya threw up her hands. "There's just so many ways, the only real protection is the gear we were wearing earlier."

"What would happen if an infected person's blood were injected into someone else's?"

"Why would anyone do such a thing?" cried Tanya. "It would be madness! Murder!"

Koroma waved his hands. "No! No! No! You misunderstand me. I mean from a needle, if you were to get pricked, through your gloves."

"Oh, sorry," apologized Tanya. "They could become infected, of course. If the needle did have some of the virus on it, and of course the more blood the better chance, then yes, they could become infected. Most likely *would* become infected."

Koroma frowned then turned toward the windows as a woman's voice called out. "Lunch is ready," he smiled. "We should eat now, while we can. There is much work left to do." He marched out of the community center, Sarah pleased to see he actually followed her instructions, leaving through the rear exit.

Tanya looked at Sarah. "Let's eat, I'm famished!"

"Me too," said Sarah, following her friend to the rear of the building, albeit a little slower as she mulled over the conversation.

She felt a chill race up and down her spine.

But she wasn't sure why.

Leroux & White Residence, Fairfax Towers, Falls Church, Virginia

Chris Leroux leaned against the acrylic shower wall, letting the piping hot water roll down his back. He had managed to get a good number of hours sleep, work only contacting him once indicating they couldn't access the Sierra Leonean databases because a power outage in Freetown had taken down the servers. He hadn't heard anything since which meant he'd be going in for his regular shift—probably at least twelve hours straight.

He didn't mind, he loved it.

And besides, it was for a good cause. They needed to track these terrorists to make sure there wouldn't be any more attacks, and they needed to try and find the Vice President's daughter and by extension the Ukrainian national. It didn't matter how many hours he had to put in, if they were successful in recovering either of them, or preventing another attack, it would all be worth it.

"Call for you."

Leroux turned off the water, quickly shaking the water out of his hair with his fingers. "Who is it?"

"Sonya."

Leroux stepped out, grabbed a towel and rapidly dried his hair and head. Taking the phone he smiled awkwardly as Sherrie took the towel and began wiping him down.

"This is Chris."

"Hi, sir, it's Sonya. We finally got into those servers. Not too much on the major that's of interest except that his wife and son died recently of Ebola, and that he's from the same geographic area as the hostage takers in Norfolk."

"That sounds like too much of a coincidence."

"Agreed. You heard about the shooting last night?"

"What shooting?"

"Sorry, the Director said to let you sleep, but I figured you'd somehow know since you seem to know everything."

"Ahh…"

"Sorry, boss, that came out wrong. Anyway, the terrorist that survived was murdered in his hospital bed last night—looks like an air bubble was injected into his IV. Anyway, security caught up to the guy who did it. Turns out he was an employee at the hospital for almost ten years. Clean record, model employee. Blew his head off!"

"Who, security?"

"No, he blew his *own* head off."

"Holy shit! Did he say anything?"

"You mean like the standard Allahu Akbar?"

"Yeah."

"No, nothing Islamic. He said, apparently in perfect English, 'For my people'."

Leroux frowned. *For my people?* That was something he couldn't recall ever being said by an Islamic fundamentalist before killing themselves. Usually they shouted the standard greeting on their way to Hell, or quoted some piece of scripture, but 'For my people' sounded political rather than religious. And he had never heard the term 'people' being used by one at all. Everything in their religion was couched in terms of Allah or Mohammed with almost all acts, whether good or evil, being done in their names.

Never 'for my people'.

"Interesting," he finally said, his voice distant as Sherrie's ministrations were momentarily forgotten.

She seemed to notice. "What?"

He didn't respond.

She yanked his junk.

He jumped, looking at her. "Huh?"

"What?"

He held up a finger. "Just a second. Sonya, I'll be there in thirty. Have the team ready for a handover to the day shift. Try to find out everything you can on this hospital worker and spread the net out. See if we can find anybody whose immigrated from that area in the past, oh let's say twenty years."

"That could be thousands."

"Could be, but at least we'll have a pool to work from."

"Got it, boss."

Leroux hung up then turned to Sherrie who playfully tossed the towel into his face. "What's the latest?"

"The surviving gunman was murdered last night in his hospital bed and the murderer blew his own head off."

"I guess I should have let you listen to the radio this morning instead of jumping your bones."

He blushed. "Yeah, well, missing the news sometimes has its benefits."

She smacked his ass cheek sending a delicious shiver through his body. "Good answer." She turned the water to the shower back on. "Give me ten minutes, I'll come in with you."

"Okay, I'll let them know."

He sent a text message to the security detail stationed outside to give them the heads up then began to dress, listening to the radio as he did so.

And still not listening.

For my people.

The connotation of those three words was eating at him.

I don't think this has anything to do with what we think it does.

Somewhere in Sierra Leone

Major Koroma sat back and belched, patting his stomach. It was the best feed he had eaten in some time. He smiled at the grandmother who had fed him.

"Fantastic as usual!"

She smiled, holding out a bowl with more food in it. "You must eat, you're still a growing boy!"

He tossed his head back and roared in laughter, his men joining in, the two female doctors at the far end of the table looking on curiously, the entire conversation in Krio. "I haven't been called that in quite a while!" he said. "But I've had enough. Save the rest for the sick, they need it more than us."

The old lady's face clouded over, the gaiety of the brief mealtime masking the dire situation they found themselves in. He turned to his second-in-command, Amadu Mustapha, who had arrived only minutes before from Freetown. "Has there been any word?" he asked, his voice lowered though still loud enough for everyone at the table to hear.

"Yes. The Americans are angry, demanding answers from our government—exactly as we expected."

"They must be going mad that there's been no demands."

Mustapha chuckled. "You should hear their news reports. They don't know what to do. Washington is denying any connection between the Vice President's assassination and the kidnapping of her"—he nodded toward the end of the table at Sarah Henderson—"but the media isn't hesitating."

"Making up the facts as usual."

"Again as we expected."

"And what is the official response from Washington?"

"They're sending a team of forensic experts, FBI, to examine the crime scene. They should be arriving later today."

"Military?"

"None that we know of."

"Any word on who killed our people?"

"No, but CNN is saying it was military, and if it was, they're also saying it could only be Delta Force."

"And what of Sekou, is he still alive?"

Mustapha shook his head. "No. I had him eliminated. We couldn't risk having him talk."

"He was your cousin, wasn't he?"

"Yes. He would have killed himself if he had the opportunity, I'm sure."

"I have no doubt. He was a good man. Family?"

Mustapha frowned. "Wife and three young children."

Koroma sighed. "The sacrifices we make today will hopefully make the lives of all our children easier in the future."

"I hope you're right, but I have my doubts."

Koroma shifted in his seat, examining his friend and confidante. "Why haven't you said anything before?"

"I have, Adofo, I have, but you would not listen. You have been set on this plan from the beginning." He raised a finger, cutting Koroma off. "Don't for a moment think that I don't support you and your plan one hundred percent. All I mean is that I don't have the same confidence that the results will be what you expect."

Koroma's head bobbed slowly. His friend was right. As a commanding officer he was used to having to express everything with confidence, as a leader in his community doubt could never be expressed. But Mustapha was right. There were no guarantees and success was a long shot. If they succeeded in what they hoped to accomplish, their names would definitely go down in history, as would Sierra Leone. The question was whether or not the infamy of their actions would spur the change they hoped.

When desperately poor people struck out at the mighty nations, not in the name of some religion but in the name of human decency and mutual respect, would it trigger a sea-change in public opinion among Westerners more concerned today with preserving their lifestyles than with the misery five billion of their fellow human beings lived in?

He put his hand on Mustapha's shoulder, lowering his voice and leaning closer. "I too have my doubts, my friend, but we must try, otherwise millions more will continue to die."

"Then let us proceed." Mustapha pushed his plate away, looking at his friend. "When do you leave for America?"

"Soon."

CIA Headquarters, Langley, Virginia

"What have you found?"

Leroux swiped the touchpad on his laptop, his palms sweating like they hadn't in months. Dating Sherrie had given him a newfound confidence that was failing him today. The Vice President himself and his wife were here, and over speaker was the commander of the Delta Force team that would be acting on his intelligence, along with untold others from the Pentagon, White House, NSA and every other agency that had been brought in to try and rescue Sarah Henderson.

It was more pressure than he could remember ever dealing with.

Except maybe that first date with Sherrie.

He thought back on how they had met, how she had been assigned to try and seduce him, to see if he would spill agency secrets, all as a test by Director Morrison to see if he could trust him.

He had passed, spurning the advances of the hottest woman he had ever met, and by far the sexiest woman who had ever tried to get biblical with him.

It had shocked him, her and the team assigned to protect her.

What he hadn't known at the time was she had been having second thoughts about her mission. She was certain he wasn't a mole and was quickly developing feelings for him, even calling her handler to try and get the mission called off before being ordered back into her living room to sleep with him, to pump him for information about his friend and CIA operator, Dylan Kane.

He had gone home with the worst set of blue-balls he could remember, but had done the right thing. The truth had crushed him—devastated him.

Learning that she was merely coming on to him as part of an assignment had been the final blow to his already fragile ego. He had never wanted to see her again, see any woman again.

It was Kane who had recognized that they both loved each other and forced them together.

And he had been happier than he could ever remember since.

But the pressure today was getting to him. His orders were to provide the results of the intel but not how it had been obtained since the Vice President's wife didn't have the proper clearances. Under normal circumstances she would never have been allowed in the room, but when the President calls and insists, you listen.

And he's probably listening in too.

Leroux pointed to the screen which now showed a picture of Sarah Henderson and Tanya Danko. "Our two subjects are Sarah Henderson and Tanya Danko. Both are volunteer doctors with Médecins Sans Frontières working out of the Hastings Ebola Treatment Center in Freetown." He clicked the button and an image of Doctor Jacques Arnaut appeared. "Yesterday evening local time the body of Dr. Arnaut was found nearly beheaded in Miss Henderson's quarters. It is believed that she and Dr. Danko were abducted together at the time of the murder."

"How can you be sure?"

It was Mrs. Henderson that asked the question, her voice cracking slightly.

Leroux looked at her then clicked a button bringing up a timeline of events. "Perhaps this will help. We know that both Dr. Henderson and Dr. Danko exited the quarantine area at approximately the same time. The log book shows Dr. Henderson completed decontamination at 7:35pm local time, Dr. Danko five minutes later. Dr. Arnaut had finished exactly thirty-two minutes before them. According to witnesses in the decontamination area, the two doctors intended to get together for dinner after Dr. Henderson made a call home."

A cry escaped from Mrs. Henderson.

"We know that call was never made, so we assume the events that took place happened within minutes of her entering her room. We also know that Dr. Arnaut had gone to the communications tent and was told of a missed call from Dr. Henderson's husband. He said he would give her the message, and we believe he then went to her quarters to deliver said message." He hesitated. "I must warn you, the next photos are graphic. I suggest you look away, Mrs. Henderson."

She squared her jaw and shook her head. "No, I'll be fine."

He nodded. "Very well." He clicked the button and a picture of the crime scene was shown, copious amounts of blood on the floor, arterial spray on the walls.

"Oh my God!"

She shouldn't be here. Neither should her husband.

"I apologize for the graphic images, but they're important." He clicked the button again and a close up of a wall was shown. "These images were taken by MSF staff under FBI direction. You can see there is a void in the spray pattern. We believe that Dr. Henderson was standing between the wall and Dr. Arnaut when the fatal blow was struck. A preliminary autopsy by MSF staff indicates he was stabbed from behind by a large blade, probably a machete, then nearly beheaded several minutes later. We believe he was waiting in Dr. Henderson's quarters to deliver the message, she entered, then the assailants arrived. They stabbed Dr. Arnaut, beheaded him, then took Dr. Henderson." He clicked again, a shot of the floor with bloody shoe prints shown. "We believe that they began to leave when Dr. Danko arrived. You can see from the shoeprints that someone headed for the door, the other two sets, one of which is Dr. Henderson's, are standing facing the door. We believe that Dr. Danko was abducted at this point."

"So there were only two assailants?"

It was a voice over the speaker, a voice he recognized as the Delta Force operator he had met before during the New Orleans crisis.

"As far as we can tell. There was so much blood on the floor in Dr. Henderson's room that it was impossible to not get it on the soles of their shoes, and there are only three sets of shoeprints visible. That doesn't mean however that there weren't more outside helping them, however we have this." He clicked again and an image outside was shown of muddy prints outside a window. "We believe they exited through this window." He clicked again for a close up of the prints. "We've found four distinct sets here, two smaller, suggesting the female doctors, two larger, suggesting the two assailants. They were the only prints around that window, and the entire area was quite muddy so it is felt there were just the two at this point."

"Have you been able to trace them?" asked Vice President Henderson.

"There's no camera footage in the area, but we did intercept some reports of three military transport trucks being stolen earlier in the day that were used to load medical supplies from the port." He clicked the button. "We were able to retrieve these satellite images." A shot of three trucks parked side by side appeared, a large cargo vessel at the edge of the shot. "We believe these are the trucks."

"What did they take?" asked a Homeland Security representative.

"Medical supplies."

"Can you be more specific?"

"Not at this time, we're trying to put together an exact list, however the three trucks were fully loaded when they left with supplies meant for one of the Ebola treatment centers."

"How are the two events connected?" asked the Delta operator.

"We weren't certain until a few minutes ago. We intercepted a report that three trucks passed through a checkpoint only hours after the abduction with two female doctors showing their IDs indicating they were transporting supplies to Port Loko Ebola Treatment Center."

"Why didn't they stop them!" cried Mrs. Henderson. "They could have saved them yesterday!"

"Nobody knew, ma'am," replied Leroux. "The body wasn't found for another hour and then word didn't reach us for several more. By the time it was realized they were missing, these trucks were well out of the city."

"Do we know where they went?"

"No, unfortunately we don't have anything on that yet, but we just received this report. We're hoping to get more satellite images before our team arrives in Freetown."

"Has there been any demands yet?" asked Vice President Henderson.

"None as of yet," replied Morrison. "There hasn't been any chatter either. Right now our only theory is that they wanted two doctors and medical supplies."

Mrs. Henderson leaned forward. "But why?"

"We're assuming there's an Ebola outbreak somewhere and they wanted doctors and supplies to help them."

"But this is Sierra Leone right?"

"Yes, ma'am."

"And the Vice President of Sierra Leone was assassinated yesterday in Washington, wasn't he?"

Uh oh.

"Yes, ma'am."

"Don't you think it's a little bit of a stretch to think this is a coincidence?"

"At this moment we have no evidence to connect the two events."

"But if their Vice President was killed on our soil, isn't it within the realm of possibility that they kidnapped our daughter for revenge?"

"We don't believe so, ma'am."

"But how can you be certain?"

"Because this plan seemed to have been well orchestrated. A group was put together, trucks were stolen, supplies were stolen, the doctors were abducted, and a definite exit strategy executed. This plan began only a few hours after the assassination. There's no way they could have put together something so quickly as revenge."

"Oh."

The wind seemed to have been taken out of her sails, and Leroux was happy she wasn't pressing it. It was his belief that the two events were indeed connected, and it was all part of the same plan. What that plan was, he had no idea, but he didn't believe in coincidences. He had little doubt the events were related, he just needed more intel to prove it.

"Do we have any leads on who's behind this?" asked the Vice President.

Leroux clicked the mouse button and a digitally enhanced photo of a man appeared, looking up at the sky as he stepped out of one of the transport trucks.

"We believe this man was in charge of the operation with the supply trucks."

"Do we know who he is?"

"Just a name. Major Adofo Koroma. He's in the Republic of Sierra Leone Armed Forces. That's all we know for now but this piece of intel is new."

Henderson pinched the bridge of his nose, closing his eyes. "I've got a son-in-law stuck in Los Angeles, taking care of my grandson, who's expecting answers from me. What am I going to tell him?"

"Tell him we're going to find out everything we can on Major Koroma, locate him, and rescue the hostages."

"How?" asked Mrs. Henderson.

Director Morrison leaned forward. "Mr. Leroux and his team are the best. They'll find him."

The Delta operator's voice came through the speaker. "And sir, once they tell us where he is, we'll do everything we can to get your daughter back."

"Please bring our baby home," cried Mrs. Henderson, suddenly bursting into tears. Her husband wrapped his arm around her shoulders and helped her up, leading the distraught woman out of the room.

"Okay, Mrs. Henderson is out of the room. Classified data can now be discussed," said Morrison. "What's the latest on the Norfolk hostage takers?"

"You're going to like this," said the Homeland Security rep, leaning forward. "They're all American citizens, all originally from Sierra Leone, some having lived here as long as twenty years. And get this."

"What?"

"They were all born within fifty miles of each other."

Somewhere in Sierra Leone

"Tell her she has to come with us."

Mustapha translated, though from the fear on the young woman's face, Sarah was certain she understood every word being said. The girl shook her head, violently, closing her eyes as if to shut out the very existence of the intruders into her home.

With their makeshift clinic set up they had begun house by house searches, looking for the hidden sick. It was the greatest way the disease was being spread. The stigma of Ebola in West Africa was so great that families would rather hide away their infected loved ones than admit someone in their household was sick.

And if they should die?

Secret burials were now common.

Which usually meant in improper burial.

Tradition had relatives washing and dressing the bodies which meant exposure to the pathogen and probable infection. The law in the outbreak countries now required all bodies of infected individuals to be collected and buried by qualified personnel wearing personal protective equipment.

And the mother this young girl was protecting from the outside world was definitely sick, but appeared to be in the early stages.

Which meant they couldn't be sure she had Ebola.

The initial symptoms were flu-like, and it was flu season, which was the very purpose of the first zone in their quarantine area. To isolate the possibly ill until their blood tests came back either negative or positive.

Sarah realized she must look terrifying to the poor girl, perhaps fifteen. Sarah was dressed head to toe in gear to protect herself from becoming infected, to take care of the sick, but it also was a barrier to humanity. But there was no choice, the risk simply too great.

"Listen, we aren't sure she has it yet. If she comes with us, we might be able to save her."

The girl opened her eyes, wide. "You save her?"

"I'll try."

She stepped back and nodded furiously. "You take, you take my mama. You save her."

Sarah stepped to the bed and helped the equally terrified woman to her feet. She clearly was having some difficulty, but at this stage seemed more tired and weak than anything else. Sarah hoped the poor woman only had the flu, but with the severity of the outbreak in this small village, she feared the worst.

The walk to the community center was short, it only a few hundred feet from the home. Tanya was working another part of the town, it decided they should split up. Sarah had asked that Koroma go with Tanya, to protect her just in case one of the men got any ideas. She was working with Mustapha who appeared to be an officer and very close to Koroma.

It confused her.

Most of the men seemed to be professional soldiers, well behaved so far with the exception of the driver. Yes they had murdered Jacques, but if what they were doing in their eyes was fighting a war, they could probably justify his killing to themselves. She could never condone it, especially the brutal way in which it had been done.

She had slept in the truck for several hours but her dreams had been nightmares, nothing but images of Jacques and her loved ones being beheaded over and over again, and she dreaded going to sleep tonight, but also looked forward to it. She was exhausted, and it was still mid-afternoon.

They put the new arrival in Zone One as they had begun to refer to it. Half a dozen were in there now, all with early symptoms that could be any number of things. Sheets from the villagers had been strung to provide for lack of a better term 'sneeze guards' between these patients. Once past Zone One, there was no need, and they would only hinder their care, a clear line of sight needed since she and Tanya were working essentially alone. But she was determined to do her best. The longer she could prove useful, the longer she might stay alive.

How can we possibly help these people? There's only the two of us!

She feared that if their captors thought they couldn't handle the job more doctors might be kidnapped and she didn't want anyone else to have to go through what they were going through.

She sighed. "I really wish we were able to test their blood," she said to no one in particular.

"What would you need?"

She turned toward Mustapha. "Well, in those supplies you managed to steal there was a portable scanning electron microscope but none of the supplies it needs. Really all we need are slides, needles. Not much. If we could do the blood tests then we could at least confirm if these people are infected or not."

Mustapha smiled. "I'll be back."

He quickly left, replaced only moments later by Tanya who was helping an elderly man into the room suffering from a cough and what appeared to be fever. She helped him onto one of the makeshift mattresses—generous piles of straw covered in blankets. She handed him some water then walked over to Sarah.

"I need to talk to you," she whispered.

Sarah could tell by her tone that it was something she couldn't risk anyone else overhearing. Tanya looked over at the door, Sarah following her gaze. Major Koroma was standing there, his hands on his hips, staring at them.

"It's time we check on the other patients in Zones Two and Three."

He nodded and left as Sarah pushed aside the sheet separating them from the infected patients. Out of sight of any of the soldiers, she pressed her head against Tanya's so they could speak quietly. "What is it?"

"I overheard their conversation at lunch."

"So did I but I didn't understand any of it. Did you?"

Tanya nodded. "Yes. The major said he's going to America soon."

Sarah's chest tightened, her eyes narrowing. "But why?"

"I don't know, but I think they killed their own Vice President while he was visiting your country. I think it's all part of a plan to get the major into the United States."

Sarah shook her head. "That doesn't make any sense. These people don't seem like terrorists to me. They seem to just want to help their people. Why go to the US?"

Tanya shrugged in her suit, the plastic rustling with the effort. "I don't know, but there's one thing I'm sure of."

"What's that?"

"Once he leaves, it will be open season on us."

Over the Atlantic Ocean

"What have you found?"

Dawson had his laptop open in front of him on the Gulf V they were using for transport to Sierra Leone. Besides his team of four there were several FBI and other agency specialists hitching a ride. It was good cover for them, they carrying Bureau of Diplomatic Security IDs themselves. It would allow them to land in Freetown and simply blend with the team then split off when they needed. The story had broken already though with the restrictions in place due to the outbreak, the Sierra Leoneans had assured them a private landing free of the press.

He wasn't counting on it.

On the laptop Master Sergeant Mike "Red" Belme was giving them an update, having taken over the stateside investigation after the hospital murder-suicide. Niner, Atlas and Jimmy were gathered near the rear of the plane, listening in.

"Not much so far. The guy you took down is Dia Conteh. He worked at the hospital for over ten years and has an apartment nearby with a wife and four kids. He got his citizenship six years ago and has a clean record, not even a parking ticket. This guy was a model citizen."

"Any links to known cells?"

"Negative. This guy had a cellphone that he barely used, no home phone, no computer or Internet access and had basic cable—none of the red flag channels like Al-Jazeera."

"I take it you've searched the apartment?"

"Yes, but the FBI got to it first. They say they found nothing. They've got a forensics team going over it and the car with a fine-toothed comb. If there's anything to find, they'll find it, but I'm not optimistic. From all outward appearances this was just a normal guy, happy to be here and good at his job."

"What about volunteer work?" asked Niner. "He had to have had some contacts with the old country in order to have been recruited."

"We've got a lead on a drop-in center that the wife mentioned. We're heading there now."

"Okay, keep us posted. This guy doesn't sound like a ringleader, which means somebody gave this guy his orders after the hostage taking. There's more out there and we need to find them."

"Roger that, BD. I'll contact you when I have something, out."

Dawson snapped the laptop shut as his team took their seats around the table, the Gulfstream V configured perfectly for quick four man meetings. "What're you thinking, BD?"

Dawson looked at Niner. "They've been able to identify all the HTs from Norfolk, plus this new guy. They all grew up within fifty miles of each other in Sierra Leone, most are Muslim but two are Christian, all but two are American citizens, and none have any significant criminal record. There was no Islamic paraphernalia found at their residences and they had no history of radicalism."

"And how do you radicalize the two Christians?" asked Niner. "The briefing notes said they weren't converts."

"That's right," said Dawson, tapping the laptop containing their notes. "And there was no evidence they were political, no evidence that they were anything but upstanding citizens, so what are they up to?"

Atlas' voice boomed. "That 'For my people' thing makes me think this is political but not religious. Could it be related to the Ebola outbreak? Maybe they want us to put more of an effort into stopping it?"

Jimmy shook his head. "Then why not make those demands? They said not word one about the outbreak. The only thing that links the outbreak to any of this is where they were born."

"Not entirely true," said Dawson. "We have to assume that the kidnapping of Sarah Henderson is connected."

"Do we?" Jimmy raised his hand. "Give me a second. I agree that they almost definitely are linked, but should we be making the assumption it is Ebola related? One of the guys in Sierra Leone has been identified, this Major Koroma. He's from the same area as the others, so it's reasonable to assume there is a link. Not only that, the timing is simply too coincidental, so I agree they're linked. But I think it's dangerous to assume this is Ebola related, because if we do, then we risk thinking their motivations are altruistic—"

"Ooh, big word!" interrupted Niner with a wink.

"Don't tease just because you don't know what it means." Niner opened his mouth to protest but Jimmy slapped a hand over his friend's mouth. "I'll dumb it down for my friend. If we assume Ebola, then we risk thinking these people are doing this for *humanitarian* reasons, so therefore ultimately have noble goals that we can identify with, rather than what we're used to—the establishment of a worldwide Islamic Caliphate. We can't assume their motives are noble."

"Agreed," said Dawson. "Clearly they're willing to kill for their cause, and die for their cause. There's too many dead hostages in Norfolk to deny that. And you're right, we can't go into this with assumptions that blind us to other possibilities. But with them taking two doctors and medical supplies, we have to assume Ebola is at least at the periphery of this. And that in my mind makes them even more dangerous than what we're used to dealing with."

Niner nodded. "They could be infected."

"That's a distinct possibility. While we're in-country we'll have to observe all protocols and avoid all unnecessary contact. No handshaking, no touching anything we don't need to touch. If we get into a combat situation, shoot them at a distance if you can."

"Man, if we start having to shoot people, and even just one of them is infected, we could all be exposed in a heartbeat."

It was Atlas that triggered the moment of reflection, none of the men saying anything as Dawson was sure they all thought of their loved ones. Thoughts of Maggie on the other side of an isolation chamber window, his mother, his sister and niece.

His brothers in arms.

A member of the flight crew walked down the aisle toward them.

"We're beginning our descent, gentlemen."

Dawson nodded. "Thanks."

And as he felt the plane begin to lose altitude, he couldn't help but look at his team and wonder if they would all make it out of this alive, this unlike any situation they had ever encountered.

For today they not only faced an enemy whose motives they knew nothing about, but Mother Nature as well.

In her deadliest form.

Somewhere in Sierra Leone

"Will this help?"

Sarah turned to see Mustapha holding open a bag, a smile on his face.

"What's that?"

"Slides and everything else I could find."

A grin broke out on Sarah's face. "Show me!" She stepped forward, eagerly rooting through the bag before Mustapha even had a chance to finish putting it on the floor. "Where did you get this?"

"There's an old clinic that was abandoned during the civil war. It was all just left to rot."

Sarah paused her inventorying for a second. "A clinic? Is it set up for patients?" She glanced over her shoulder at her own makeshift treatment center, wondering if it had all been a wasted effort when there was something else nearby.

Mustapha shook his head. "No, Doctor, its roof was torn off years ago in a storm. The only reason this stuff survived was because it was in a storage locker."

"And no one stole it?"

Mustapha smiled, shrugging his shoulders. "Everything of value was looted over a decade ago. Nobody's paid it any mind since."

"But these supplies, they're worth a lot of money."

"If you can't eat it or barter it to someone else who thinks they can eat it or barter it, it's not worth anything."

Sarah nodded, realizing that electron microscope supplies in rural West Africa were only valuable to a medical professional, and those were few and far between here. But one man's junk…

"This is fantastic," she said as she finished rifling through the bag, it containing everything she would need to test at least one hundred people. The only problem now was finding the time to do the tests, it something she couldn't really trust to anyone but her or Tanya. She stood up, looking around. "I don't want to do the testing in the treatment center because of possible cross-contamination. Is there another room or building we could use?"

Mustapha nodded, picking up the bag. "Follow me." He led her to another door of the community center. Inside there was an office area, simply furnished with several desks, chairs and cabinets. "Will this do?"

"Perfect," she said. "We'll need to have this room cleaned with a water-bleach solution, just in case anyone came in here infected."

"No one has been in here for days, I assure you."

"A single drop of blood can contain a massive amount of the virus and be infectious for days if not weeks. We can't take any risks."

Mustapha nodded. "I'll take care of it right away."

Sarah yawned, stretching, catching a whiff of her own body odor from the protective suit she had been wearing for hours earlier. "I need to get some rest and to bathe somewhere."

Mustapha nodded. "We've got showers. No hot water, but nothing's really cold around here," he said, smiling. She followed him down a hallway to another side of the building, away from the main hall where their clinic had been set up. "Can I ask you a question?"

Mustapha seemed almost hesitant, raising a red flag with Sarah's subconscious. She felt her stomach flip in fear of what might come. "Yes."

"If I were to be exposed, like from a needle prick or something, anything I guess, how long would it be before I could infect someone else?"

Sarah breathed a sigh of relief. "Well, it depends. You're not contagious until you start to show symptoms, and those can start to show anywhere from two days to several weeks after. It all depends on the individual." She stopped. "Why, do you think you've been exposed?"

He shook his head. "I hope not. I mean, I've been careful and fortunately my family hasn't been affected yet, but I guess I'm just curious. If I were infected today, for example, would I, or you I guess—a doctor—be able to tell?"

Sarah shook her head. "Not without a blood test."

"Then how do they screen people at the airport?"

"They check for an elevated temperature and unfortunately rely on the honesty of the passengers."

"What do you mean?"

"They interview everyone to see if they've been exposed in some way. Unfortunately as we saw with the case in the United States, people will lie just to get out of here. If they aren't exhibiting any symptoms yet, then there's no way without doing blood tests on every passenger to prevent them from leaving."

"Sounds insane."

Sarah smiled. "Agreed, but there's not much else we can do. Locking the country down would simply mean it would be harder to get medical staff in and out along with supplies."

"I would think you just restrict the civilians. I mean, we've got tourists still coming here, people from your country coming here to visit family."

Sarah frowned. "I know. Unfortunately it's hard to regulate stupidity."

Mustapha laughed. "No, that is true in your country I guess as much as it is here." He opened a door, showing her a shower and change room. "What do you think would happen if you had a large outbreak in your country?"

Sarah stepped inside, pausing. "Define large?"

Mustapha shrugged. "I don't know, fifty, hundred?" He pointed to a locker. "There are clothes in there. You'll have to share with the other doctor, we were only expecting one of you."

Sarah opened the locker and nodded, several sets of medical scrubs sitting in a pile. "These will do perfectly. We're going to need to launder them every day though."

"Some of the women in the village will take care of that."

"It will need to be done in boiling water."

"Of course."

Sarah smiled, slightly embarrassed. "Sorry, I didn't mean to—"

Mustapha cut her off with a raised hand. "You didn't." He pointed to the showers. "There's a tank on the roof that has been pumped full of water. It works on pressure. Try not to waste it because someone has to refill it." He pointed to a nearby sink. "There's soap and shampoo. It hasn't been used and that's all there is."

Sarah stepped over to the shower, it from all outward appearances looking like any other simple shower except that the red and blue temperature dots were meaningless. "Understood."

"I'll go wake your partner," said Mustapha.

"No!" Sarah raised her hand apologetically. "Sorry, I mean, let me do that. I'll only be a few minutes."

"Very well." Mustapha stepped out of the room, closing the door behind him. She noticed a small pushbutton lock on the door and pressed it, the comfort it provided slight. She stripped out of her sticky clothes, piling them on the floor by the door, then turned the knob for the shower. Cool water flowed from the showerhead, the pressure excellent. She stepped under the blast of water, her eyes closed, and simply stood there for a minute letting the water run over her naked body, the stress and sweat of the day slowly rinsing away.

She thought of Mustapha's question and wondered herself what would happen if there was a significant outbreak back home. If fifty or a hundred people were to become infected somehow, what would happen?

Mass panic.

The economic damage would probably be worse than the human toll. The disease was difficult to spread if proper protocols were in place, and with modern communications and good medical support systems, the infected would be isolated quickly and anyone they had contact with traced.

But all it would take would be one person, infected and contagious, to be working at a restaurant, dealing with customers, handling food, for it to spread to possibly hundreds more over the course of their being infected and undetected.

For there was a fatal flaw in the capitalist system when it came to the spread of infectious diseases.

Those who handle our food and clean our buildings are the lowest paid workers, meaning they were also the same people who could least afford to take a day off sick. They were most likely, due to simply being poor, to force themselves to go to work when sick, and all it would take would be one to have the disease, be contagious, and handle the food that went out to the customers.

And at the onset of an outbreak, those newly infected customers would assume they simply had the flu, and instead of isolating themselves and contacting the authorities, they too would quite often force themselves to go to work for the same economic reasons or because they had an important project due at the office.

It would spread for the same reasons the flu spread—people simply didn't stay home when they should.

She wasn't concerned about some sort of zombie apocalypse. If the spread continued curfews could simply be declared—it wasn't like the infected would be dragging themselves through the streets, moaning "Brains!" while the uninfected tried to remember their Walking Dead episodes.

It would be the panic created that would probably hurt more people in the end. The public would stay home, the economy would grind to a halt, and it would last for weeks, possibly months, until the authorities could convince people the outbreak had been halted.

She paused working the shampoo into her hair and thought back to Mustapha's questions, and again felt a chill run down her spine.

And still wasn't sure why, the questions innocent and nothing she hadn't heard dozens of times before.

You're being paranoid.

She resumed washing her hair, frowning.

And you have every right to be.

She rinsed the shampoo out of her hair and tossed her head back, wiping her eyes clear. She opened them and gasped, a face pressed against a window high on the wall quickly disappearing. Instinctively she covered her exposed flesh as best she could, but at that moment, she had never felt more vulnerable or exposed in her life.

And Tanya's words echoed in her mind.

"Once he leaves, it will be open season on us."

Hastings Ebola Treatment Center, Freetown, Sierra Leone

Dawson was careful not to step on any of the bloody footprints on the floor as he surveyed the scene of the crime. The body had been moved but everything else had been left in place, at least according to the Sierra Leonean authorities. The evidence certainly seemed to match that already provided in the briefings he had been privy to, and he saw little value in being here, but as part of their cover, he had to at least feign interest.

"Agent White."

Dawson looked over his shoulder and saw Niner beckoning him. He stepped back into the hallway and saw a well-built man standing with the rest of his team sporting a fashionable suit, dark sunglasses despite being indoors, and a brilliantly white smile. He extended his hand. "Lamina Margai, Agent *White*. I'll be your liaison while you're here." Dawson looked at the hand, leaving his own clasped behind his back. Margai quickly withdrew it, smiling. "Sorry, old habits are hard to break."

Dawson had little doubt this man was military or at least former military—definitely security of some type. He wouldn't want to scrap with him in any case. "Mr. Margai, pleased to meet you. How about we let the forensics team get to work while we discuss the latest updates outside."

Margai smiled. "Of course. Follow me." They strode quickly down the hallway, the rooms off either side repurposed classrooms from the former police training center. Exhausted and nervous medical personnel coming off shifts shuffled past, the entire treatment center subdued since they had arrived.

He couldn't blame them.

One of their own had been murdered in the most gruesome manner possible, and two kidnapped. Not to mention that day in and day out they dealt with death by one of Mother Nature's most perfect killers, too often powerless to save those brought to them too late.

Yet not a single person had asked to be reassigned or to go home.

Impressive.

He had a tremendous amount of respect for these people. Hundreds of them had died despite their protective gear and training, and hundreds more probably would die before this was over, yet they kept coming, they kept volunteering.

They were soldiers in the fight against an invader that couldn't be seen.

He didn't envy them, preferring his targets viewable under the sight of his weapon rather than a microscope.

But the true misery was not inside this relatively sedate cluster of buildings, it was outside the makeshift hospital that was devoid of laughter, devoid of even the sounds of innocent children so often unavoidable no matter how serious the warzone.

Here there was only misery and death, hope drummed out of the population despite the fact in some of these clinics nearly fifty percent were surviving.

Which meant fifty percent were dying.

The insanity of the disease, of the situation, was obvious outside the walls. People would arrive, some under their own power, some dropped off by relatives, and most were turned away, the clinic full.

And instead of going into isolation, they would cross the street and wait at a bar for a position to open, either through death or a rare success, while spreading the disease further.

It was ridiculous.

Margai saw where he was looking. "It's sad, isn't it?"

Dawson nodded. "More needs to be done."

"Yes. We are doing all we can, but we are a poor country. Perhaps when we have oil, we will get more attention."

Dawson didn't take the bait. In his briefing notes he had read about Sierra Leone's economic situation and of how they were hoping to develop possible offshore oil, but that was years away. And the sad thing was the man was probably right. If this country had resources that the rich countries of the West were dependent upon, it would have most likely received a more rapid response. "Have there been any leads?"

"No, nothing of consequence. Three supply trucks were signed out with the proper paperwork by Major Koroma, they were driven to the port, loaded with medical supplies, then last seen clearing a checkpoint as they left the city with the two missing doctors claiming to be delivering supplies to the Port Loko Treatment Center."

"And I assume those supplies never arrived."

Margai shook his head. "Obviously a ruse. We're checking reports that they were spotted at another checkpoint heading south but we haven't been able to confirm those yet. Outside of the city things are unfortunately pretty lax."

"Understood. What can you tell me about Major Koroma? Any idea why he'd do this?"

"I never knew the man, but I've spoken to several of his colleagues and all are shocked by this. Frankly, they can't believe he'd do this. He's a family man, dedicated soldier, well respected by his men and superiors, and non-political."

"Religious?"

"He's Muslim if that's what you're asking."

Dawson smiled slightly. "No, I mean could he be motivated by religious reasons, regardless of whether or not he was Christian or Muslim?"

Margai smiled broadly. "Of course that's what you meant. And no, I've heard nothing suggesting he has any type of extremist leanings. If anything he was considered quite moderate by his Imam."

"You spoke to him?"

"Yes, but his Imam here in Freetown; what happens back in his home town, I honestly couldn't say. He may be a completely different man there."

"Either he *is* a completely different man when back home, or he's *become* a completely different man. Something has caused this apparently upstanding soldier to betray his country."

Margai frowned. "It may be that he thinks he's doing this *for* his country."

Dawson nodded as he watched a body being carried out of a nearby tent, a poignant reminder of the danger they were under just being there. "Whatever his motivations, his actions are what concern me. We need to find him and rescue the hostages."

"May I ask *you* a question?"

Dawson tore his eyes away from the body bag and the small procession carrying the anonymous victim, all clad in protective gear. "Of course."

"Have *you* discovered why our Vice President was killed?"

Dawson shook his head. "I was hoping you could tell us."

Margai's eyes narrowed. "I don't understand."

"He was murdered by people from your country, all who grew up within fifty miles of your Major Koroma."

Margai's eyebrows shot up. "You are certain of this?"

Dawson nodded. "Yes."

Margai bit his bottom lip, appearing slightly concerned. "How—" He paused, as if debating whether or not to continue.

Dawson decided to press him. "How?"

Margai looked at Dawson then away. "How did you find out so quickly?" The words were delivered slowly, as if he were reluctantly delivering each syllable.

"Our government can be very efficient when it wants to."

Margai smiled, seeming to regain his composure.

"If only it had been efficient on the important things, then perhaps all of this could have been avoided."

Somewhere in Sierra Leone

Sarah frowned. Another positive test. Tanya had worked all evening getting blood samples from those they suspected might be infected so they'd be ready for her when she took over. Tanya was now finishing her shift in the isolation wards before getting as much sleep as she could. They had no idea how long they'd be here, but they had both discussed it and decided it was best to try and maximize their usefulness but also to spend as little time alone as possible.

Sarah wasn't sure who had been watching her in the shower, but she thought she recognized the driver who had groped Tanya. She just couldn't be certain, it only being a brief glimpse. She hadn't told Tanya, her friend's grip on sanity hanging on by a thread, but the house they were sleeping in, apparently Koroma's family home, had a bedroom door that didn't lock. She had slept lying in front of it so no one could enter without having to push her aside.

Fortunately exhaustion had her to sleep quickly and soundly.

And now sample after sample was showing the virus, the outbreak worse than initially thought. Fortunately—or unfortunately—these people were in the early stages, and with proper care could be saved. She just wasn't very confident in their ability to provide that care. They had no IV equipment which meant all they could do was try to feed them and have them drink plenty of well water.

She marked the result on the list of patients compiled by Tanya and prepared the next sample, looking up as Koroma walked into the nearly spotless administrative office, Mustapha true to his word.

"What have you found?" he asked.

"See for yourself." She pushed the sheet toward him. "Out of the eleven tested so far I've found seven infected."

Koroma frowned. "We just received word that the government has announced house to house searches in the cities."

Sarah for a moment felt a surge of hope. If the authorities were searching house to house for them, her father must be placing a tremendous amount of pressure on the government here. But Koroma's apparent lack of concern had her second guessing that hope. He had said cities, and they were in a small village of several hundred at best.

They'll never find us.

"I guess they're hoping to find all of the infected before they can spread the disease further." Koroma pushed the list back toward her as she realized he hadn't been talking about a search for them at all, but a search for the infected. "They won't bother with us until they eradicate it in Freetown. Do you think they can?"

She was almost overwhelmed with disappointment, the one shred of hope, dangled out there purely based on a misunderstanding, yanked out from under her, the delicate balance she had been able to maintain crumbling around her.

"Doctor?"

She looked up at Koroma, her eyes unfocused as tears threatened to spill down her cheeks. "Wh-what?" she finally managed, looking away.

"Do you think they can stop the spread?"

She nodded slightly as she blinked the tears out of her eyes. "If they're thorough, then yes, but only if they've got enough room for the sick. We know how to stop the disease, we just need the resources to fight it, and the people to stop hiding the sick."

"Resources. I keep hearing that word and it makes me sick. That's what they told us when I brought my wife and son to the clinic. Not enough resources. Not enough room. My wife and son died because there weren't enough resources."

Sarah turned toward Koroma, the villain seeming a bit more human if only for a moment. "I'm sorry about your family."

He nodded, then pointed at a name on the list, a name she hadn't tested yet. "My daughter."

A pit instantly formed in Sarah's stomach, words escaping her. She pictured her own son and how she would feel if he were infected. Then she wondered what she would do if she lived in a poor country like Sierra Leone.

Would I kill to save my own son?

She would like to think that she wouldn't. She couldn't imagine justifying killing another human being to save her own son.

Unless that person were directly threatening her child.

But if that were an exception, what constituted a threat? Would someone withholding medicine that could save her child justify her killing that person to get the medicine? Her moral side said no, it couldn't possibly be used as a justification for murder, but her logical side said it could. If someone were denying her access to something that could save the life of her own flesh and blood, then yes, killing them would be justifiable.

And wasn't that what Koroma was doing? Trying to save the life of his child, the lives of his village?

"How old is she?"

"Five."

A lump formed in Sarah's throat. "I-I'm sorry to hear that. I'll test her next."

"No."

Sarah looked up from her chair at Koroma's shaking head. "Why not?"

"She shouldn't get preferential treatment just because of who her father is. That's what's happening in Freetown. Those who have the connections, those with money, they're the ones getting the treatment and it's disgusting—they should all be left to rot like those of us who are poor have been left to."

"We don't discriminate at our clinic, that I can assure you."

Koroma laughed, dropping into a nearby chair. "You are so naïve. You apply your Western way of thinking to everything you see. You assume because someone smiles and is polite that they are honest by your standards. And that is the key—*your* standards. You Americans always express shock and outrage when you are asked to pay a bribe to get something done, but what you don't realize is that the vast majority of the world works that way—it is simply common practice. You go into a store and pay the price on the tag, but in the markets of my country it is an insult to not try to negotiate the price down. You apply your values to us, and that in itself is an insult and one of the reasons so much of the world hates you."

"Do *you* hate us?" Sarah nearly peed her pants at the words that had come out of her mouth on reflex.

She held her breath.

Koroma smiled slightly, as if impressed she had the balls to ask the question given her situation. "Yes. But not in the way you probably think. I hate your politicians for doing nothing while our people were dying. It wasn't until your own might die that you took action. I hate your people collectively for ignoring our plight and not insisting their government do something to stop the horror we've been living with for months. But I don't hate the individuals."

"I don't understand. How can you hate the people but not the individuals who *are* the people?"

"I make the distinction because the *people* act as a collective, the individual as himself. The people collectively did nothing, but individuals did do something, like yourself. And I think that individual Americans or Europeans, when shown the horror, would demand something be done. The problem is that your culture is so wedded to your television sets and your Internet that unless someone does a cute viral video with a cat in it, you don't pay attention. If one of your Hollywood stars came down with Ebola, maybe then you'd demand action, but when your own CDC says there could be a million cases of Ebola here within the next few months, and the only *collective* reaction is 'what happens if it comes here?', then your society has a serious problem. You care deeply about yourselves, individually you claim to care deeply about the downtrodden around the world, but collectively you do little." He sighed. "And that is why I hate you, the people, but not you, the individual."

Sarah didn't say anything for a moment. There was nothing she could say. He was right. Doctors like her had been begging their governments to do more but their pleas had fallen on deaf ears until the first case was reported on US soil. Then there had been action, but still not enough. Why had it taken only one sick person on American soil for the government to react, when thousands of Africans had died already? It was indifference. No one cared unless it affected them personally and politicians only cared about what their voters cared about.

"I understand." She put the next slide under the microscope and looked, shaking her head, the virus clearly visible yet again. She marked the sheet.

"Another one?"

She nodded.

"These samples. What would happen if you came into contact with them?"

Sarah pulled away from the microscope and the blood samples, suddenly nervous. "I could become infected. A single drop of blood can contain over a million copies of the virus." Her eyes narrowed and her mouth-brain barrier failed her. "You know that. Why do you keep asking these questions?"

Koroma rose from his chair. "Let me know what the test result is for my daughter."

"And if she's positive?"

He paused, looking over his shoulder but not making eye contact. "Then I will have a decision to make." He walked out of the room, leaving Sarah to wonder what decision he could possibly be talking about.

She looked back at the list and at his daughter's name. Biting her cheek, she debated for a moment on what to do, then decided she had to know. She took his daughter's sample and prepared it, her hands almost shaking in anticipation and fear. If she were positive, how might he react? He could go crazy, but she thought that unlikely. The man had already lost his wife and son and had maintained control.

Control? He beheaded Jacques!

But he had done that with some end goal in mind. If his daughter were confirmed sick, it just might give him the reason he needed to keep her and Tanya alive to try and save her, and if they were lucky, she might survive the ordeal, or at least survive a couple of weeks, long enough perhaps for her father to find them.

You're hoping a little girl suffers for as long as possible to save yourself?

Her mouth filled with bile at the thought, guilt almost overwhelming her as she leaned back in her chair, her shoulders slumping.

What's happening to me?

She thought of her own child then this sweet little girl who had never done anything to harm anyone in her life, who had already lost her mother and brother, who was now in a strange room with the sounds of the sick and dying on the other side of a soiled sheet with strange people in suits like nothing she had seen before tending to her.

Shame overwhelmed her, her chest heaving with sobs as she prayed to God for forgiveness, her selfishness so out of character, it shocked her to her core.

Sucking in a deep, slow breath, she calmed herself, blinking the tears out of her eyes otherwise she'd need to remove her gloves. It took a few minutes but gave her the time to think and she came to a decision. If Koroma's daughter was infected, she would do everything she could to save the little girl despite Koroma's objections. Self-preservation aside, she was an innocent, the youngest of the victims so far, but her survival could mean their survival, and she would be a fool not to recognize that.

She loaded the slide and looked.

"Oh no."

CIA Headquarters, Langley, Virginia

"What's that?"

It was Marc Therrien that vocalized what Leroux had already spotted—three dots on a road clearly visible on one of the Operations Center displays. They had been poring over satellite imagery from the hours during and after the kidnapping, and beyond spotting the trucks at the Port of Freetown, they had found nothing. Police reports from their point of contact in Freetown had suggested the trucks had been spotted heading south but nothing had been found. It was Leroux who had redirected the search north, toward the geographic region all of their suspects had come from.

And this might be their first hit.

"Zoom in."

A mouse pointer dragged across the image, selecting the portion showing the dots and a segment of road. A pixelated image appeared then quickly resolved into a crisp new image.

Clearly showing three transport trucks heading north, not south.

"Do we have any shots from an angle?"

"Give me a minute."

Leroux began to type a quick communique to his boss warning him of possible false intel, the reports of them heading south appearing to be a red herring. He glanced up at the main screen as Therrien ran a search to see what satellites might have images of the exact coordinates the trucks had been spotted on.

Suddenly a shot was displayed that looked like it was a view from the north, lower on the horizon.

Are you kidding me?

He jumped out of his seat, rushing forward. "Zoom in! Clean that up!"

Therrien was way ahead of him, everyone in the room forgetting what they were working on, instead all eyes now focused on the screen. The image changed, the large pixels resolving into the ridiculously fine imagery possible with modern spy satellites.

"Is that what I think it is?" asked Alice Michaels, one of his analysts.

"That's definitely four people in the front of that lead truck," said Therrien. Leroux agreed, but what wasn't clear was *who* was in the truck, it still a nighttime image seen through a specialized filter that gave a greenish glow to everything, the occupants almost outlines of themselves, no features distinguishable.

He snapped his fingers. "We know the two hostages are white, and most likely their kidnappers are black. Can you enhance that image to at least see if two of them are white?"

"Give me a second!" Therrien was clearly excited by the idea, his fingers expertly flying over the keyboard, his mouse clicking on icons furiously as the image slowly changed, moments later showing exactly what Leroux was hoping for.

Two white faces flanked by two black faces.

"That must be them," said Michaels. "And they look much shorter than the driver and the one on the far left."

"I think we've found our two missing hostages. Good work people, scratch that, *excellent* work. See if we can track where they went and cross-reference this with any records we have of legitimate shipments. We don't want to send an armed team in unless we're sure. And I want to know if there were any checkpoints along the way, see if you can pick up any chatter about them passing through. I'm going to go see the director and let him know." He turned to Therrien. "Print those out and email them to me, CC the Chief."

"Done and done," said Therrien, pointing to a nearby printer.

Leroux grabbed the sheaf of papers off the high-speed color printer and headed for Director Morrison's office, leafing through the pages. When he reached the office Morrison's assistant was expecting him.

"He said to send you straight in."

Leroux nodded, knocking on the door.

"Come!"

He stepped inside, closing the door after him.

"Is this what I think it is?" asked Morrison, pointing at one of his monitors.

"Yes, sir," said Leroux, standing in front of Morrison's desk, leaning over briefly to see what his boss was pointing at. "We found three transport trucks heading *north*, not south like we were led to believe. That enhanced image is showing four people in the front of the lead truck, two we believe are Caucasian."

"And these aren't just a regular transport?"

"We're checking that now, sir, but I doubt it."

"Your gut?"

"My gut. And the fact that they're heading toward the area where all of our known suspects are from, and that there are no clinics in that area."

"When will you know for sure?"

"It could be hours, sir. It's a little bit like the Wild West out there. Three trucks, heading into this particular area, with two white people in the lead vehicle, exactly as described at the Freetown checkpoint? That's too much of a coincidence and I don't believe in coincidences."

"Neither do I. Get the intel to our team in Freetown. Warn them of the possible false intel as well. I assume you're trying to find out where these went?"

"My team is on it as we speak."

"Excellent. Pass on my compliments."

"I will, sir." He turned to make for the door when Morrison stopped him.

"Oh, and Chris?"

"Yes, sir?"

"Now you see the power of having a team. With the right supervisor, they can work twenty-four-seven." He motioned at the screen. "And look at the results."

Leroux felt himself flush, uncertain of what to say, the Director well aware of his reluctance to have a team. "Uh…"

Morrison chuckled, flicking him away with his fingers. "Go. And keep me posted."

"Yes, sir."

Leroux beat a hasty retreat, his cheeks burning as he quickly walked back toward the Op Center, his mind split between processing what Morrison had said, and the possibilities of this being a false positive in their search.

He's right. I couldn't have done this without my team.

Well, that wasn't entirely true. He could have, but most likely it would have taken longer because sleep would have been an absolute necessity. But with his team large enough to do two shifts, it meant he could leave them working under his orders while he rested his brain.

And he had a good team.

Actually, he had a great team.

Most in the CIA were the cream of the crop when it came to minds. In his business those who just couldn't cut it were quickly weeded out, tossed either to less mentally tasking jobs or out of the Agency completely. And it wasn't just IQ that mattered—it was mental toughness. Could you think clearly for 24 or 48 hours? Could you deal with images of torture and mutilation, the pressure of innocent lives in the balance, or the ramifications of delivering that piece of intel that could result in the deaths of the guilty?

He had passed all those tests, all those pressures. It had actually been quite the surprise since he had never considered himself brave or even much of a man. He was a shy loner who took a job working with computers and data, two things he loved. The CIA had approached him, he having done well on some aptitude test he had taken online on a whim.

And he'd never looked back.

Now thanks to his job he had a stable income, a good if infrequent friend back in his life, and a girlfriend who was way out of his league.

You have to stop thinking like that!

Sherrie would kick his ass if she knew he still thought that way. He used to always say 'I don't deserve you' to her and she had ignored him at first, but finally turned on him one night. In his mind it was true, he didn't deserve her, and by telling her so, it was a compliment, but apparently she wasn't taking it that way.

"How do you think it makes me feel?" she had screamed. He had merely stared at her blankly. "Every time you say that you're putting yourself down! You're telling *me* that I've chosen poorly! Well, I don't think I have, and you better realize that you *do* deserve me pretty damned quick, or you're never going to see me again!"

She had stormed into the bathroom and taken a long shower while he cried into his pillow.

And he never said those words again, though his feelings had barely changed. He realized now that she truly did love him, and he her, and that they really were a great couple. They liked a lot of the same things, and since they both had top security clearances, they could be honest with each other, though sometimes that merely meant saying, 'Sorry, classified.'

He thought of what Morrison had said and realized the man was right. And as he entered the Operations Center, his team and other support staff looking at him expectantly, he realized for the first time that he had become a man, despite his best efforts. He was a boss, and apparently good at it, his team respecting him and looking up to him, despite his age. His supervisors and peers treated him as an equal, no longer talking down to him as if he were a pimply kid fresh out of college, trusting him to make life and death decisions on a daily basis.

He sucked in a deep breath, pride and confidence swelling inside him, a rare feeling with so many eyes on him.

And decided that tonight when he got home, he was going to tell Sherrie how he truly felt.

That he did deserve her.

He pointed at a map of Northern Sierra Leone on one of the displays. "Let's get some drones over that area ASAP."

West African Drop-In Center, Baltimore, Maryland

Master Sergeant Mike "Red" Belme pulled open the glass door of the West African Community Drop-in Center, Spock behind him, Control jacked in through his earpiece and a hidden mike on his jacket. The center had opened about ten minutes late and they had observed from their car parked across the street seven people enter since, five of them still inside, all male.

Photos had gone to Bragg for identification but nothing had come back yet. The order had come down the pipe to proceed, a possible sighting of the Vice President's daughter reported by Langley only minutes before.

Time was of the essence, the location of the sighting over 24 hours cold and the intent of the kidnappers still unknown, except that they were willing to kill and die for their cause.

Assuming the group here were connected to those in Sierra Leone.

Intel suggested the one suspect in Africa was born in the same vicinity as the terrorists here, a tenuous connection at best, but a connection nonetheless. And the timing was simply too coincidental. Red, like the others, was convinced everything was connected, though the end-game was still a mystery.

And if their experience so far was any indication they were about to discover absolutely nothing that might help them.

A rattle above the door signaled their entry, three men visible inside turning their heads to stare, Red's pale redhead British heritage setting him distinctly apart, Spock's lineage not much better though at least he could tan.

Red pulled out his wallet, flashing his fake FBI ID. "I'm Special Agent Grey, this is Agent Brown. Can we speak to whoever's in charge?"

Nobody said anything for a moment, the stares continuing though the eyes were a little wider, a hint of fear clearly evident.

Maybe we have *stumbled onto something.*

He stepped toward the group, just a single step, and they all turned to face him, eyes darting about as if looking for somewhere to run. Intel had already provided them with floor plans. There was the front entrance now at their back, a rear entrance through three adjoining rooms, and a fire escape if they were to go up the stairs, accessed through the next room, to the second or higher floors.

"Are one of you in charge?" he asked pleasantly, a smile on his face as he continued forward, subtly nearing the rear door so he could cut them off should they try to flee. "We just have some questions about Mr. Dia Conteh. I understand he came here often."

Looks were exchanged and words whispered in what he assumed was their native tongue of Krio, a language he was nearly completely unfamiliar with. He and the others had been receiving crash courses in the language as soon as the Norfolk incident had begun, but it was impossible to learn a language in a couple of days, and their knowledge transfer had been more the key phrases like "hands up" and "drop your weapon".

Panicked conversation hadn't been covered yet.

His comm squawked. "The one on the right is telling the others not to say anything. The one behind the counter agrees."

Fortunately for them someone back at Control spoke Krio perfectly and could see and hear everything thanks to the hidden comm gear both he and Spock were wearing.

"Listen, nobody's in trouble, we just have a few questions." He looked at the man on the right who had told the others to say nothing. "Did you know Mr. Conteh?"

The man quickly shook his head. "Good, you do speak English." Red knew damned well the man spoke English, English was the official language in Sierra Leone, and even though their version of it was quite often unrecognizable when overheard by an American, these men could certainly understand the version spoken in their new country.

He simply hoped to goad them into a reaction.

"Of course I speak English."

And it had worked.

"Good, that will make this much easier. I assume of course your friends here speak English."

His comm squawked. "The man on the right is Ahmadou Ballo. He's the founder of the West African Immigrant League. No criminal record, American citizen for six years. He works nights as a janitor, volunteers at the center during his off hours."

"I'm looking for a Mr. Ballo. Is that you?"

The man's eyes flared almost imperceptibly. The others leaned away slightly.

"Yes."

"Good, then I'm sure you can definitely help us." He stepped over to the counter, leaning on it, his body angled in such a way that he could easily block the rear exit from the room, Spock covering the front and hanging back at the opposite corner of the room, forcing the men to continually turn their heads if they wanted to watch both of them. "When was the last time you saw Mr. Conteh?"

Ballo shrugged. "I'm not sure. Not for a long time." His English was heavily accented but excellent, good enough for Red to be able to sense the tension in his answers.

"Really?" Red pointed at the counter, a pile of leaflets advertising some sort of mixer next month, the same leaflet stuck to Conteh's fridge with a Domino's Pizza magnet. "New flyers? Kinko's?"

The man behind the counter shook his head. "Staples."

Red picked one up, pretending to read it but instead watching their reactions through his peripheral vision. "Looks like it might be fun." He rubbed the paper between his fingers, detecting nothing. "Feels new. Last week?" The man behind the counter nodded. "First batch?" Another nod. "That's good, then we're getting somewhere."

"What do you mean?" asked Ballo.

"Well, this flyer was on Mr. Conteh's fridge, so we now know that he was here after you had these printed last week."

Ballo glared at the man behind the counter for an instant then caught himself. "Perhaps someone gave it to him."

"That's always a possibility." Red was impressed, Ballo clearly quick on his feet. "Which means someone that frequents this place saw him recently." He suddenly changed tactics. "Where are you from?"

Ballo's eyes narrowed. "Sierra Leone."

"Where in Sierra Leone."

"Kamakwie."

"That's fairly close to where Mr. Conteh is from, isn't it?"

Ballo nodded, though he appeared reluctant to do so. He looked at the other two. "Are you from the same area?" The man behind the counter nodded, the other shook his head.

Someone from the next room yelled something in Krio, Ballo responding.

"He just told the person in the back to tell the others to leave."

Red pretended to not know what was going on, Jagger and Sweets covering the rear exit and listening in. "Can you tell whoever is back there to come out here, please?"

Ballo shouted something to the back.

"He just told them to arm themselves. Sending backup to your location now."

Red stepped back, drawing his Glock 22, aiming it directly at Ballo's chest, Spock covering the other two. The man in the middle's face visibly sagged, a small yellow puddle forming at the soles of his shoes. "Now everybody is going to remain calm and get on the floor," said Red. The soiled man hit the floor immediately, but Ballo didn't budge, neither did the man behind the counter who seemed to be taking all his cues from his boss.

And his hands, on the counter, seemed to be twitching, as if ready to reach for something.

"Now listen," said Red, moving slightly so Spock would have a clearer shot at the man behind the counter, "nobody has to die here today. The rear exit is covered, nobody's leaving here. Tell your friends in the back to lay down their weapons and nobody has to get hurt."

"The man behind the counter is named Camara Okeke. He's got a wife and a daughter."

Red looked at Okeke. "Do you have a family?"

The man nodded.

"Any children?"

A rapid nod, his eyes flittering between his boss and interrogator.

"Son? Daughter?"

"D-daughter."

"What's her name?"

"Tell him nothing."

Red turned to Ballo. "What harm could there be in telling me his daughter's name?"

"We will tell your government nothing."

Red pursed his lips, his eyes narrowing slightly. "You're an American citizen. Isn't it *your* government too?"

"It ceased being my government the day they let my homeland die."

Bingo! Motive determined, now for the endgame.

"I assume you mean Ebola?"

Ballo nodded, lowering his slightly raised hands and turning to face Red's weapon directly, as if making certain there was no way a bullet could miss the large target now provided. "You let our people die while wasting billions on your wars over oil, and only react when someone shows up here sick. You spend millions to save two of your white volunteers, but barely a penny on the thousands of blacks suffering in Africa."

"Ahh, so it's a race issue."

"It is, and it shouldn't be."

"I agree." Red was pretty certain where this was heading, but he had to make one last effort to diffuse things before the ending Ballo seemed committed to was triggered. "Listen, just because I work for the government doesn't mean I agree with everything they do. Between you, me and the lamppost, I think our government should have gone all out in fighting this disease at the outset. Thousands of lives would have been saved, and in the end, hundreds of millions if not billions of dollars as well. By ignoring it thousands of your people died needlessly, and now it will just cost that much more to try and stop it." Red shrugged. "Washington is filled with assholes who only care about getting reelected. There's nothing I can do about that except vote against them in the next election. And as an American citizen, that's what you can do too. You though have a luxury I as a public servant don't. You can publicly criticize your government, organize rallies, protest, and change people's opinions so they change their elected representative's opinion. There's nothing more terrifying to a politician than the thought of losing the next election. But this"—he motioned with a turn of his head at the room—"is not the way. You will never gain sympathy from Americans by killing innocent people in the name of your cause. Lay down your weapons and tell your story. Americans will listen to you. If you're dead, your people lose what is obviously an impassioned voice."

Ballo seemed to be taking in Red's words, and for a moment Red had a sliver of hope that they might just be able to shut this impending disaster down when shouts from the back erupted, the thunder of a shotgun piercing the tense silence of the front room.

Okeke's hands dropped below the counter. Spock put two in his chest as Ballo lunged for Red. Red shot him in the shoulder, spinning his body in mid-air. Ballo cried out in agony as he hit the floor on his back, the third man, already on the floor, begging not to be shot.

Red pushed Ballo over then stepped on his back as Spock quickly zip-tied the man's hands and feet, moving on to the pisser. Sirens in the distance signaled that the local backup response status had been upgraded to lights and sirens now that shots had been fired. Red advanced, his weapon aimed at the door to the rear of the building as the shotgun continued to pump rounds, a second one joining in.

The distinctive sound of an AK47 upgraded the situation. "Bravo Zero-Eight, Bravo Zero-Two, preparing to enter through door Alpha, over."

"Bravo Zero-Two, Bravo Zero-Eight, we'll provide suppression fire, keep left, over."

"Roger that, keeping left. Proceed in three, two, one, execute!"

The sound of two Glocks opening up on the rear of the building momentarily silenced the opposition's weapons as they took cover. Red advanced, Spock on his six, taking a quick glance around the doorframe, finding what looked like a meeting area, threadbare couches surrounding the walls, an old CRT television against one wall and one man crouching near the door to the back room spinning toward them, a Smith and Wesson .357 Magnum gripped in his hand.

Red double-tapped his chest.

Shouts from the next room indicated their approach had been discovered and rounds from the AK47 ripped through the thin gyprock. Red hit the floor as did Spock, both opening up on the wall. Somebody screamed on the other side, the AK47 silenced if only for a moment, but it was enough time for Red to jump to his feet and approach the final door, it closed with several bullet holes in it.

"Approaching Door Charlie, over."

"Roger that, continuing suppression fire, over."

The steady stream of fire from Jagger and Sweets minimized the response from what should have been only one gunman but sounded like two. Somebody had obviously already been in the building when it was unlocked less than half an hour ago.

Red kept to the left and low, Spock directly behind him as they continued to pump their own rounds through the wall, suddenly switching to the door as Red reached forward and grabbed the knob, shoving the door open. Spock surged past, firing three times, taking down the man holding the AK47, Red firing, eliminating an already wounded man gripping a shotgun. A third man was dead near the window, his own shotgun under his body.

"Clear!" announced Spock, still hugging the wall, suppression fire continuing.

"Clear!" said Red, activating his comm. "Hold your fire, situation is secure, over."

The gunfire from the rear of the building stopped immediately. "Roger that, approaching Door Delta, over."

"Opening door," said Red, nodding toward Spock who opened the rear door, waving at their approaching comrades. Red immediately headed for the front of the building, there still two hostiles alive, Spock close behind. He found Ballo almost at the door, having wriggled his way across the floor, the urinator unmoved.

Ballo rolled to his side, twisting his body so he had a view of his whimpering partner, shouting something at him.

"He just said if you tell them anything you're dead."

Red smiled.

Good to know he knows something.

Somewhere in Sierra Leone

Sarah Henderson double-checked her gear in a large mirror that had been brought in from one of the houses. One of Koroma's men was helping with a checklist that she had written down from memory, but without another trained eye to inspect her personal protective equipment, she had to rely on herself when Tanya was sleeping. It was nerve racking knowing she might have missed something, Tanya already having caught an improperly Velcroed seal, something the "trained" men were supposed to catch.

It showed the system was flawed.

At least their hobbled together system.

Back at the clinic she wasn't concerned. She paid attention but two other people who did this type of work day in and day out were there to make sure no one screwed up. When she entered the isolation wards she was confident everything had been done to protect her.

Here she had no such confidence, especially when Tanya, with two months of experience, wasn't with her.

And now she was about to do something already making her stomach sick with the thought of it. She stepped into Zone One, it a little emptier now than it was earlier, those who had tested negative to the blood test immediately moved into another part of the building where they would be tested again until she was certain they weren't infected.

But it was at least a little encouraging. The village had been thoroughly searched and all symptomatic people had been brought to their makeshift clinic. Koroma's soldiers would be searching the village every day now, looking for previously asymptomatic people. If they could contain things for three weeks, then they might just beat the outbreak.

But dozens more would die before then, of that much she was certain.

Including perhaps the patient she was about to move into Zone Two.

She pushed aside the sheet protecting her patient and felt tears flood her eyes as the innocent little five year old girl looked up at her, fear in her own.

"I need you to come with me," said Sarah, her voice cracking as she held out her hand. She knew the tiny creature didn't understand her but her intent was clear, and with the innocence only a child could possess, she quickly rose from her makeshift bed where she had been playing with a threadbare homemade doll, and took Sarah's gloved hand. They stepped out from behind the sheet and Sarah looked toward the entrance to Zone One, the squeak of its door drawing her attention.

"Papa!"

The little girl darted toward Koroma who stood in the doorway, but Sarah tightened her grip as her captor dropped to his knees, the anguish clear on his face. He held up his hands, urging his daughter to stay back.

"Pickin!" he gasped. "Stay!" He said something in Krio and the little girl's tugs on Sarah's hand eased somewhat, finally subsiding as her shoulders slumped in defeat.

Koroma looked up at Sarah, his eyes pools of tears. "Will she live?"

Sarah shook her head. "I don't know. I'll do everything I can to save her."

Koroma rose to his feet, a single tear racing down his left cheek. "You do nothing for her you wouldn't do for anyone else."

Sarah's stomach felt hollow, bile filling her mouth as his words echoed in her head.

She nodded then turned, pushing the sheet aside separating Zones One and Two, leading the now sobbing little girl into a chamber filled with the sights and sounds of the sick and dying. She put her on a donated mattress nearest Zone One, the tiny bed separated from the others with a hanging sheet she had set up earlier to help protect the child from the visual horror surrounding her.

"You'll stay here," she said with as much reassurance as she could muster, pointing to the bed. The little girl wiped her tears away with the back of her hands then lay down on the mattress, curling into a little ball, hugging her doll and squeezing her eyes shut.

Sarah adjusted the sheet to try and provide as much privacy and protection as she could. Taking one last look at the little girl, she made for the rear of the building, quickly checking on each patient to see if there was anything she could do to help them, but beyond filling water glasses, there was little.

And one more was dead in Zone Three.

She exited the rear of the building and waited while she was sprayed down with a bleach and water solution by one of Koroma's men then removed her equipment, a check list read out by the same man in heavily accented English. She at last headed for the showers, locking the door behind her. Stripping out of her clothes she turned the water on, leaning against the wall as the cool liquid spilled down her back, then turning around and sliding to the floor, she began to sob as selfish thoughts flooded her mind.

Please God, let that little girl live long enough for them to find us.

A cry erupted from deep within and she bent over to her side, vomiting with shame.

FBI Washington Field Office, Washington, DC

Master Sergeant Mike "Red" Belme sat across from a clearly terrified man he had come to think of as "The Urinator"—at least until his identity had been established. Tutu Magoro. Not a citizen yet, but in the process of getting it. He was a legal immigrant with a valid green card and worked as a taxi driver for the past two years as well as the nightshift manager at a drycleaner. Clean record, no wife or kids, just a young man struggling to scrape out a life for himself.

A poor man in a rich country.

He often wondered if immigrants thought of this fact. In their own countries they might be poor, but they were equal to most of those around them. Any opulence or excess was usually limited to the ruling class, the other 99% living in true abject poverty—not Western style poverty.

But in America, or any other Western democracy, if they came here with no relevant skills, they quite often were relegated to minimum wage jobs that barely paid enough to live on, and didn't in the big cities where immigrants tended to congregate. When Walmart's own employees cost the taxpayer over six billion dollars in government assistance every year, there was clearly a problem.

Minimum wage in high cost of living areas simply didn't cut it.

Which meant those occupying these low paying jobs, quite often immigrants, were poor.

Dirt poor.

Surrounded by opulence and excess.

Ignorance is bliss.

He often thought it had to be worse knowing you were poor compared to most of those around you than actually being just as poor as everyone else and never knowing any better. If you were safe with your belly full, happy in your ignorance, was emigrating really the best thing to do? If you never knew what a flat screen television was or had lived all your life not knowing that high speed Internet access and McDonalds drive thrus were the norm elsewhere, were you really any worse off not having them?

Fleeing war, oppression, hunger—those were always legitimate reasons. Trying to provide a better future for your children? Always. But to come to America just to be poor in a rich country? He saw so many people simply scraping by but unwilling to improve themselves—both American and foreign born. He knew people who would work two, three even four jobs to try and make as much money as they could to support themselves and their families, trying to set a little bit aside so that one day they might start their own business, buy a small home or put their kids through college so they wouldn't suffer the way their parents had.

He admired those people.

Greatly.

Like this man sitting in front of him. He was working two jobs, keeping his nose clean, even had accumulated several hundred dollars in a Chase savings account despite sending a sizeable chunk of his weekly paycheck back to Sierra Leone to help support his mother.

A poor woman in a poor country.

The uncooperative, confrontational manner displayed by their other suspect, Ahmadou Ballo, contrasted sharply with Magoro. Red had been trained to read people, and all his training and intuition was telling him that this man was either completely innocent, or an unwilling participant.

He was betting on the former since unlike the others, Magoro came from Freetown.

"You know why you're here?"

The man shook his head, his eyes darting away for a moment, the sweat beaded on his forehead trickling into his eyes.

He squinted, the salty liquid clearly causing his eyes to burn.

Red turned to the FBI guard standing at the door. "Why don't you get our friend a glass of ice water and a towel?"

The guard nodded and stepped outside, returning a moment later having apparently passed on the request. Red made a show of reading over the file on Magoro, using his pen to highlight several points of little interest, merely toying with Magoro's mind, making the man think there were things in the file that were of concern.

There was a knock followed by the guard opening the door, a pitcher of ice water with two glasses carried in on a tray by the poor lackey not senior enough to pass the request down to an underling. It was placed shakily on the table, the man clearly never having spent any time as a waiter, then the towel, held over his arm almost giving him a touch of class, was handed to Magoro.

The man tentatively took it, almost scared to look at the man.

"Th-thank you."

The delivery boy didn't say anything, instead leaving with a bit of an annoyed glance at Red. Red merely smiled and nodded, pouring out two glasses of water. He put one in front of Magoro then took a long drink from the other.

He gave a satisfied sigh, the sound enough to encourage Magoro to drink from his own glass then towel off his face.

"Better?"

The man nodded, still averting his eyes.

"Good. Now, you said you don't know why you're here, but I think we both know that's not true. I *highly* recommend you simply tell me what you know. If you're guilty, we're going to find out anyway, so not telling us simply makes things worse for you in the end. But if you're innocent, *not* telling us will get you in trouble that you don't deserve to be in. And if you get a criminal record for not cooperating with Federal authorities, then you can kiss your Green Card goodbye, because you'll be on the first flight back to Sierra Leone." Red leaned forward slightly. "So what's it going to be?"

The man gulped, the sweat already returning to his forehead. "I-I want—"

He stopped then looked at the door, shifting in his chair uncomfortably.

"Listen," said Red, his voice lowered. "Between you, me and the lamppost, your friend, Mr. Ballo, the one who threatened you, is going to prison for a very long time. Any threats he made against you are worthless, he'll never be able to touch you."

"He has friends."

"Good, that's good. If you tell us who they are, they too won't be able to touch you."

Magoro shook his head. "They'll kill my family back in Sierra Leone."

"Not if we take them all down, and believe me, we will. Nobody commits a terrorist attack on our soil then lives to tell about it for very long."

Magoro leaned forward, his head dropping as he stared at the floor. "I don't know what to do. I have nothing to do with this, all I did was go to the center to get the name of an immigration consultant who could help me with my citizenship application. Then you showed up."

"That sounds completely innocent to me." Red leaned back in his chair. "Then what do you think Mr. Ballo was talking about when he told you to say nothing?"

Magoro shrugged. "I don't know."

He didn't sound convinced.

"Oh, I think you do. Perhaps you overheard something?"

Magoro tensed, his sudden, momentary inhalation catching Red's ear.

Bingo.

"What was it you overheard?"

"Nothing," Magoro mumbled.

"Listen, this can all be over very quickly if you just tell me what you overheard. They'll never know you told me anything, and we can put you in Witness Protection if you want."

Red wasn't sure if that last part could actually be done—he didn't have the authority. But lying to witnesses withholding information on possible terrorists gave him a lot of leeway. And judging by Magoro's interested expression, it might have just been the right inducement.

"I heard them talking in the back when I came in."

"What were they saying?"

"They were talking about the kidnapping of the Vice President's daughter."

We have a connection!

"What did they say?"

"Nothing, really. I heard one of them yelling that they should kill her now so the Americans—I guess you—stop looking for her. That's when they heard me talking to Camara in the front and they got quiet. This Ballo guy came out to see who I was, then you came in."

"And you heard nothing else?"

Magoro shook his head. "No, nothing. I don't know these people. I've only gone there maybe three or four times since I arrived in America. I didn't join the center because I wanted to become American, not a hyphenated American."

Hyphenated American. I think I like this guy.

"So you can't tell me of anyone else who might go there?"

"No, except my friend who got me the job at the drycleaner. He's the one who told me about the center."

Red pushed his pad of paper and pen toward Magoro. "Write down his name, address and phone number. We'll want to talk to him."

Magoro hesitated, his mouth open but no words coming out.

"We won't tell him about you, we'll just say he was seen at the center while it was under surveillance."

Magoro seemed satisfied, quickly scribbling the information down, pushing the pad back. "When can I get into that Witness Protection thing?"

Red rose, picking up the pad and files. "I'll get back to you on that."

He left the room, leaving Magoro alone with the guard. Spock was in the hall waiting for him.

"Anything?"

Red nodded. "Not much, but we know for sure they're connected to the kidnapping of the VP's daughter."

But how that helped them he wasn't sure.

Somewhere in Sierra Leone

Sarah took Tanya by the arm and led her into the office area where their electron microscope had been set up. Closing the door, she quickly swept the room with her eyes, making sure they were alone.

"What is it?"

"It's Koroma's daughter."

Tanya gripped her chin between her thumb and forefinger. "Oh no! Did she test positive?"

"Yes. I moved her into Zone Two a little while ago."

"Does he know?"

Sarah nodded. "Yeah, but he said not to give her any special treatment."

Tanya's eyes popped wide. "Are you kidding me? We have to do everything we can to save her! She could be our ticket to survival for the next few weeks!"

Sarah sighed in relief, happy Tanya was thinking the same way she was, it making her feel a little better that she wasn't alone in her morally questionable thoughts of self-preservation. "I agree. That's why I put her in the very first bed on the left side. We'll always treat her first to limit the risk of further exposure. I hung a sheet to give her some privacy and additional protection."

"Why? Is there any doubt she's infected?"

Sarah felt a knot in her stomach at the thought of a false-positive. But the test had been conclusive. "I just want to make sure she doesn't accidentally pick up another strain, you know how this thing is mutating."

Tanya nodded slowly, squeezing her chin harder, the tanned skin turning white. "Yes, yes, we need to do everything we can to save her." She tugged at her chin in frustration. "But we don't have the supplies we need to save any of them!"

"I know. We'll keep her well hydrated and fed, but if the infection takes over, there's not a whole lot we can do without IV supplies."

"Can they get them?"

"I asked that Mustapha guy and he said he would look into it, but I'm not confident."

Tanya dropped into a nearby chair, her death-grip on her chin released as she lowered her head between her knees, her long, curly blonde hair dangling toward the floor, hiding her face. Sarah sat across from her, in front of the microscope, looking at her friend. Tanya's skin was a healthy looking golden brown, or at least what used to be considered healthy looking in the West. Now the paranoia of skin cancer was scaring too many people into avoiding the sun. She glanced at her own hands, the California sun she lived under having turned much of her regularly exposed skin light brown. She had to confess she loved the look and other than avoiding getting a sunburn, she made no effort to shun the sun when she had the chance to get outside of the ER.

And in the Ukraine, the skin cancer scare hadn't taken hold yet, Tanya on her rare time off basking under the African sun, soaking up every ray she could, her skin after two months California gold, her naturally blonde hair even more so.

She's a beautiful woman.

Sarah wasn't one to obsess about looks, but she did take care of herself and according to her husband, who could be faulted for being a little biased, she had "a crackerjack ass and a great rack". At least that's how she had overheard him describe her to one of his buddies on the phone recently when discussing an upcoming high school reunion. She had felt disgusted and titillated at the same time, and while cooling her jets in the bathroom, found herself looking at her body in profile, smiling at her pleasant bumps.

And forgave him, putting her "crackerjack ass and great rack" to good use as soon as he got off the phone.

He didn't know what hit him.

She smiled at the memory.

"What?"

Her eyes returned their focus to Tanya who was now looking up at her. "Huh?"

"You're smiling."

"Was I?" She paused as her daydream quickly faded, trying to hold on to it for one more moment. "Just thinking of home."

"Me too." Tanya sighed, leaning back in her chair. "If we can keep this little girl alive, it might give them time to find us then we can both get home."

At least she hasn't given up hope.

Sarah hadn't either, but she had to admit with each passing hour what spirit she had left was being gradually drummed out of her. The pressure of dealing with the sick and dying, of having no support team, of worrying about what might happen if they were left without Koroma to protect them, and of worrying about when Koroma would decide he didn't need them anymore, it was all quickly getting to her.

"I don't know how much longer I can last," she finally whispered. Her head dropped as she rested her elbows on her knees. "I just pray they find us soon. You said Koroma was leaving for the United States. I'm afraid he's going to kill us before he does."

Tanya shook her head. "There's no way. As long as that little girl is alive, we're alive."

Sarah looked up at her friend. "I wish I had your confidence."

"Think about it. He lost his wife and son and look what he did! He's kidnapped us, killed Jacques, stolen supplies from his government and committed God only knows what other crimes. There's no way he's going to let his daughter die after doing all that!"

Sarah sat back up. "Or, he's going to let her die, or worse, kill her, so that she's not left alone when he's gone. He's going to do something back in the States, something bad, and my guess is he won't survive whatever it is. And if he's leaving soon, he can't wait for her to die. I wonder..." She paused for a moment, thinking back on her conversation with him.

Then I will have a decision to make.

"He said he'd have a decision to make if she tested positive," she murmured, her eyes meeting Tanya's with a look of horror.

"You don't think..." Tanya's voice trailed off in shock as her eyes opened wide, her jaw dropping. "You don't think he'd kill her, do you?"

It had to be what he had meant. What other possible kind of decision could he have been referring to? The very thought was inconceivable to her, but from her experience, she knew it was possible. "I've seen enough murder-suicides in my life to know that some people, in a moment of weakness, will kill their children before they kill themselves so they won't be left alone with no one to take care of them. We don't know this man, we don't know if he's mentally unbalanced, but I wouldn't put anything past him."

"My God, what have I done?" cried Tanya, gripping her hair and pulling at it viciously.

Sarah felt her chest tighten, a sense of foreboding crawling up her spine. "What do you mean?" she asked, terrified of what the answer might be.

"It never occurred to me, I never thought he'd kill her! I mean, what kind of maniac does that?"

Sarah's chest was like a vise and she felt herself going cold. She gripped the arms of the chair as her mouth filled with bile. "You switched the samples!"

The words smacked Tanya like a two-by-four to the chest, the distraught woman shoving herself back in her chair, her eyes, red and wide, staring at Sarah as she let go of her hair and began to beat her thighs with balled up fists. "It was the only way to save us!"

Sarah turned in her chair, unable to look at Tanya. She swallowed the saliva quickly building in her mouth and jammed a thumb in the pressure point on her left wrist, slowly massaging it, trying to fight off the urge to vomit. What her friend—and could she even call her that anymore?—had done was unbelievable. Inexcusable. Unimaginable. To risk the life of a little girl to save your own?

"How could you?" she murmured, still not looking at Tanya.

"I-I—" No more was forthcoming, instead sobs filled the room eventually accompanied by pleas to God for forgiveness. As Sarah listened, she thought of her own rationalizations when she had been doing the testing, and couldn't help but realize that she had been secretly happy that the little girl had tested positive as her illness would most likely lead to their survival.

"We have to get her out of there," she finally said, pushing herself to her feet. "Now!"

Tanya reached out and grabbed her arm. "But she's been exposed now. We can't take her out."

"We don't know that. I put her behind a curtain and nobody has touched her."

"But how will we explain it? If he finds out what I've done, he'll kill me!"

Sarah wanted to tell her she deserved to die for what she had done, but couldn't. She knew deep down that she herself had debated what she would do if the blood test had been negative, and a small part of her had decided she would claim it was positive just so they'd have this poor, innocent child to use as leverage in their struggle to survive.

But she hadn't had to make that decision. She had been saved from that by Tanya switching the samples.

A thought dawned on her.

"Do we know for sure she was negative?"

Tanya's sobs stopped for a moment. "Wh-what?"

"You switched the samples but we tested her because she was symptomatic. What did you do with her real sample? Did you test it?"

Tanya shook her head, a sudden look of hope appearing. "No, I mean, I just—" She stopped, the look of hope replaced by one of shame. "Oh God, I'm doing it again." She stood and picked up her gloves, pulling them on as she walked over to one of the desks. Opening a drawer, she reached inside then held up a vial. "This is hers."

Sarah rushed over to the electron microscope, flicking the switch to turn it on, this building one of the few actually with power, solar panels and batteries making it by far the most modern structure she had seen here. The microscope hummed to life as she pulled the chair out from the desk. "Test it."

Tanya nodded and quickly donned her head gear then sat down and prepared the sample. Sarah felt like she was holding her breath the entire time. She kept eyeing the door, terrified someone would come in to wonder where they had gone. They were supposed to only come here for a few minutes so she could brief Tanya on Koroma's daughter. It had never occurred to her that this woman, this mother, would risk the life of another child just to save her own.

Yet she couldn't condemn her and she found herself placing her hands on Tanya's shoulders, squeezing them gently. Tanya looked up at her through the goggles and facemask, smiling tentatively.

The machine beeped and they both looked at the display then each other.

"Oh no," they echoed.

Embassy of the United States, Freetown, Sierra Leone

"How sure are you of this?"

Dawson sat with the rest of his team in a small conference room provided to them after their arrival. It had been decided there was no point in remaining at the clinic and risking continued exposure since the FBI forensics team were the needed expertise, not Spec Ops. Right now they were in a holding pattern until additional intel came in, and by the sounds of it, it was finally arriving.

"Not a hundred percent, but it's highly probable that these are the trucks we've been looking for."

Dawson recognized the voice of the CIA Analyst he had dealt with on several occasions, but hadn't been certain for the first few minutes since the voice seemed to sound slightly different, as if there was something there that hadn't been before.

Confidence?

If so he was happy for the kid. *Kid!* He wasn't that much younger than Dawson, certainly not anywhere near young enough to be his son, but his demeanor, the way he carried himself, had always suggested insecure teenager. How he had ever managed to land the honey he was dating he'd never know, but he obviously had some confidence somewhere in order to hold on to her. And now it sounded like the young man might have finally found where it had been hiding.

"Two short Caucasians accompanied by two black taller people in a truck heading north. That's all you've got?"

There was a pause filled with quiet white noise coming from the speaker. "Yes."

"Sounds good to me. Have we got eyes in the sky there?"

"UAVs should be starting overflights shortly but it's a huge area," replied Leroux. "We're concentrating on the area where all of our suspects have come from which might help narrow the search."

"Okay, we'll make arrangements to head into that area. Any word on the outbreak there?"

"Only that it's bad, but the population is sparse. There's hardly any medical facilities in the area so we suspect most of the sick have moved away. There's really nothing beyond a three month old report from the World Health Organization so you're going in pretty much blind."

Niner elbowed Atlas. "We're used to that."

"Not with this kind of enemy," boomed Atlas. And he was right. Heading into a situation blind with an unknown number of hostiles in unknown locations wasn't the preferred option, but wasn't unheard of if it were absolutely necessary. But a disease? It was just something they hadn't encountered before. They trained for it, though rarely for viral outbreaks like Ebola. It was more for biological, radiological or chemical warfare situations.

Not a pissed off Mother Nature.

"We'll arrange transport through our liaison here. As soon as you have something from those UAVs, let us know. I'd prefer to not be going in completely blind."

"Yes, sir," replied Leroux. "Another piece of intel has just come through that suggests the northern connection is more plausible. We've linked one of the Norfolk hostage takers to Major Koroma. He's his brother."

Niner slammed a fist on the table. "Now that's simply too much of a coincidence!"

"That pretty much settles it," agreed Jimmy. "Even Vegas bookies wouldn't touch those odds."

Dawson had to agree. There was no way these two events weren't connected now that they had this familial link. Cousins were one thing. Brothers? No way.

Leroux continued. "There's one more thing I've been asked to warn you about."

Dawson glanced at the others, leaning in. "What?"

"You're still secure?"

Dawson knew they were, but glanced about regardless. "Yes."

"The intel you were provided indicating they had gone south, well, we could find nothing to corroborate it, and the fact that we found them going north suggests an intentional false flag."

Dawson's head bobbed slowly. He had already picked up on that little discrepancy, but what he didn't know yet was who was responsible. Their liaison Margai had told them of the southerly sightings, but had he made it up, or had he been provided the bad or false intel? Either way it didn't matter. All that he could say for certain was that any intel provided by Margai, or the Sierra Leoneans, couldn't be relied upon.

Now he had to determine what side Margai was playing for.

"Understood. I want you to dig a little deeper into our contact here. See if there's any connection with Koroma or any of his men from Norfolk."

"Will do."

"Good. Keep us posted, Freetown, out." He hit the button killing the call then turned to his men. "What do you think?"

Atlas cleared his throat. "The intel sending them south never made sense to me—almost intentionally opposite of what was to be expected with all the connections pointing north. If you really wanted to throw us off, why not east? An exact one-eighty just seemed too convenient."

"Not to mention I don't trust anyone in a suit," added Niner. "That guy just came off as too slick. I wouldn't trust him as far as I could throw him, and he's a big bastard so that wouldn't be far."

"Pussy!" coughed Jimmy who was rewarded with a none-too-gentle punch to the shoulder from Niner.

"Agreed," said Dawson.

"What, that I'm a pussy?"

Dawson deadpanned Niner for a moment, saying nothing. "I don't think we can trust any intel provided by the locals until we determine the source of the bad intel."

"He thinks I'm a pussy," hissed Niner as an exaggerated aside to Jimmy who was still massaging his shoulder.

"Agreed," said Jimmy in response to Dawson, quickly leaning out of reach of Niner's fist. "Do we trust this guy to make our transportation arrangements?"

"We don't really have a choice." Dawson tapped the table. "That doesn't mean we don't take precautions, though."

Somewhere in Sierra Leone

Sarah woke to the sounds of a car horn honking. She looked at her watch and frowned, her shift not due to begin for another two hours. She lay her head back down and tried to will herself back to sleep, but some excited shouts from outside had her curious and a bit afraid.

To hell with it!

Wiping the sleep out of her eyes with some well-placed knuckles, she rose from her makeshift bed, looking around to make sure she was alone. Satisfied, she pulled her hair back, tying it with a rubber band she had found in the administration office, then slipped into her shoes, stepping out of the room given to them in Koroma's home and heading toward the noise of gathering people.

Idiots. Don't they know crowds are how this disease is spread?

Stepping into the morning sunlight she squinted, letting her eyes adjust for a moment as she shielded them with her hand. She spotted Tanya standing in the rear doorway to the clinic as she was hosed down by one of Koroma's men. She waved, Sarah smiling at her as she walked toward the road that passed in front of the community center.

Several cars and trucks were present, including one large black Mercedes with Sierra Leonean flags flying from the front corners of the hood.

Government?

Her heart leapt with hope as she realized they might be here to rescue them, armed soldiers and men in suits with dark glasses in abundance, none of whom she recognized from Koroma's cadre. She began to walk toward one of them when she stopped, spotting Koroma shaking hands and laughing with a large, rotund man in what appeared to be an expensive Italian suit.

The way ass was getting kissed here, it was clear Koroma thought this man was important, and the size of the security detail certainly suggested it. A briefcase was handed over to one of the new arrivals by Koroma's letch of a driver, unfamiliar words in Krio exchanged with some laughter then suddenly silence, somber expressions replacing the jovial ones. Hugs were exchanged, foolish in this epidemic, but if these men were friends, she had no sympathy for either of them.

The man glanced in her direction, pausing. He said something to Koroma who looked at her before replying. He seemed completely unconcerned that she had been spotted, which proved her suspicions that this man was in on whatever Koroma was planning.

And this man was government.

Which meant whatever was going on appeared to be far bigger than one major betraying his country.

For if his actions involved this obviously important man, who seemed to be a member of the government, then perhaps he wasn't betraying his government at all.

Perhaps he was acting under their orders.

Which means there's no way they're helping find us.

The man climbed into the back of his Mercedes as the security detail quickly loaded into their own vehicles, most of the procession leaving within moments, leaving nothing but a cloud of dust and shattered hopes.

And two vehicles with four men standing in front of each.

I wonder why they stayed behind.

Koroma walked over to her, his expression grim.

"Why aren't you working?"

Sarah's mouth went dry. "I'm not due for another couple of hours. A horn woke me up then I heard a crowd gathering. I thought I should remind whoever was gathering that they should avoid contact."

Koroma stared at her for a moment then motioned for the new arrivals to join them.

"I have a job for you."

Tanya stood near the far corner of the building and watched as Sarah was led away by Koroma, the new arrivals following. She was terrified for Sarah, images of gang rape filling her mind as her chest tightened. If it were to happen to her she knew she would try to kill herself, there no way she would want to live through an ordeal where in the end they were most likely going to kill her anyway. She had read enough horror stories of the Janjaweed and other like-minded Muslim groups raping and pillaging their way across Africa, repeatedly sexually assaulting women and children until they were dead.

It was something she had said she'd never let happen to her.

Yet here she was.

Kidnapped by murderers with an unknown agenda who had already promised to kill them rather than let them go, and with at least one man among them that had already put his hands on her, and if Sarah were correct, spied on her in the shower.

She didn't know why Sarah had been led away but she had to somehow tell her what she had overheard. It was the only ray of hope that she had felt since Koroma's daughter had been admitted to Zone One with possible symptoms. She still felt sick to death with what she had done, but in a moment of weakness she had pictured her own child without his mother. It had overwhelmed her. She had switched the samples and had been sick with the knowledge ever since.

She knew Sarah well enough to know she would do whatever it took to make certain the little girl was well treated and isolated. They had already discussed isolating the young children from the sights of the dying around them and the protocol they had developed also dictated that the newest arriving children would get the beds nearest Zone One to try and minimize what they would hear from Zone Three.

Which meant in her desperately confused mind she had felt even if the child was actually negative, she would have been reasonably protected from infection.

Reasonably!

It was probably the greatest regret of her life, a shame she would take to her grave, a decision she could never take back and right here, right now, if she could switch places with this innocent little girl she would, even if it meant her own death.

For Koroma's daughter had tested negative.

The question now was whether or not she was *still* negative, something they couldn't know for days, and with every minute she spent in that clinic, her chances of contracting the disease rose exponentially.

Yet they couldn't move her.

Not without having to explain what they had done.

What *she* had done.

Which meant certain death.

But if what she had overheard was true, there might still be hope to save the little girl even if she had become infected.

The Americans are coming.

The man who had arrived in the Mercedes had told Koroma after he had arrived. And they had laughed. It was as if they had no concern over the news.

Which meant whatever they had planned didn't rely on them being dead or alive.

Or they're just suicidal like all those insane terrorists.

She wasn't sure what was in the briefcase, but Koroma's words had sent a chill racing up and down her spine.

She confirmed it would work just like we thought.

That was when all joviality had left the conversation, as if a darkness, pushed aside for the reunion, had reasserted itself, sucking all the joy out of the meeting. A foolish meeting.

They shook hands and hugged!

She couldn't believe the foolhardiness, after everything she and Sarah had told them repeatedly about avoiding all unnecessary contact. But then there was something in their tone, in their demeanor, that told her these people didn't care whether they lived or died.

If only we knew why!

Clearly Koroma was upset at the West for their lack of response to the Ebola crisis, that much was clear from the conversations related by Sarah. And he had also lost his wife and son, which had to affect anyone. Which was why when Sarah had suggested he might actually kill his daughter rather than let her suffer and die alone, it had seemed completely plausible.

And horrifying.

It had brought home the reality of the crime she had committed, though in the court of law she'd probably be found not criminally responsible due to her mental state.

That did little to comfort her now.

These new events had her mind reeling with new possibilities. Something big had just gone down, that much was evident. The car was flagged as if government or diplomatic, and there was simply too much security for the man to not be important. She had seen the man look directly at Sarah, and it hadn't prompted any questions. He *knew* who she was, of that much she was certain.

And he hadn't cared.

None of them had cared that the Americans were apparently coming, and if they were coming, she had to assume they'd be here soon.

Which meant whatever was going down was going down in the next few hours, perhaps even minutes.

Which meant Koroma might murder his own daughter at any time.

I have to save her.

She turned to head toward the clinic rear entrance, part of her satisfied that this act might in some small way make up for the unspeakable one she had committed when she cried out in shock, a large hand suddenly slapped over her mouth, silencing her scream.

"You listenin' to tings you should na," hissed a voice in her ear, the breath hot and foul, Koroma's driver wrapping his other hand around her front as his groin shoved into her side, his free hand finding a breast and squeezing painfully. "I tink it be time to teach you a lesson."

She screamed into his palm but it was no use, her voice too muffled. And even if she could scream aloud, would anyone who heard it care? With a rough jerk she was spun around on her heels and pulled toward the rear of the building, her shoes making two long lines in the dirt, pointers to where her ultimate humiliation would come to pass.

I deserve this!

It was God's way of punishing her for what she had done. Sacrificing the safety of an innocent child to save her own neck. She could imagine no worse sin, not even murder or suicide.

Suicide!

She had sworn she would kill herself if something like this were to happen, if she found herself powerless to stop her attackers. She wondered if Koroma had given the order, if the eight other men who had followed Sarah were now doing to Sarah what was about to happen to her.

You poor girl!

They reached the rear of the building, it backing onto a sparse area of yellow grass with no one in sight. He let go of his death grip on her chest and a gun was suddenly placed against her temple.

"Get on your knees."

She knew what was coming and her mind began to shut down. As she dropped to her knees, shoulders sagging in resignation, she listened for Sarah's screams but heard nothing. Instead all she heard was the sound of her assailant's zipper opening, a musky, unwashed stench immediately causing her to gag in disgust.

"You know what to do."

And she did. She gripped him, tight, and began tugging. The man's moans were nearly instantaneous and the gun left her head, resting at the man's side as he tossed his head back in ecstasy. Reaching into a pocket on the thigh of her scrubs, she pulled out a large scalpel she had found among the stolen supplies. Gripping it tightly, she pulled hard on the man, exposing the thick member then sliced, tossing away the resulting flesh as blood spurted from what remained, her assailant screaming in agony. She jabbed the scalpel deep into his inner thigh, yanking it downward, toward the knee, slicing vertically along the femoral artery, blood gushing over her hand, a pool of blood pumping onto the ground as the enraged man shouted at her in Krio.

"What have you done!" he cried, the gun swinging toward her. She knew it was now only a matter of moments. If she could survive long enough, he would be no match within thirty seconds. She launched herself from her knees, her right hand still gripping the scalpel, her left hand reaching for the arm with the gun, her countdown begun the moment she sliced the artery still ticking in her head.

Seven…eight...

Her hand wrapped around his wrist, still powerful, he easily overcoming her attempt to deflect the weapon. She sunk the scalpel into his stomach, jerking up.

Another cry of pain, this one turning into a whimper then a growl.

Twelve…thirteen…

His free hand wrapped around her throat, squeezing tight. She pulled the scalpel out, jabbing upward, catching the bottom of his chin, hitting hard bone. The grip tightened around her throat as she struggled to pull the blade free, it jammed in tight.

Sixteen…seventeen…

Her left foot slipped in the blood and she dropped to the ground, the grip on her throat loosening, her own on the scalpel lost. She grabbed at the gun hand with both of hers, the barrel now pointing directly at her head.

Twenty…twenty-one…

She pushed it aside, the man's strength weakening. His grip on the gun loosened and she did what all of her training told her could be a death sentence, but covered in the man's blood, she knew it was already too late for her if he were infected.

Yanking down on his gun hand, she sank her teeth into his wrist, clamping down as hard as she could.

Twenty-three…twenty-four…

The gun dropped and he collapsed to his knees. His free hand swatted at her face, making contact, the sheer mass of it still enough to stun her, but the energy behind it now weak.

She held on tight as another blow landed, this time even weaker.

Twenty-seven…twenty-eight…

He fell over to his side and she loosened her jaw, letting go of his hand, instead scrambling back in the large pool of blood, grabbing the weapon and pointing it at him.

Thirty…thirty-one…

His hand slowly reached out for her, his eyes wide with fear, then slowly closing as every muscle in his body relaxed, the outstretched arm finally hitting the ground with a splash of his own blood.

Tanya looked to her left then her right. She was still alone, it appearing the man's screams had brought no one. But for how long, she couldn't know. She jumped to her feet, wiggling the scalpel free from the now nearly dead lump of flesh and rushed to the corner of the building. Peering around the corner, she saw no one. The door that led to the showers was only twenty feet from her. She rushed back to her attacker and grabbed him by the arm, attempting to drag him toward the side of the building but she soon gave up, the man simply too heavy, especially as a deadweight.

I'll need Sarah's help.

If she's still alive.

She peered again around the corner then darted toward the doorway leading to the showers. Stealing a glance through the glass, she yanked it open and jumped inside, racing for the shower room. Pushing the button to lock the door, she immediately stepped under the shower and turned it on, the cool water soaking her still clothed body as she collapsed to the floor, shaking uncontrollably as her rapist's blood washed off of her then spiraled down the drain.

As she lay on the tile floor, curled in a ball of shock and self-pity, she thought of that little girl and how scared she must be, all because of the selfish actions taken by a coward.

And she pushed herself to her feet, determined to make sure they all survived until the Americans arrived, even if it meant Sarah had to endure an unspeakable horror.

Northern Sierra Leone

Dawson sat in the passenger seat, their liaison officer, Margai, driving. Atlas, Jimmy and Niner sat in the back, the conditions cramped with Atlas' broad shoulders, but complaints were few. The alternative was splitting up and driving in vehicles occupied by their escort who they couldn't be sure weren't infected. It was a new dynamic having to think of such things, and he would have preferred to have two vehicles, driven and occupied only by his own men, but that wasn't an option here.

In fact, initially Margai didn't want them to even come.

"I'm afraid I cannot agree to that. You are my responsibility, and I cannot risk you getting lost, injured or worse, infected. My men will check it out. If we find anything, we will let you know."

"Unfortunately I cannot agree to *that.* Your government promised us full cooperation. We *will* be investigating these sightings. You can drive us there yourself, or we will arrange our own transportation. Either way, we're going."

Margai had smiled. "I'm afraid you wouldn't get far. There are many roadblocks and checkpoints."

Dawson had pointed skyward. "Where we're going, we don't need roads."

Niner had stifled a snicker nearby at the obvious Back to the Future reference, Margai either not noticing or choosing to ignore it. They were soon on the road with two troop transports accompanying them, half a dozen men in the lead vehicle, the trailing vehicle almost empty, it to carry back any prisoners.

They had been travelling for several hours, their vehicles and Margai's ID clearing them through checkpoints very quickly, little time lost. The sun was low in the west, to their left, their direction a mix of north and east jaunts along the windy road, long straight highways not something easily afforded in a poor country.

It didn't matter. According to Dawson's phone they were already nearing the area in question, a cluster of small villages all within approximately fifty miles of each other, all the original homes to those involved. Several drones were in the air and satellites had been re-tasked to try and provide as much coverage as possible, but nothing yet had been reported.

There was a squawk in his earpiece. "Bravo Zero-One, Control, maintain radio silence on your end." Dawson felt himself tense up slightly, it clear their minders back home didn't want Margai to know they were communicating. "We've got a UAV over you now. There's a road block ahead, just over the next rise, heavily armed. It looks like they're prepping for your arrival. ETA two mikes, over."

"It would be nice if we had some help when we got there," said Dawson, turning toward Margai and smiling.

"My men can handle anything we might encounter," said Margai confidently, his right hand loosely on the wheel, his left holding a cigarette, his arm half out the open window.

"We've got Royal Marines inbound by helo now, ETA fifteen mikes, over."

"I need to hit the head, can we stop? I'd hate to enter combat with a full bladder."

Margai laughed. "Just ahead there's a village with a good restaurant. We can stop and get something to eat and drink there."

"How far?"

"About two minutes."

"There's nothing for the next fifteen minutes on this route, over."

"Can't wait that long," said Dawson, his right hand sliding to his hip as he turned toward the back of the vehicle. "You guys up for a piss break?" He made direct eye contact with each of them, all privy to the conversation with Control.

His message was delivered.

"Oh you can wait two minutes," came the cheery reply.

"'Fraid not." Dawson pulled his weapon, jamming it against Margai's ribcage. "Stop the vehicle."

"What are you doing?" cried Margai, his cigarette dropping from his fingers as he grabbed the steering wheel with both hands.

"Stopping whatever it is you've got planned," replied Dawson as Niner's gun pressed against the back of the man's neck. "Now come to a nice, easy stop."

Margai hammered on the gas, his hand shoving against the horn, the loud sound causing the troops in the lead transport to poke their heads out from under the canvas. Dawson pumped two rounds into Margai's ribcage, scrambling the man's heart and lungs. Margai collapsed into the steering wheel, the soldiers ahead of them raising their weapons. Niner reached forward and grabbed Margai's collar, yanking him backward allowing Dawson to reach over and shove the door open. Pushing Margai's body out of the vehicle with one hand, the other on the wheel of the rapidly slowing vehicle, he climbed over the console and dropped into the driver seat just as the first rounds from the lead vehicle tore into the windshield.

"Return fire," ordered Dawson as he slammed on the brakes, throwing the vehicle into reverse. Niner and Atlas leaned out their windows and opened fire on the rear of the lead vehicle as Jimmy climbed into the passenger seat.

"Cover the rear!" he shouted to Atlas as he took over firing at the lead vehicle, Atlas spinning in his seat, taking out the shocked and confused driver of the now stopped trailing vehicle. Another shot and the passenger was eliminated. Dawson expertly continued to reverse the vehicle, swerving around the trailing vehicle as he updated Control.

"Control, Bravo One, we've been engaged by our escorts. Liaison has been eliminated, over."

"Bravo One, Control Actual, are you intact, over?"

Dawson always felt a sense of comfort when he heard Colonel Clancy's voice—it meant the big man was aware of what was going on and had their backs. "Affirmative."

"Someone must have radioed in the situation. The vehicles at the roadblock are scrambling, heading your direction, over."

"Numbers?"

"Four vehicles, at least two dozen hostiles."

"Lovely," muttered Dawson. "Ammo check!"

"Two mags!" shouted Atlas.

Niner leaned back in for a moment. "One plus one just loaded!"

"Three!" replied Jimmy as he ceased firing, the lead vehicle no longer moving, it apparently waiting for reinforcements.

"We've got movement behind you, two vehicles. Possibly hostile, over."

Dawson slammed on the brakes.

"What's up, boss?" asked Niner as Dawson shoved the vehicle into first, hammering on the gas and popping the clutch.

"The only weapons and ammo are in those trucks and we're about to be surrounded." They surged forward, racing back toward the trailing truck. He looked back at Atlas as he hit the brakes again. "Get their weapons and ammo."

Atlas jumped out, the tires already spinning as they raced toward the lead vehicle. Nothing moved in the rear, his team's shots true, but most likely the driver and at least one additional man in the cab of the truck were still alive.

"ETA sixty seconds on the vehicles in front of you, two mikes on your six. Marines updated on your status, ETA now ten mikes, over."

"This will be over by then," said Dawson as he brought the vehicle to a halt, Niner and Jimmy jumping out, racing up either side of the stopped transport vehicle. Two shots rang out from either side before he was even out of the vehicle.

"Clear!" shouted Niner, immediately echoed by Jimmy.

"Weapons and ammo!" shouted Dawson as he jumped into the rear of the transport. Someone moaned to the left resulting in a double-tap to the chest. He began tossing weapons, mostly AK-47s, out the back then patting the bodies down for ammo, finding two magazines on each of the six men.

"Look, BD, RPG!" Dawson turned to see a grinning Atlas holding up the weapon in one hand, two AKs in the other. "Got four mags, too."

Dawson jumped back to the ground, pointing to Niner. "Block the road with this," he said, slapping the side of the transport. "Flatten the tires."

Niner nodded, yanking the body of the driver out of the cab and climbing in as Dawson surveyed the terrain. There were plenty of low trees with a taller grove several hundred yards to the east but there was no way they could make them in time; they would be sitting ducks if their opponents could actually shoot.

The hiss of air filled his ears for a moment as Niner and Jimmy used their knives to flatten the tires rather than waste valuable ammunition. "Weapons and ammo in our vehicle, let's head south. We'll intercept the smaller force, take out one of the vehicles with the RPG, the other by surprise. That should allow us to continue retreating. If we can stay ahead of the approaching reinforcements long enough, the Brits might just get here before it's too late."

Armfuls of weapons were grabbed and dumped into the back seat as Dawson jumped into the driver seat, turning the key, the engine merely turning over but not starting. And he already knew the reason.

He could smell gas.

He jerked a thumb at Atlas. "Check the other transport, see if it starts."

Atlas, not yet in the vehicle, tore off toward the only other vehicle that might still be functional, climbing inside and turning the key. It roared to life.

But too late.

"They're here," shouted Niner, pointing ahead as a column of vehicles crested a ridge, single file.

"Hit the lead vehicle," ordered Dawson as he stepped out of the vehicle, cranking the wheel to the left. He pushed, the vehicle inching forward then finally gaining some momentum as he directed it toward a shallow ditch at the side of the road. Stepping away the truck rolled into the depression, its front bumper slamming into the embankment with a crunch.

The distinctive sound of an RPG launching to his right was ignored, the resulting explosion and cheer from Niner telling him all he needed to know. Reaching into the back seat, he pulled the weapons out, tossing them to Jimmy and the returning Niner as Atlas attempted to turn the massive transport on the narrow road behind them. He leaned out the window.

"There's just no room!" he shouted. "We'll have to back out of here!"

Dawson nodded, stuffing his pockets with magazines. "Let's go!"

They ran toward the rear transport, Dawson pointing toward the passenger side. "Jimmy, with Atlas! Cover the front!"

Jimmy broke off as Atlas straightened the truck, adjusting the side view mirror as Dawson and Niner jumped into the back of the vehicle. It began to reverse as gunfire erupted from the front, Jimmy's AK-47 responding. They began to pick up speed as Atlas expertly guided them toward the smaller enemy, all Delta Operators trained in high speed driving in both directions.

Dawson braced himself, sprawled on the floor of the transport, his AK-47 at the ready.

I wish I had my MP5!

But he'd have to make do. The AK-47 was a fine, reliable weapon, and it killed quite effectively if well-aimed.

"Control, Bravo Zero-One. ETA on those Marines?"

"Six mikes."

"Direction of arrival?"

"From the south."

"Good, we're heading toward them. Hopefully that'll shave a few seconds off."

At the speeds the helicopters would be travelling, their barely ten-mile-per-hour retreat would literally result in mere seconds of savings, but in a gun battle that could mean the difference between life and death.

"New arrivals from the south are around the next bend, over."

"Did you hear that?" shouted Dawson.

"Affirmative!" replied Atlas as the bend in question appeared.

"Control, type of vehicles?"

"Two troop transports, just like you're in, over."

"I'll hit the passenger side of the windshield, that should cause the driver to swerve left, exposing the rear of the transport. I'll take out the driver and any front seat passengers, you empty your mag into the back."

"Got you."

The lead vehicle suddenly appeared from behind a stand of trees.

"Engaging," said Dawson into his comm as he placed two shots into the passenger side windshield, conveniently eliminating one of the enemy. The truck jerked to the left, as predicted, giving him a clear shot of the driver through the passenger side window. He let out a short burst, the AK-47 not known for its sharp-shooting abilities.

But his aim was true.

Beside him Niner's AK pumped death at the rear of the rapidly nearing vehicle as Atlas continued to reverse. Jimmy's gunfire had ceased, enough distance having been placed between them and the stalled column. He could hear the shouts and cries of panic as those in the back of the lead vehicle were torn apart by Niner's well-placed shots.

Dawson took a bead on the driver of the second vehicle as the man brought his vehicle to a stop, the soldiers in the rear pouring out. A short burst shattered the windshield, leaving a bloody mess behind it as Dawson turned his attention to the scrambling soldiers, Niner reloading and quickly joining in.

Dawson felt the vehicle slow as they approached the lead vehicle now blocking the road, gunfire being returned by the survivors.

"Control, status on northern column, over!"

"Just underway now, over."

"Atlas, move forward, take us back around the bend then we'll use that stand of trees as cover!"

"Roger that!"

The truck jerked forward, the engine roaring in the low gears as they surged away from one enemy and toward a greater. The bend in the road quickly took the southern force out of sight and Dawson slapped his hand on the metal floor, signaling Atlas to stop. He swung out onto the road as Niner handed him the weapons then jumped down himself. Dawson looked around the driver side of the vehicle at Atlas.

"Put it in the ditch, we'll use it as cover."

Atlas gave a two fingered salute with his left hand and cranked the wheel as Jimmy joined them in the shallow ditch in front of the small stand of trees. Dawson pointed to the southern side as the truck's bumper crunched against the embankment. "Jimmy, Niner, you two cover the rear, Atlas and I will cover north. Control, ETA on the Marines?"

"Three mikes, over."

"Okay, we just need to hang in for three minutes. No heroes today, we're just delaying. Keep them pinned down, and keep your own heads down. One-hundred-eighty seconds, that's all."

He dropped to the ground, taking up a position behind the wheel of their truck, a clear view of the road ahead. Atlas lay on the road, the rear wheels providing valuable protection as he took aim under the truck.

Gunfire erupted behind them, single shots, as Niner and Jimmy engaged the enemy.

"Report!"

"I'm counting six hostiles still moving," shouted Niner. Another shot. "Make that five!"

The distinctive sounds of AK-47s responding were ignored by Dawson, his main concern the approaching larger force. His guys could take out six—scratch that, five—men with little problem. But they had almost two dozen ahead of them.

Atlas opened fire, a group of four hostiles foolishly clustered together cut down, causing the others to scramble for safety, the vehicles they had been in just coming around a bend slightly down the road. "Hit the engine block!"

Atlas and Dawson opened fire on the lead vehicle, tearing into the engine compartment, Dawson briefly raising his weapon to take out the driver. Steam erupted from the hood, the vehicle jerking to a halt as they redirected their attention to the soldiers on foot.

"Conserve ammo! Just keep them pinned down for now!" Dawson's mental count had the Brits less than two minutes away. "Control, Bravo Zero-One. ETA on those Marines, over?"

"Less than two mikes, over."

"We've got hostiles at our twelve and five o'clock, over."

"Roger that, Marines have been briefed as to your situation, over."

Dawson fired two rounds at someone stupid or brave enough to attempt closing the distance. He dropped, writhing on the ground with a new hole in his leg. Two of his buddies scrambled forward to carry him to safety but Atlas took them out with leg shots as well.

It takes two healthy men to carry out one wounded man.

The three were left to cry for help, the others keeping their heads down.

"Niner, status!"

"Two left, hunkered down. They're not going anywhere."

"Good! Keep them that way!"

"Do you hear that?"

Dawson cocked an ear and smiled, the distinctive thumping of helicopter blades approaching.

"Bravo Zero-One, this is Alpha-One-Zero-Alpha, do you read, over."

The distinctive Limey accent was music to Dawson's ears. He exchanged grins with Atlas who fired a couple more rounds to keep the enemy heads down.

"Alpha-One-Zero-Alpha, Bravo-Zero-One, reading you five-by-five, over."

"Keep your heads down, chaps, we're coming in hot, over."

Dawson looked to the south and saw two Merlin HM1 helicopters racing toward them, one breaking slightly to their right, mounted L7A2

GPMG's opening fire on the remaining southern position, Niner waving a thumbs up at them. "Ground beef!" he shouted to Dawson with a grin, returning to covering their flank, just in case someone had survived. The second chopper opened fire on the column, explosions drowning out the screams as the first chopper touched down behind them for a moment, the Marines jumping out, rushing toward Dawson's position as their ride rose into the air, its guns belching lead at the hostiles.

Dawson gave them a wave, returning his attention to the battle ahead as the Marines advanced in full combat gear, Dawson and his team content to sit back in their thin shirts as the helicopters ceased fire.

An eerie silence settled over the area, pierced only by the occasional sharply issued order by the platoon commander. In less than two minutes the Marines had the site secure, the second group exiting their own chopper to the north, cutting off the escape of what turned out to be three survivors.

It was a bloody day for the enemy.

Just like it should be.

"Careful, men, we don't know if any of them are infected so keep your distance." Dawson strode toward the man obviously in charge. Salutes weren't in order since Dawson was in civvies. "Are you Mr. White?"

Dawson nodded.

"Captain Grimshaw, at your service." A slight bow was provided, which Dawson knew wouldn't have been offered if the Captain knew Dawson's lowly rank.

"Much appreciated, Captain. You arrived just in the nick of time."

Grimshaw looked about. "I got the impression you had things well in hand."

"I was two minutes away from calling you off."

Grimshaw tossed his head back, roaring in laughter. "You Yanks, I've missed your sense of humor."

"Served with us before?"

"Too many bloody times in Iraq."

"Yeah, been there a few times myself."

Grimshaw pulled his shades down slightly, revealing his eyes. "Just a few, *Mr.* White?"

Dawson winked. "Whatever do you mean, Captain?"

"I'm sure I have no idea." He pointed toward one of the helicopters that had landed. "Shall we give you a lift back to base?"

Dawson shook his head. "Negative. We've still got a mission to complete."

A smile slowly spread across Grimshaw's face. "You have no idea how happy you just made me."

"Bored?"

"You have no bloody idea."

Dawson's comm squawked. "Bravo Zero-One, Control Actual. Sit rep, over."

"Control Actual, Bravo Zero-One, situation is secure, over."

"Good to hear. We've got intel from Langley. They just might have found our doctors, over."

Dawson smiled at the others, Grimshaw not privy to the conversation.

"What is it?"

Dawson tapped his ear. "Eye in the sky. Up for some more action?"

Grimshaw's smile spread even further. "Absolutely."

Samaia, Sierra Leone

"Infect these men."

Sarah froze, uncertain if she had heard Koroma correctly. *Infect them? Was he crazy?* Suddenly everything that had been said to her, everything that had been overheard, made sense. The constant questions about infection, needle pricks, how long to show symptoms, Koroma's leaving for America.

They are *terrorists!*

Her stomach suddenly flipped and her vision blurred as she tried to come to grips with what was going on. She had spent her entire time here trying to survive, trying to prove her usefulness so that she might be rescued. It had never occurred to her that the real reason for her kidnapping had little to do with who she was.

It was *what* she was.

A doctor.

They had needed someone who could answer their questions then infect them.

But that makes no sense!

Why would they kidnap her, such a high profile doctor? Her father was the Vice President of the United States. If they had taken someone like Tanya, or better yet, a local doctor, no one would have even blinked.

No, there was more going on here than just needing someone to infect them. She was still connected to this somehow, but how, she had no idea. But she had the distinct feeling that after she did infect these men, she'd have served her purpose and would be killed.

And how she'd prevent that, she wasn't sure.

"I-I can't do that."

"You must."

"But I'm a doctor! I swore an oath to do no harm!"

Koroma pulled his weapon from its holster and pointed it toward the clinic. "I will put a bullet in every single one of those people if you don't."

"You'd kill your own daughter?"

Koroma squinted slightly, sucking in a deep breath. "To spare her from the suffering to come? Absolutely."

"But she can be saved!" Sarah wanted to tell him his daughter might not even be infected, to tell him there might be no suffering at all, but she was certain telling him this would get her, or at least Tanya, killed for certain.

She bit her tongue.

"You and I both know the chances of that are slim. And even if she is saved, she will be alone."

Sarah looked at him. "So you are going to kill yourself."

He nodded toward the men. "I ask nothing of my men that I'm not willing to ask of myself."

Sarah's head was shaking in disbelief. He *was* mad, he *was* crazy. He wasn't a religious zealot like most terrorists, but he was a zealot nonetheless. If his plan was to infect himself and these men with the Ebola virus, then travel to the United States, he was clearly insane.

And she told him so.

He chuckled. "Doctor, I admire you. You speak your mind even though you are faced with certain death." He sighed. "No, I am not insane. What *is* insane is your Western governments allowing what is happening here to have continued on for so long. It is time they tasted the fear and heartache we've been experiencing for over a year."

"But what do you hope to accomplish?"

He shrugged. "Nothing."

"What do you mean? Don't you have any demands?"

He shook his head. "No, no demands. It's too late for demands. The dead are dead and they will remain so. The dying are already dead. Our own government is locking down the country, taking the measures necessary to eventually stamp out this plague until it rears its head again months or years from now. Your money and medicines will merely speed up the inevitable process. Anything I do will not stop that flow as you are now too scared to have it arrive on your own doorstep again. You will do whatever it takes to stop this outbreak from reaching your shores." He paused, looking at the clinic for a moment then back at her, his voice slightly lower. "But it doesn't excuse you for what you did."

"So this is revenge?"

"This is payback. You sat back and did nothing in Rwanda. Almost one million were killed in one hundred days and the world did nothing but talk. Why? No oil. No white people. It's time you were taught a lesson for your depraved self-interest."

"Aren't you scared you'll just piss us off? That those very people you blame for not urging their politicians to take action will instead be the same people who demand their politicians pull the help we're now providing?"

Koroma smirked. "If that is the reaction, then they definitely deserve what they get. Why punish an entire people for the actions of one man?"

Sarah couldn't answer him. "Because" wasn't a reasonable response, but angry, scared people weren't always reasonable. If people linked to the Sierra Leonean military and government were implicated in a horrific biological attack on America, what would the response be?

She suspected nothing. There were no terrorist bases to destroy, no weapons of mass destruction to find, no oil fields to secure.

Instead she expected the response would be nothing beyond demanding the perpetrators be brought to justice.

Koroma was right. The West would still fund the efforts to stop the outbreak at its source so it couldn't be used against them again, and in the end he would have won. His country would be saved, and he would have his revenge.

And deep down, she empathized.

She could never condone it though.

She could tell from Koroma's expression he felt he had won the argument. He flicked his gun toward the clinic. "Enough talk. You will draw blood from the sickest patient and inject us all with it, starting with me." She was about to open her mouth when he aimed his weapon at the clinic again. "Do it, or they all die."

She nodded. "I have to suit up first."

He shook his head. "We don't have the time and besides, there's no need."

Her chest tightened as if someone were sitting on it as she realized this was it. He was going to kill her as soon as she had finished. Her purpose will have been served.

She nodded, thinking quickly. "At least let me put gloves and a facemask on so I'm not cross-contaminating people."

He acquiesced, the little lie bought, bare hands or gloves making no difference in this situation—it was only to protect her in case she managed to think of some way to survive the next few minutes.

She stepped into the front of Zone One, snapping on the gloves then quickly donning the goggles and facemask. She felt naked as she took the syringe from Koroma, pushing the sheet aside to Zone Two. She glanced at Koroma's daughter, the little girl looking at her curiously, smiling at the first human she had seen in some time who didn't look terrifying.

Sarah waved at her then let the sheet close behind her as she continued toward Zone Three, her mind racing as she tried to figure out what to do.

Then she smiled. She eyed the syringe then her exposed arms and realized that she couldn't stop what was going to happen here, couldn't save her life or that of Tanya's, but she might be able to save thousands back home. She stepped into Zone Three, those inside too weak to even raise their heads to look at her. Looking behind her, she squeezed her left hand tight, extending the arm as she looked for a vein.

"Once again you surprise me, Doctor." She yelped as Koroma stepped up behind her, grabbing her arm. "I must admit my admiration for you continues to grow. I promise that your death will be painless."

She stood, staring at the floor, shaking, the syringe now at her side, her brilliant attempt to thwart Koroma's plans stopped in its tracks. He pointed at a man near death, blood seeping from every orifice. "Take his blood. Now."

She nodded as he let go of her arm. She stepped over to the man and knelt down beside him, taking his arm in her hand. She quickly filled the syringe's barrel with the deadly fluid, each drop enough to theoretically infect thousands if not more.

It terrified her.

And there was nothing she could do.

She rose, the man too far gone to have felt what she had done. She handed the syringe to Koroma but he refused it. "Come with me." He began to head to Zone Two when she grabbed him by the arm.

"No!"

Koroma turned, a look of mild surprise on his face.

"We never go backward."

"It hardly matters now."

"And if your daughter were to become infected by us breaking protocol, would you feel the same way?"

Koroma paused, his eyes narrowing slightly. "What do you mean?"

"What if the blood test was wrong? What if the samples were mixed up? What if she had a mild strain that she could easily survive? Didn't you notice how we've kept her isolated more than the others? We're giving her every chance she's got to survive. Don't risk her life for the sake of an extra few seconds going around the building."

Koroma said nothing, seemingly evaluating what she had said. She decided her best bet to encourage him to follow protocol was to simply give him no choice.

She headed for the rear exit and shoved open the door, stepping outside. The man who would normally hose her down looked confused, surprised. Even a bit scared.

She placed the syringe on a table then held out her gloved hands, determined to keep them on as long as she had to handle the syringe. "Just spray my hands and my feet."

The man nodded, carrying out the unusual orders as Koroma stepped outside.

She pointed at Koroma's boots. "Spray his feet too."

The man looked terrified, almost too scared to even look at his boss let alone follow through with the order.

Koroma shook his head. "There's definitely no need for that."

Sarah decided it was best to pick her battles. If she was right, Koroma would soon be gone, surrounded by infected men who once displaying symptoms, would be infectious to those around them whether some of the virus were on the soles of his shoes or not.

They rounded the building, returning to where the men were waiting, Sarah filling the seconds with encouraging words about how his daughter was very likely to survive with proper care, a feeble attempt to reinforce the need to leave her and Tanya alive.

Koroma said nothing, instead holding out his arm as soon as they were with the other men. She said nothing, instead injecting him, not even half a CC, but more than enough to infect him in the days to come.

"Thank you, Doctor."

Her automatic response was said before she could stop herself. "You're welcome."

She closed her eyes for a moment, shaking her head, then injected the other men, none to a man showing any hesitation. She wondered if the Kamikaze pilots of World War II were as stoic in their resolve, if the Islamic terrorists heading out on a suicide bombing mission were as steadfast. As she finished with the last man, she made it a point to make certain the syringe was empty lest Koroma turn it on her.

I'd rather die from a bullet than Ebola.

"Very good." He said something in Krio that sent the men running to their vehicles. Koroma turned toward her, pulling his gun. "I'm afraid it is time."

Her stomach tightened and her heart slammed against her ribcage as blood rushed through her ears. Thoughts of her husband, her parents, her family filled her mind, of the sick and the dying, of the lives lost and saved over the years, and of one trembling lip, her last memory of her son, a memory she had never dreamed she would be taking to her grave.

Her breaths were shallow, rapid, as she began to hyperventilate. She stepped backward, bumping into a table holding supplies. She gripped its edge. Tight. A splinter from the worn table made its presence felt, jarring her back to reality if only for a moment. Koroma stood in front of her, a blur, her eyes filled with tears.

"I'm sorry, Doctor, but I can't risk someone finding you and you telling them of our plans."

She sucked in a sharp breath and held it, blinking rapidly. She refused to wipe her eyes dry, her hands still gloved and possibly still contaminated from the patient she had taken the blood from.

And besides, it would only give her a clearer view of the man about to shoot her.

"Is there anything you want to tell your father?"

"Wh-what?" The question caught her by surprise. What did he mean? Was he going to send him a message, or worse, actually see him?

"Do you have a message for your father?"

"I-I don't understand. Are you—are you going to see him?"

Koroma didn't reply. "Do you have a message? Last chance."

She nodded, hesitantly. "Y-yes. Tell him, tell my husband and son, and my mother, that I love them and that—" She stopped, the words caught in her throat as she choked out a sob. "Tell them all that I'm sorry, and that I love them, and that my last thoughts were of them."

"They will receive your message." He stepped closer. "Now close your eyes."

She gasped out a cry, her entire body shaking like a leaf as she squeezed her eyes tight, her hands trembling at her sides as she turned her head slightly, cringing with the anticipation of her impending death.

God forgive me for all my sins. Please take care of my son.

A horn honked, the grinding of gears causing her to open her eyes and look toward the road. "I got it!" a voice shouted, "I got it!" She saw the blurred form of Koroma turn toward the voice, a voice it took her a moment to recognize as Mustapha's.

The truck he was in skidded to a halt, a cloud of dust rolling toward them as he jumped out, the man clearly excited.

"Got what?" asked Koroma, stepping away from Sarah, giving her a moment's reprieve she wasn't sure she was happy to have, it merely giving her more time until her impending doom.

"The IV supplies they said they needed!"

This statement snapped Sarah's survival instinct back into play. She yanked off her face mask and gloves, tossing them aside then wiped her eyes dry. "Did you say you got IV supplies?"

The suddenly in focus Mustapha nodded, a genuine smile spread across his excited face. "We hijacked a supply heading for Port Loko. That's where I've been for the past few hours." He jerked his thumb over his shoulder as two men began unloading boxes of supplies. "We've got a whole truck full."

She chose to be bold, to take the initiative and ignore the danger, since the worst that could happen would be for Koroma to shoot her, something she had been seconds away from regardless. She walked swiftly to the rapidly growing pile of boxes and tore one open. Inside were precious bags of IV fluids, the exact type she needed to help save the people in her makeshift clinic.

She flashed a smile at Mustapha then whirled on Koroma, pointing at the boxes. "With these I can save your people."

Koroma said nothing, the gun still out, but now at his side.

"You can kill me now and all of this will go to waste, or you can let me put this to use. I can save your people, not all of them, but many of them." She stepped toward him, lowering her voice. "I can save your daughter."

This got a reaction as his eyes finally met hers. "Are you sure?"

She decided telling the truth was the best option, any hint of deception possibly sealing her fate. "No, I can't guarantee it. But she's young, strong and has just started showing symptoms. She's been isolated early and hasn't begun to dehydrate yet." She pointed at the boxes. "Let me save her. With proper, prompt intervention, over half can be saved. Let *this* be your legacy."

He said nothing for a moment, then suddenly holstered his weapon, walking briskly toward the idling vehicles. He stopped, turning toward her. "Save my daughter."

"I-I will."

He nodded then turned to Mustapha. "If my daughter survives, give her to her grandmother."

"Of course, Adopho."

"And if the Americans come, you know what to do."

Mustapha bowed slightly, closing his eyes for a moment. "It will be done."

Koroma opened the passenger door to the lead vehicle, looking at Mustapha one last time. "Good bye, my friend."

Mustapha snapped a rigid salute, Koroma returning it as the vehicle pulled away, leaving Sarah to wonder what Koroma's final instructions were.

She could think of only one thing.

Kill the doctors.

But she had to ignore that inevitability for now. She turned to Mustapha.

"I have to get Tanya. I'll need her help to get everyone hooked up as quickly as possible."

Mustapha nodded and she headed toward the showers, assuming that's where Tanya had disappeared to, she not having seen her since the new arrivals had first appeared. Stepping inside the building, she pressed against the wall, her entire body shaking with relief as she looked up to the heavens, thanking God for one more chance.

CIA Headquarters, Langley, Virginia

"What are we looking at?"

Chris Leroux used a laser pointer to indicate an L-shaped building surrounded by a loose cluster of houses in a semi-circle on three sides. To the right, only several hundred yards from the tiny village was a small winding river, the entire area cleared of trees leaving pale yellow grass and dried dirt covering the open areas.

"This is a community center in the town of Samaia in northern Sierra Leone, population less than five hundred. When these photos were taken several hours ago, you can see two transport vehicles that match the description of those missing here and here," he said, moving the pointer. "What's interesting though is this." He hit a key on his laptop and the photo changed to a zoomed in and enhanced photo of the southern side of the building. "Here you can see two individuals, one appears—"

"Is that biohazard gear they're wearing?" asked Donovan Eppes.

"We believe so. It matches the personal protective equipment that those dealing with the Ebola outbreak are wearing."

"So they have an outbreak in this village," said Cindy Fowler, the testiness in her voice suggesting she was pissed off at somebody, probably Eppes. "Should we be surprised by that?"

"Of course not," said Leroux, ignoring her attitude, it getting tiring. "We've confirmed however that there are no clinics in this area, no workers assigned to this village, and that this village, Samaia, is the hometown of our prime suspect, Major Adopho Koroma."

"Now those are just too many coincidences," said Morrison with a slight smile of approval directed at Leroux. "Anything else you can tell us?"

Leroux nodded, flicking through several more enhanced photos, each showing different armed men around the village. "Clearly there is a significant armed presence for this small a village. We've got a UAV heading for the area now and our Delta team along with British Marines are ready to enter, but the Sierra Leonean government is refusing permission. They want to handle it themselves."

"When?" cried Vice President Henderson. "How long will it take them to get there?"

"Hours. They're proposing leaving the operation until tomorrow morning as it will be dark before they get there."

"No goddamned way are we waiting until tomorrow!" Henderson jabbed his finger into the tabletop. "I want Delta sent in, now!"

This demand was above Leroux's pay grade. He turned toward Morrison who said nothing. He began to wonder if his boss was expecting him to respond when he was finally saved by someone jacked in over the speaker.

"Proceed."

Henderson's shoulders slumped in relief.

"Thank you, Mr. President."

Samaia, Sierra Leone

"Tanya, it's me!" Sarah knocked on the door to the showers again, this time a little harder. She could hear the water running inside, but the door was closed and locked. She put her ear against the door and swore she heard sobbing inside. Pushing on the door, she twisted the knob as hard as she could to no avail.

She slammed on the door with the palm of her hand.

"Tanya, open the door!"

The sound of the water changed inside, then the squeak of the knob being turned was followed by the water stopping. She stepped back slightly, not sure of what to expect, but when the door finally opened, she gasped, stunned at what she saw.

Her friend was soaked from head to toe, her clothes stained dark red, the water pooling at her feet mixed with what was clearly blood.

She resisted the urge to grab her, her fear of the virus too great, but when her friend started to collapse, she leapt forward and grabbed her, helping her to a nearby bench in front of the lockers then kneeling at her feet. "What happened?" she asked, quickly checking her body for wounds, finding none. "Whose blood is this?"

"It-it's not mine," she finally said, her eyes at last looking at Sarah. "It's the driver's."

Sarah's jaw dropped. The amount of blood was significant, despite her having been under the shower. If she had stabbed him, they were dead.

Or maybe he's *dead?*

"What happened?"

"He tried to rape me."

"Oh my God, are you okay? Did he…" She couldn't bring herself to say the words, the very idea of vocalizing them sickening, as if it would make it that much more real. But Tanya was suffering, and she needed her help. "Did he hurt you?" she finally managed, the words a whisper.

Tanya shook her head, vehemently. "I cut it off."

Sarah fell backward, looking up at her friend. "You what?" She knew what the words meant, but she wasn't sure if 'it' was really *'it'*. She secretly hoped 'it' meant what she was thinking.

"I cut it off. Clean off. With a scalpel."

Sarah bit her knuckle, hard, trying not to laugh with delight, the horror of the situation still not lost on her, but still she couldn't help herself. "You mean…his penis…you cut it off?"

"I sliced the goddamned thing off and tossed it away like a piece of gristle." Tanya looked at her and smiled bashfully. "Was that okay?"

Sarah finally let herself laugh, pushing herself back up on her knees, grabbing Tanya by either side of her face, touching foreheads. "Oh you brave, brave, girl. Of course it's okay!" Tanya suddenly hugged her, sobbing and laughing, and the two of them sat there for a moment without saying anything. Sarah finally gently pushed her friend away, holding her shoulders and looking into her eyes. "Where did he go?"

And it was the critical question. If he had time to get away and tell someone, they'd be looking for them and if the wrong person found them, they'd be dead, or worse, raped like originally intended.

But not by that bastard.

"Nowhere. He's still behind the building."

"Really? Didn't he run away?"

Tanya shook her head. "I sliced his femoral artery. He was out cold within thirty seconds. I'm sure he's dead by now."

Sarah felt her chest tighten. "We have to hide the body, now."

Tanya nodded. "I tried but he's too heavy."

"We'll do it together." Sarah pushed herself to her feet and helped Tanya to hers. "Show me."

Sarah stepped into the hallway, looking both ways to make sure they were alone, then led Tanya out by the hand, heading quickly for the rear exit. Opening the door, she looked outside and saw no one, the community center backing onto a cleared area then trees. Running toward the back, Tanya in tow, she rounded the corner and gasped. The amount of blood was incredible. The driver she remembered as Mohammed lay in the center of it, one hand gripping his groin, the other outstretched in front of him, his eyes closed, his skin a sickly color she had seen too often in her line of work.

There was no doubt he was dead, drained of blood.

She let go of Tanya and grabbed the outstretched arm, beginning to pull. "Help me!" she grunted, Tanya frozen in place. "Tanya, help me!"

Tanya finally moved, taking the other arm. Between the two of them they managed to drag the deadweight to the rear entrance when Sarah stopped.

"What?" asked Tanya. "We have to hurry before someone sees us!"

"They'll be searching for him."

Tanya looked at her and nodded. "Which is why we need to hide him. Now!"

Sarah shook her head. "If we put him inside they'll find him and know we did it."

Tanya looked over her shoulder at the distant tree line. "There's no way we can get him all the way over there. And besides, they'll find him anyway."

Sarah motioned toward the front of the building. "We'll put him in Zone Three." Tanya's eyes opened wide then she smiled slightly as she too realized it was the perfect hiding place. "I'll make sure it's clear." Sarah let go of the body and walked toward the front of the building. Nobody was at the rear entrance to Zone Three. The only problem now was the lack of protective gear.

They'd have to risk it.

She rushed back to Tanya and grabbed Mohamed's loose arm. "It's clear." She began to tug when she noticed Tanya not helping. She turned. "What?"

"We don't have any equipment."

"I know. We'll have to chance it, we have no choice. If they find him, we're dead anyway. If we catch Ebola, there's at least a fifty-fifty chance we'll survive. I prefer those odds to certain death."

Tanya nodded, beginning to pull again. "We need to survive until the Americans get here."

"Koroma had me infect him and eight others with the virus," grunted Sarah as they pulled the two hundred pound man in jerks. "He was going to kill me when Mustapha arrived with IV supplies."

"Really?" Tanya sounded excited. "With those we might actually save some of these people."

"Agreed." The word was strangled out, her muscles screaming for relief. She moved two hundred and even three hundred pound men around in her daily life, but it was always on a gurney or at least with some of their own power helping her.

Never had she pulled a deadweight across dirt for a couple of hundred feet.

She was exhausted.

She peered around the corner and they were still clear. In one last, all-out effort they pulled him as quickly as they could toward the door. She opened it, looking inside, seeing no one but the dying. Trying not to touch anything with her hands, she took a deep breath and yanked the body inside, eying an empty spot nearby. A few more tugs and the body was flopped into place.

They raced outside.

She gasped for air, her lungs screaming in protest. Tanya already had the hose pumped, the bleach solution spraying on Sarah's feet then her outstretched hands, Sarah returning the favor before they sprinted to the other exit that led to the showers. Inside they stripped and shared the shower, Sarah's discomfort over being completely naked with another woman forgotten.

Tanya turned the water off and hugged Sarah, tight. Sarah returned the hug, her discomfort slowly increasing as she remembered they were both buck.

"The Americans are coming," whispered Tanya.

Sarah's heart leapt. "What?"

"I overheard them. The Americans are on their way. We just need to keep alive until they get here."

Sarah pushed Tanya away, holding her by the arms, a huge smile of doubtful hope on her face. "Are you sure?"

Tanya nodded, a huge grin on her face. "I'm positive. I overheard them talking. That's why he was going to rape me then kill me."

Sarah rushed toward the change area. "We need to get into the clinic and act as if nothing is happening. They could be here any minute, or it could be hours." As she quickly toweled off she began to think about the blood at the rear of the building and decided to go back outside and at least kick some dirt over it. If someone walked in it there would be no hiding it, but if a casual observer were to look in the general direction, they at least wouldn't see anything.

She froze.

"We forgot the penis!"

Tanya looked at her, stunned, then suddenly a snicker escaped. And another. Sarah giggled, and within seconds both were laughing uncontrollably, the nervous energy they had been operating under now out of control.

Somebody hammered on the door, silencing them.

"What's taking you so long?" demanded Mustapha from the hallway.

"I had to shower. We'll be there in one minute!" shouted Sarah, the moment of levity abruptly over, fear once again the order of the day.

But they're coming!

Samaia, Sierra Leone

Abdallah pulled a long drag of his cigarette, his last one. He was determined to savor it himself, which meant he had to make sure none of the others saw him—they'd ask him to share.

Not my last damned cigarette.

He had no idea when he'd get more. Mustapha had just arrived with a truck load of bagged water. What the hell they needed bagged water for, he had no idea, though one of the others had said it was actually medicine.

They're all dead already. We should just kill them now so they don't suffer.

Both his parents had died months ago and he had no family of his own. It meant he had nothing to lose when Major Koroma had approached him for help. He had been more than willing to. Koroma was like a big brother to him, someone he had known as a little boy, Koroma at least ten years older. He had tried to model himself after the man, joining the army and trying to get assigned to his unit.

He had succeeded, and now was prepared to die to support his childhood hero.

Though he secretly hoped to avoid that.

He was too junior to have been chosen to head to America as part of the strike force, instead he had been chosen to be a decoy, to keep the authorities occupied here should they be found. It would most likely mean his death, but as long as the doctors were dead first, then his job would be done, the authorities hopefully thinking they had killed all involved.

At least long enough for the others to complete their task.

He kicked at something on the ground, it rolling in the dirt, dried grass sticking to it.

What the hell is that?

He bent over and picked it up, his cigarette, dangling out of his mouth, forgotten. Standing straight, he turned it around in his hand.

Then gagged.

Tossing it away, he bent over and heaved, his cigarette hitting the ground before his lunch, as the realization of what he had just picked up set in. He stepped away from it and felt his feet slip out from under him, sending him backward, landing hard on his back with a splash, something soaking through his shirt. He pushed himself into a seated position and looked at his hands.

Oh my God!

"Something's going on," rumbled Atlas, lying prone beside Dawson, looking through the scope on his MP5. "Guard at the two-three corner."

Dawson watched as the man bent over to pick something up, examining it. "What the hell is that?"

"Day old sausage?"

Suddenly the man threw it away as if it were crawling with maggots, jumping back as he did so. He slipped, falling on his back. As he sat up, the back of his uniform was soaked in something dark.

"Is that blood?" asked Atlas.

"I think so. Take him out."

A single, muffled shot rang out, the man, not yet standing, crumpled to the ground. "Move! Move! Move!" hissed Dawson as he leapt to his feet. Charging forward, using the back of the community center as cover, he and Atlas along with half a dozen British Marines raced across the field toward the small village. It was hot, hard work, all of them dressed head-to-toe in bunny suits and gasmasks, the internal temperature through the roof.

Intel suggested less than 500 lived here on a good day, yet it appeared almost abandoned other than soldiers lazily walking through the streets. Not a single civilian had been spotted since they arrived, most likely all hiding inside out of fear of the soldiers and the disease ravaging their country. If the civilians just stayed inside, this might be a cakewalk.

"Bravo Zero-One, Bravo One-One. I've got activity at the front of the community center, over."

Of course.

"Any sign they've made us?"

"Negative, but I've got eyes on our two hostages."

Dawson smiled. "Roger that. Control, did you copy that?" Dawson pressed his back into the wall of the community center, using hand signals to send four of the marines to the three-four corner.

"Confirmed, Bravo Zero-One, relaying information, over."

Dawson peered around the two-three corner toward the front of the building, no one in sight, then signaled for everyone to advance.

Somebody shouted.

Shit.

"So you think you can save my people?"

Sarah drew in a slow, deep breath, slightly shrugging her shoulders. "I hope so. At least now there's hope, thanks to you."

Mustapha smiled, looking at the large stack of supplies standing by the side of the clinic, some of his men moving it inside and out of the sunlight. So far it appeared that no one had discovered that Mohamed was missing and though Koroma was gone, she felt safe from the others with Mustapha here. He seemed to be an honest man who genuinely wanted to help his people, who seemed to understand the need to help those inside the clinic medically. According to Tanya he had apparently expressed doubts about

Koroma's ultimate mission, which gave her hope that he may actually let them live.

He had already saved their lives just by arriving with the supplies, and these past several hours of bought time she had put to good use. All of Zone Two were already hooked up to IV's, including Koroma's daughter, and they were now taking a little rest before they tackled Zone Three where there was much less hope of saving anyone, but they had to at least try.

Somebody shouted.

Sarah spun toward the outcry to see one of the soldiers sprinting toward them, yelling something in Krio and pointing toward the rear of the building. Sarah's heart leapt into her throat as she realized the pool of blood must have been discovered.

Tanya grabbed her arm, trying to will a message to her with only her eyes, a message that didn't seem to have any fear it, only hope. And that's when she realized what was being shouted.

They're here!

She stepped back, away from the approaching soldier when Mustapha's hand darted out and grabbed her by the arm. He pulled his weapon from his holster as their eyes met.

"I'm sorry, Doctor."

He raised the weapon to her head and she closed her eyes.

"He's about to eliminate one of the hostages, taking the shot."

Niner squeezed the trigger and the target dropped, the two doctors jumping up and down in a panic for a moment, their screams reaching the tree line he was hiding in. They bolted for a door in the community center as other hostiles rushed toward the building, firing blindly at their unseen enemy. He and Jimmy along with two other Brits were covering the northern approach to the village, a British unit of four the south. The river to the east blocked any escape or risk of reinforcements, and the west was where Dawson and the rest were executing their insertion.

He scanned for his next target as Jimmy's weapon fired a single shot, it now open season on the hostiles. The orders of the day were to eliminate from a distance and not approach. There were only enough bunny suits for the insertion team which meant he and the others had to sit things out on the sidelines while trying to make sure the hostages stayed alive long enough to be reached.

Someone had spotted the team, which meant all hell was breaking loose.

He could hear disciplined shots coming from the other side of the village, the British team engaging the enemy. He squeezed the trigger, another hostile getting too close to the building dropping. Suddenly a group of four burst from a set of doors in the community center and shoved through the other set the doctors had just gone through, no one able to get a shot off before they disappeared.

"Four hostiles just entered the building after the doctors, over."

Sarah jumped then screamed as she realized the shot she heard was too far away to have been from Mustapha's weapon. She opened her eyes and looked down as his grip on her arm loosened then gave way, a rapidly growing stain in his chest indicating where he had been hit. More shouting and she saw more of Koroma's men running toward them, Tanya screaming beside her.

Grabbing Tanya by the arm she rushed toward the clinic doors, pushing them open just as several bullets tore into the ground behind them. Yanking Tanya inside, she shoved the door shut, looking for a lock.

There was none.

She pointed at a nearby table. "Help me move this in front of the door."

She grabbed it and a still shaking Tanya took the other end. They quickly moved the far too light table to the door as Sarah searched for a better alternative. She spotted a broom standing in the corner and grabbed it, sticking the wooden pole through the door handles.

She knew it wouldn't hold.

"Gear up, they might not follow us."

Tanya nodded, rushing over to the area containing their protective gear and quickly shoved her legs inside the bunny suit as Sarah did the same. She zipped up the front of her suit, snapped on her gloves and pulled on her boots as the gunfire and shouting continued from outside. This was it, the moment they had been waiting for, and it could be all over in minutes.

More than enough time for just one of Koroma's men to execute their final orders.

Kill the doctors.

She snapped her goggles in place then pulled the hood over her head, shoving the plastic visor over her face just as somebody slammed against the door.

Tanya grabbed her by the arm, pulling her through the curious onlookers of Zone One, tossing the sheet to Zone Two aside as the broom splintered behind them, the table shoved aside. Sarah stole a glance over her shoulder to see at least four men rushing inside after them.

"Run!"

Tanya let go of her arm and sprinted as fast as her gear would allow her toward Zone Three, flinging the sheet out of their way. Sarah rushed after her, stealing glances over her shoulder, spotting the men following them without hesitation as they burst into the quarantine area, unconcerned with the risk to their lives.

The door ahead of them burst open, armed men rushing toward them. Tanya dropped to her knees, screaming as she raised her hands, covering her head. Sarah skidded to a halt and cringed, protecting her head as gunfire erupted from the two men in front of them, their weapons belching lead at them, their muzzles flashing in the dimmed light of this abattoir of Mother Nature.

But she wasn't hit.

She opened her eyes to see the men rushing past her, still firing. She spun, seeing their pursuers dropping as the shots she thought meant for them found their mark, and within seconds they were all down.

One of them turned back toward them as the rest rushed forward. He was wearing some sort of gas mask obscuring his features.

"We're American and British soldiers. Are you Doctors Sarah Henderson and Tanya Danko?"

She nodded, her chest suddenly beginning to heave as sobs of relief escaped, tears flooding into her goggles as she turned and hugged Tanya, the two of them collapsing into a heap on the floor, exhausted physically, drained emotionally, as the dead and dying around them watched, too weak to react.

"Let's get outside," said the man, urging them to their feet with a helping hand. They exited the rear of the building and on instinct Tanya grabbed the hose and began spraying Sarah as several soldiers gathered around, taking covering positions. The gunfire was sporadic, the sounds of several guns firing rapidly, other weapons, fired in single bursts, seemed to be coming from all directions.

She ignored it all, the possibility of being killed by a stray bullet not even crossing her mind as the horrors of the past days were quickly pushed aside with the realization they had been rescued.

Thank you, Daddy!

She took the hose from Tanya and returned the favor, her shoulders still shaking from her sobs of joy and relief, and when done, she ripped her headgear off, tossing it aside as she unzipped the suit, having to catch herself as she momentarily forgot protocol. She took a deep breath and looked at Tanya.

"Protocol."

Her friend nodded, sniffling inside her facemask as they completed the deliberate process, the last thing they needed now an accidental infection after having survived everything that had happened to them. When they were finally done, she realized she hadn't heard any gunfire for minutes.

She looked at the soldier that had burst through the doors and saved them, then grabbed the hose, spraying him down from head to toe, finished, she handed the hose to Tanya who began hosing the other soldiers down who had entered the building.

"Is it safe to take this thing off?" asked the soldier who had entered the clinic first.

She nodded.

"Good." He pulled it off revealing a face she wasn't expecting to see. He didn't look like any soldier she had ever seen, his hair disheveled and longer than the usual buzz cut she was anticipating. And the week's worth of facial hair looked at once sexy and also court martial worthy.

Could he be civilian?

"I'm Agent White, Bureau of Diplomatic Services." He pulled a satellite phone out of his pocket and dialed a number. "Go for Henderson?" He nodded, then handed her the phone. "Someone wants to speak to you."

She took the phone, holding it up to her ear, curious. "Hello?"

"Sarah honey! It's Daddy!"

She dropped to her knees once again, her shoulders heaving at the sound of a voice she thought she'd never hear again.

Gateway Village Apartments, Baltimore, Maryland

Red walked through the small apartment, it cluttered with the necessities of life stolen an item at a time, closets jammed with individual toilet paper rolls, paper towels and feminine hygiene products, along with cleaning supplies in bulk containers. The urinator's cousin worked as a cabbie but also a janitor at a local hospital, it clear he was pilfering supplies to supplement his family's meagre existence.

He could have been stealing much worse.

There appeared to be little by the way of luxuries here, a few hand crafted items that looked like they were either carved in his homeland or made by local artisans originally from there, along with an old CRT television and a $30 DVD player.

And no phone.

Red turned to FBI Agent-in-Charge McKinnon. "Does he have a cellphone?"

McKinnon nodded. "Yeah, we're trying to trace it now but it looks like it's been turned off." He held up an evidence bag with a piece of paper inside. "But we found this."

Red took the bag and frowned as he read the letter from their suspect to his wife and child, apologizing for what he was about to do, but justifying it as punishment for what had happened to their native Sierra Leone. He shook his head.

"This isn't over yet."

McKinnon took the bag back, handing it to one of his underlings. "Definitely not. Unfortunately we've found nothing yet that tells us where he went. There's not a single document here or piece of paper here, no computer, no internet access. These people were poor but up until now, law abiding.

"Just like all the rest." Red pursed his lips, walking into the single bedroom, a double bed wedged in one corner, a single at the foot of it with a bright pink blanket adorned with hand-stitched lions, zebras and giraffes.

Whoever sewed this has skills.

It was too bad those type of skills were no longer valued in mainstream America today. A person who could create such a masterpiece could make an excellent living if they knew how to market those skills, and more importantly, if they knew those skills were actually worth marketing. In today's America most people looked for the cheapest bed covering, made by slave labor in China or Bangladesh, rather than an expensive handmade item that would last a lifetime.

It was sad that so many immigrants came to America with basic skills that we no longer valued as a society, but cooed over at the local antique shop as quaint and worth top dollar.

And of course we told them their skills were worthless.

A commotion from the main living area drew him out of the bedroom. A woman carrying a small child, maybe Bryson's age, was shouting at the police guarding the entrance in heavily accented English.

"Who are you? What are you doing in my home? I demand you get out! I know my rights!"

McKinnon quickly headed for the door to try and defuse the situation. "Ma'am, I'm FBI Agent-in-Charge McKinnon. Are you Mrs. Buhari?"

"FBI?" Anger turned to fear very quickly as the woman took a step back, gripping her child a little tighter, tears already running down the little girl's cheeks.

"Yes, ma'am. Are you Mrs. Buhari?"

She nodded, hesitantly, turning slightly, placing her shoulder between McKinnon and her child. "Why? What has happened? Why are you here?"

"We're looking for your husband, ma'am. Do you have any idea where he is?"

Her eyes narrowed, but Red could see almost every muscle in her body tense up.

She knows why we're here.

"No, I don't know."

"Shouldn't he be at work?"

She hesitated, realizing she had been caught in a lie. "Well, yes, I mean, of course he's at work."

McKinnon held out his hand, inviting her inside. "Why don't you come inside, ma'am, so we can do this in private. Your neighbors don't need to hear this."

She looked over her shoulder and Red suppressed a smile as several doors could be heard slamming shut. Mrs. Buhari stepped inside and McKinnon motioned at one of his men.

"Why don't you get Mrs. Buhari a glass of water?" he said as he motioned toward a threadbare chair that would have looked at home on the set of Archie Bunker. She sat down, still trying to direct her child's face away from the gathered strangers. Remarkably the little girl hadn't made a sound.

McKinnon sat on a vinyl couch, the wheeze of air squeezing from the cushion an almost comic relief to the tension in the room.

"Now, ma'am, we need to find your husband as quickly as possible. We believe he may be in serious trouble."

"Wh-why? What has he done?"

Interesting choice of words.

"As far as we know he's done nothing, yet." McKinnon motioned for the letter to be brought over. "He wrote you this." He showed her the letter and Buhari quickly read it, tears rolling down her face by the time she finished. "Do you know what he's referring to?"

She shook her head, quickly. A little too quickly.

McKinnon caught it.

"I think you do, Mrs. Buhari. If we find him before he does anything serious, he'll be in a lot less trouble than after."

Buhari looked about the room, most eyes on her, clearly making her discomfort nearly unbearable. It was a tactic that could work, but it could also backfire. She might spill her guts under the pressure, or she might fight back by clamming up if she supported her husband's actions in any way.

And her quick head shake seemed to suggest there was at least tacit support there.

Red turned to Spock. "Wait outside," he said quietly, hoping McKinnon would take the hint.

He did.

McKinnon made a slight motion with his head and most of the room emptied out into the hallway, Red taking up the rear, staying near the door so he could hear what was being said.

"Now, ma'am, it's clear you love your husband, and I'm sure you don't want anything bad to happen to him, especially with such a pretty little girl depending on him so much." There was a murmured reply he couldn't hear. "Good, then I need you to help me. Do you have any idea where he might be?"

"No."

"Do you know who he might be with?"

There was a pause. Red leaned into the apartment, trying to hear if there was no reply, or just a quiet reply.

"He might be at the drop-in center."

"We were just there, he wasn't."

"Mommy, he's with Uncle Bai!"

Out of the mouths of babes!

"Who's Uncle Bai?"

This time there definitely wasn't a response.

"Listen, we'll find out eventually, and then it might be too late to save your husband and a lot of innocent lives. If your husband is involved in this, he's already partly responsible for over a dozen deaths. As far as we know he hasn't pulled the trigger on a single person yet. If we get to him in time, he'll get a slap on the wrist, especially if he cooperates."

Slap on the wrist, my ass.

"What was the name the kid said?" whispered one of McKinnon's agents.

"Uncle Bai," said Red.

The agent held out a tablet computer with phone records obviously from their suspect's phone. He pointed at one. *Bai Gondor.* "That's a pretty unique name if you ask me. Could be him."

Bai could be like John in Sierra Leone for all we know.

But it was something.

Red nodded. "Better tell him."

The agent stepped into the apartment, disappearing around the corner, returning a moment later without the tablet.

"Your husband seems to have made a lot of phone calls with a Bai Gondor. Is that 'Uncle Bai'?"

Again no reply.

"I think it is, and now that we know your husband thinks he's going to die, we'll have to treat it as a terrorist situation, meaning your husband will most likely die long before he achieves whatever it is he felt was worth dying for. Do you want that?"

There was a long pause, then finally Buhari replied, a hint of defiance in her voice. "Of course I don't want my husband to die. But do you know how many of my family have died back home? Do you know how many of my countrymen have died? All for the lack of money? Thousands! And thousands more will die! It should never have happened and yet it did, all because your country did nothing to stop it."

Funny, I thought this was your country now, too.

"So this is about the Ebola epidemic."

"Of course it is you stupid, stupid man. Your very words show how stupid your country is, how ignorant it is. How you can go about your daily lives while tens of thousands are dying on the other side of the ocean sickens me. I wish I had never come to this country! I wish I never knew how horrible America is! I thought this was a land of dreams, of possibilities, of people who cared for their fellow man! I never knew that they only cared about their own, and *that* they don't even do well. Look at how many poor people there are, how many homeless, and yet you do nothing. As long as they don't interfere with your day, you pay them no mind. And if the disease is thousands of miles away, you don't care about them either. Yet one man is infected in America and the news coverage is constant, the money flows freely without thought." There was a spitting sound. "You all disgust me!"

Red could just imagine what McKinnon was thinking right now. How do you respond to a tirade grounded in reality? It was true to a certain extent. Little had been done. Much was being done now, but she was right, it wasn't until the epidemic threatened to spread beyond the borders of the poorest of African nations that the West took action.

He did find it disheartening though that a woman who had been a citizen for almost ten years, lived in the country for fifteen, hated her new home so much and felt a complete disconnect with her fellow citizens and countrymen.

It's the new multicultural reality.

Encouraging people to hold on to their old ways was already destroying the European nations, the multicultural doctrine that all cultures are equal and all cultures are equally good was bullshit, but it was politically incorrect to say so.

"Your reaction tells me that this is the man we're looking for. We'll have someone from Child Services come to take your daughter unless you've got someone she can stay with. You'll have to come with us to the Field Office for further questioning."

A burst of Krio erupted, the little girl finally crying aloud.

He felt sorry for the woman, she clearly not involved. He understood her desire to support her husband, and even understood the anger. It was the killing of innocent people he couldn't condone, and with this effort so well coordinated thus far, he could only imagine what horror they had planned next for his country, her new and hated country.

Off the coast of Guinea

Koroma lifted the wide-brimmed hat covering his face while he lay down in his cabin, the gentle sway of the ship on the waves and the constant drone of the engines about as peaceful an experience as he could recall having in a long time.

The knock was repeated.

"Yes?"

The door opened and the ship's captain entered, cigar clamped between his teeth, a thick curly gray beard stained yellow from a habit formed years ago. Koroma had never met the man before today, but Mustapha had arranged passage several days before for a non-trivial amount of money with one condition.

No questions asked.

Koroma had boarded in Conakry, Guinea, only hours after leaving his village, his travel greased by a diplomatic passport provided when the motorcade had arrived. It had been an uneventful yet stressful journey, this the most difficult part of his plan, it being almost completely out of his control.

He just hoped bad news wasn't about to be delivered.

Pushing himself up on his elbows, he swung his legs out of the bed, the captain waving him off before he could stand. Instead, the man, at least twenty years his senior, plunked himself down in the tiny cabin's single chair.

"I've got news."

Koroma felt his heart hammer out a few extra beats. "What?"

"Your men are dead. Apparently the Americans and British raided your village and killed them all."

"That's unfortunate. And the hostages?"

"What hostages?"

"Never mind."

The captain tapped the ashes from his cigar into an ashtray Koroma would never make use of, smoking a nasty habit he had never started—mostly because he had been too poor to. "You seem unaffected by this news of your men dying."

"They died for a cause they believed in. A cause I believe in."

"And just what is that cause?"

Koroma wagged a finger at the man, a slight smile creeping across his face. "Remember, no questions asked."

The captain shrugged, pushing himself to his feet. "No matter. It's none of my business as long as it doesn't affect the operation of my ship. Once I've offloaded you in Senegal I'm done with you and we'll never see each other again."

"Of that you can be certain."

The captain frowned. "You're not a terrorist, are you?"

"Are you asking if I'm a Muslim terrorist?"

The captain waved his hands back and forth in front of him, turning away and closing his eyes. "No, no, no, I don't want to know. Your business is your business and none of mine. That was the agreement." He opened the door then turned back toward Koroma. "Oh, there was one other thing they wanted me to tell you."

"What's that?"

"They've arrived."

Koroma smiled. "Thank you, Captain."

The door was closed and he lay back down in his rack, placing the hat once again over his face, blocking out the light coming through the small porthole window, the thin curtain covering it doing little beyond changing the colors splashed around the room.

And as the events he knew would take place over the coming hours played out in his mind, his smile turned into a sneer as hatred filled his heart.

America will pay for what it has done to my country.

He drew in a deep breath, wondering if Mustapha had executed his final orders. Part of him hoped he hadn't, the doctors the best hope his daughter had of surviving, then again, if the Americans had arrived in the village, surely they would provide care for the sick which would save her regardless.

If she can be saved.

He felt a tightness in his chest as he thought of her all alone. She was so young she'd forget about him quickly, and in time, she'd have no memory of her father or beloved mother, just the legacy of his actions, which he hoped would go down in the history of his people as a heroic action, rather than the demonic actions of a crazed man.

It would all depend on who she listened to.

Her people, or the Western press.

Her grandmother will tell her the truth.

He was sure of it.

He thought of the brave doctor and how she had fought him every step of the way. In another time, another place, perhaps they could have been friends.

But she instead was a pawn, a means to an end, her father signing her death warrant the day he had cast that vote, and today, Vice President Henderson would begin the long, painful journey to his own death. But not before Koroma delivered a dead daughter's final message while he rotted away from the very disease he and his government had done nothing about until it was too late.

And that was only the beginning.

Massachusetts Apartments, Washington, DC

"A little nicer place than the last one."

Red nodded at Spock's comment, looking up at the apartment building "Uncle" Bai Gondor lived in. A quick records check and they had his address but had been waiting for a warrant to search the premises, a warrant that had just arrived. Special Agent-in-Charge McKinnon was standing beside them as an FBI SWAT team entered the building, Gondor's unit on the third floor. It didn't take long before they had the all clear, and word the apartment was empty.

Spock cursed. "Why am I not surprised? It seems these guys are always one step ahead."

Red followed McKinnon into the building, Spock at his side. "In-theatre they had an inside man, here I think it's just dumb luck. They're ahead of us in their plan, and we're still playing catchup."

"Assuming this isn't a dead end."

They followed McKinnon onto an elevator, Red's phone vibrating as his comm activated. "Bravo Zero-Two, Control. We just sent you intel on Gondor. He works for the Sierra Leonean embassy, over."

The doors opened as Red repeated what he had just been told, opening the file.

"Why are you hearing about this first?" asked McKinnon as Red held up a photo of their suspect.

"Our Kung-Fu is stronger than yours?" suggested Spock with a cocked eyebrow.

McKinnon wasn't amused.

Lighten up buddy, it's not like you're under fire.

"It doesn't matter," saved Red as they entered the apartment. "What does matter is this guy has inside connections. We know there was a security breech in Freetown, and this might prove it extends to their government reps here."

"Or this guy could just be Uncle Bai."

McKinnon looked at Spock and nodded. "Let's hope not, otherwise our trail goes cold until the next person dies."

"Got something!"

They all turned toward the voice coming from a room down the hall and to the right. One of the FBI agents stepped into sight, holding a bag with a cellphone in it.

"I assume that's his?" asked McKinnon.

"Yup. There's packaging in here for a burner, so he's gone off the grid. This one's been stomped on. Explains why we couldn't pick it up. SIM card's gone too."

"Shit," muttered McKinnon, pointing at the phone. "Get our lab guys on that ASAP."

"Will do." The agent stepped past them, hurrying out of the apartment as they stepped into the kitchen.

Spock whistled. "Either this guy's planning on running against Vice President Henderson in the next election, or he's got a man-crush on him."

Red pursed his lips as he slowly walked around the kitchen table, surveying the piles of papers, photographs and newspaper clippings. Headlines about Ebola, CDC warnings, lack of funding, the response to cases here at home and in Europe certainly indicated the direction of the man's obsession.

But it was the photos of Vice President Henderson, some of which looked like surveillance photos, that had him more worried, especially when they seemed to include Henderson's top aides and members of his security detail.

"I think he's planning a hit," he finally said.

McKinnon nodded. "But when?"

"I don't know," said Red, pointing at one of the headlines. "But I think I know why."

The room gathered around the large headline across the Washington Post's front page from months ago.

VP VOTES AGAINST INCREASED EBOLA FUNDING IN SPLIT SENATE

"Jesus," muttered Spock. "This has been about Henderson the entire time."

Red stepped out of the room, activating his comm.

"Control, I think we found our motive."

Samaia, Sierra Leone

"Hi, honey, it's mommy, how are you?"

Tears poured down Sarah's face as she heard her son's voice, the poor kid crying uncontrollably. According to her husband they had tried to shield him from the news of what was happening but the cruelty of youth with the anonymity of the Internet had conspired against them and word had reached him.

They had been forced to tell him the truth.

Since then he'd been inconsolable.

"I th-thought you we-were d-dead!"

"Oh, honey, I'm not dead, I'm perfectly safe, perfectly fine. You know that now, don't you?"

"A-are you s-safe?"

"I'm surrounded by American soldiers. All the bad guys are gone."

She looked over at the four Americans standing in front of the community center, one of them taking photos of the bodies, apparently sending them to someone for identification purposes.

"This one's Koroma," said an Asian looking soldier, pointing at one of the bodies.

Sarah's eyes narrowed as she turned toward them, trying to listen to what was being said while her son continued to talk, telling her everything that had happened, excitement replacing fear as he finally spoke to his mother after days of torment.

"Mommy?"

"Yes, honey?"

"Are you listening?"

"Of course I am, honey. Listen, I'm going to have to let you go. Tell your daddy that I will be home soon and I can't wait to see you both and hug and kiss you until you're sick of me."

"I'll never be sick of you, mommy."

She gasped as she tried to stifle a cry, her heart hurting from the innocence of youth.

"I love you, honey. Good bye."

"Bye, Mommy."

She walked over to who she assumed was the head of the American team. He had identified himself as some sort of agent, but she could tell just by the way they carried themselves they were soldiers, and now that she had had time to think about it, their appearance suggested Special Forces.

"Agent White?" The man turned and she handed him the phone. "Thank you for arranging the phone call."

"No problem," he said, nodding toward Tanya. "We just got through to her family as well."

Sarah looked over at Tanya who was sitting against the wall of the clinic, tears pouring down her cheeks as she spoke rapidly and excitedly in Ukrainian. Tanya spotted her looking and smiled widely, waving and pointing at the phone.

Sarah grinned, giving her a thumbs up. She turned back toward the soldiers. "Did I hear you say that Koroma's body was here?"

White nodded, pointing at one of the bodies. "Intel confirms this is him."

Sarah stepped closer to make sure of what she already knew then shook her head. "I'm sorry, Agent, but that's not Koroma. That's Mustapha."

"What!"

The shock in his voice was clear as he motioned for the Asian to hand over a tablet. He showed her side-by-side photos, one of Mustapha in uniform, looking up at the sky from beside a truck, the other of his dead face taken minutes ago. "You're telling me these aren't the same people?"

There was no doubt they were. "No, that's not what I'm saying. I'm saying that man is *not* Koroma. Koroma looks nothing like him. This is his second in command, Amadu Mustapha. I think I heard him called Captain at one point, but I'm not sure."

"Did you meet Koroma?"

"Yes, he's the one who kidnapped us."

"When did you last see him?"

"Earlier today, first thing this morning. I don't know, maybe ten, twelve hours ago. What time is it now?"

"Almost midnight local."

"Really? Then probably closer to fifteen, I guess. I'm not sure."

"And you're positive this isn't Koroma."

"Absolutely."

"Maybe they just switched names to confuse you?"

She shook her head. "No. Koroma's daughter is inside that clinic. Tanya took her from her home where his name was on the front door, and we've been sleeping there. There's no doubt the man I knew as Koroma was Koroma."

"Shit!" he muttered as he stepped away, activating some sort of radio. "Control, Bravo Zero-One. We've got a problem here."

Dawson stared at the satellite image taken from the docks when the supplies had been stolen, then their corpse. There was no doubt.

It's definitely the same guy.

Yet their hostage was adamant this wasn't Koroma.

Which meant the intel was wrong.

Which wouldn't be the first time.

"Bravo Zero-One, Control. We've patched in Langley and Homeland Security. Repeat what you said, over."

"Doctor Henderson has confirmed that the man we've identified as Koroma is *not* Koroma, I repeat, *not* Koroma. His name is Amadu Mustapha, apparently his second-in-command."

"This is Leroux. How certain is she?"

"Absolutely. Apparently Koroma's daughter is in the clinic they created here and Doctor Danko took her personally from his home where his name was on the door. I think we have to assume the man we've thought was Koroma isn't."

"Which means we have no clue what Koroma actually looks like," added Niner, shaking his head. "This is a Charlie-Foxtrot if I've ever seen one."

"She says he left about fifteen hours ago, but she's not sure exactly. Did we have drones in the air anywhere near here?"

"Negative," replied Leroux. "We'll have to go to the satellites. It's going to take some time, but at least we have an exact location for where he was and a time window."

"Maybe you can see who the VIP was," said Sarah Henderson, listening in on a comm provided by Niner.

Dawson's eyebrows rose slightly. "What VIP?"

"Some guy was here before he left. Lots of security and a Mercedes with flags on the hood. He looked important. Koroma handed him a briefcase." She motioned for Tanya Danko to join them. "She overheard the conversation. She speaks Krio."

Tanya jogged over, all the while saying goodbye to her family on the phone. She hung up and handed it to Niner. "Yes?"

"Tell them what you heard them say, when the VIP was here."

"Oh, that! Yes, well, Koroma told this guy something like 'she confirms it will work just like we thought', but I don't know what he was talking about. Or at least I didn't then."

"What do you mean?" asked Dawson, not liking where this was heading.

Sarah responded. "They had me infect them with the virus."

"What?"

Even Langley echoed the outbursts on this end, Dawson leaving the comm open so everyone could hear the civilians.

"Eight of them that arrived with this VIP," said Sarah. "And Koroma. Apparently they're going to commit some sort of attack on the United States as payback for us not helping them sooner."

"Jesus Christ," muttered Dawson. "Did you guys copy that?"

"Affirmative," came Clancy's subdued voice.

"Yes," said Leroux. "I think we need to focus on that VIP. I've already got my team trying to track anybody who left that village today, but the VIP might be faster. If he was senior enough, then we might have a much narrowed list of people to go through. I'm going to pull what we've got and have their photos pushed to you. Give me a few minutes."

"Roger that," said Dawson, handing the tablet back to Niner. He turned to Sarah. "How quickly will they become infectious?"

"In as little as a day or two, but it could be longer. But that's just them being contagious. If they decide to use themselves as transport devices, the virus is in their blood. They could simply take their own infected blood and use it to infect others."

"This is unbelievable," muttered Niner. "And we have no idea who the target is?"

Sarah's mouth opened slightly, then snapped shut.

It wasn't missed by Dawson.

"You've got an idea?"

She nodded, slowly. "Well, he asked if I had a message for my father."

Dawson's eyes narrowed. "Really? That suggests he's going to see your father."

"That's what I thought."

"Control, did you hear that? The target might be the Vice President."

"We've confirmed that on this end," replied Clancy. "Bravo Zero-Two and the FBI just hit a suspect's apartment. It looks like this is all about him voting against an Ebola funding bill months ago."

"Do you have him in custody?"

"Negative."

Niner waved the tablet. "First photos are coming through." He handed the tablet to Sarah who began to swipe through the images, Tanya at her side. They had flipped through several dozen before they both cried out in excitement. "That's him!"

"Who?" asked Dawson, taking the tablet and looking at the photo.

"The VIP."

"Langley, it's photo ID Alpha-six-four-seven."

"Are you sure? Can you repeat that?"

"Alpha-six-four-seven."

"If your witnesses are correct, then they've just identified the new Vice President of Sierra Leone, Mr. Ibrahim Kargbo."

"Do we know where he is?" asked Dawson.

"Yes. He's at a reception at their embassy in Washington right now, meeting Vice President Henderson."

Republic of Sierra Leone Embassy, Washington, DC

"I'm Special Agent Savalas, head of Vice President Henderson's detail. What the hell's the problem here?"

Red's quick assessment of the new arrival already told him he didn't like the man. Savalas appeared arrogant and already on the defensive, his tone and language walking into this situation speaking volumes to his character.

Now we know why Henderson is still here.

He and Spock along with FBI Agent-in-Charge McKinnon had been left cooling their heels in the security office at the Sierra Leonean embassy for ten minutes, impatiently waiting for Savalas to grace them with his presence, all the while working the phones as they tried to get an update on why their security warnings were going unheeded.

McKinnon flashed his badge. "I'm Agent-in-Charge McKinnon, FBI. There's a threat to the Vice President's life."

"I'm aware of that."

"Then why is he still here?"

"The Vice President is quite secure. Thank you very much." Savalas turned to leave when Red reached out and grabbed him by the arm, yanking him back toward them.

"Obviously I'm misunderstanding something," said Red, his eyes narrowed slightly as he glowered at the arrogant asshole. "You are fully aware of the threat to the Vice President, the fact that this threat involves the very man he is meeting here today, and that this threat involves infecting the Vice President with Ebola, yet Vice President Henderson remains. I am going to assume that this is on his own orders, rather than the supreme idiocy of the head of his security detail, because if I'm wrong, and you haven't informed him of this threat, and the fact that the intelligence comes from his very own daughter, then I'm going to put two bullets in your chest right now, because you, sir, are a threat to national security."

Savalas stared at him, sweat beading on his brow as Red's iron grip continued to tear into his arm.

"Come with me," he finally said, Red's grip immediately loosening. "But you leave your weapons here."

The three of them disarmed then followed Savalas into the embassy, two Sierra Leonean guards accompanying them. Red heard a squawk in his comm.

"Bravo Zero-Two, Control. We've got more intel on Vice President Kargbo. Apparently he's Koroma's wife's uncle and was his commanding officer until about five years ago when he went into politics. CIA has also confirmed that Koroma's records were altered in the Sierra Leonean mainframe to replace his photo with that of one Amadu Mustapha. We still have no photo on Koroma, but if the Vice President was at the village and is now at your present location, Koroma may be with him, over."

"Copy that, Control." Red turned his head slightly toward McKinnon, Spock having heard the conversation. He relayed the intel in a low voice. "This new VP was Koroma's wife's uncle and his former commanding officer. There's also the possibility Koroma may be here."

"And we have no idea what he looks like," hissed McKinnon, shaking his head.

"We need to get the Vice President out of here. With this virus the threat may be indirect. They might infect him somehow without ever touching him."

"Agreed."

They stepped into a large conference room, the tables and chairs having been removed so they could fit a decent sized crowd of about fifty dignitaries. It was fairly tight, everyone having some elbow room but little else. He noticed several cellphones out as people took video of the dignitaries. He turned to Spock. "Start sending video to Control and keep an eye out for Uncle Bai." He activated his comm as Spock pulled out his phone. "Control, Bravo Zero-Two. We're sending you footage now. Request you push to Bravo Zero-One so the witnesses can pick out Koroma if he's here, over."

"Roger that, Bravo Zero-Two. Receiving footage now and relaying, over."

They followed Savalas through the crowd, weaving between the guests as they neared the rear of the room where it appeared the guests of honor were standing. Red spotted Henderson and his wife, huge smiles on their faces now that they knew their daughter was alive and safe. He was impressed that they were here, but apparently it was to thank the Sierra Leonean government for their assistance in the recovery of their daughter.

Despite their best efforts.

He was pretty certain from Savalas' reaction that Henderson had no idea the man he was glad-handing with was involved in the kidnapping and that their end game had been to kill her. It was clear to him Savalas hadn't passed on all of the intel that he had been provided, or, if he were to give the asshole the benefit of the doubt, Henderson hadn't been willing to let him, instead dismissing him.

God knows I've had enough politicians ignore me.

But still, Savalas' reaction made him think he hadn't told Henderson everything on purpose. Either way, Henderson was going to listen now.

"Wait here."

Savalas went ahead, leaving Red and McKinnon cooling their jets not ten feet away from the man. Red took the opportunity to scan the crowd, spotting Spock in the thick of things with his phone, pretending to be taking selfies, instead getting the faces of those behind him.

"Both witnesses have confirmed the man identified by them as the VIP is standing beside Vice President Henderson." It was Dawson's voice passing on the intel. He could only imagine how terrified Henderson's daughter must be right now knowing her father was two feet away from the man that had been involved in her kidnapping. "Still no sighting of Koroma, over."

He personally didn't think Koroma was here, but the possibility couldn't be ignored. If he were Koroma, out for revenge against a country whose people he apparently hated, he wouldn't be targeting one man. He'd be targeting hundreds or thousands. And with his body an incubator for a disease that could do just that, multiplied nine fold with the others that were infected along with him, this contained venue made no sense.

But according to the witnesses, something had been given to the new Vice President, a briefcase containing God knows what, but when handed over, a reference being made to "it" working like they thought it would.

And that had to be the virus.

He knew from his briefings that a single drop could last for days or even weeks, depending on the conditions, and the handover was only earlier that day, the time difference and haste of the meeting meaning tight timeframes.

They had no idea where Koroma and his accomplices had gone, but he was willing to bet they weren't in a hurry, instead wanting to give the virus time to be truly contagious before unleashing themselves on an unsuspecting American public.

Savalas waved them over as Henderson appeared to excuse himself, the four men gathering in a corner of the room.

"Now what's this about," asked Henderson. "I'm in the middle of a very important gathering."

Red took the lead, he the only one of the four jacked in directly to Sierra Leone through his comm. "Mr. Vice President, I'm part of the same unit that rescued your daughter earlier today."

"You're Delta?"

Henderson seemed to immediately realize the gaffe he had just committed, but with the secret spilled, Red noticed an immediate change in Savalas' body language suggesting he was ready to defer to him.

And a touch of fear.

"I can't say. What I can say is that according to your daughter, Vice President Kargbo visited the village she was held hostage in earlier today, was friendly with our prime suspect, Major Koroma, and was fully aware your daughter was there, looking directly at her."

"Impossible! How could he have gotten here so quickly?"

"Your daughter was only a three hour drive from Freetown and the flight was ten hours, sir. With the time difference, he had plenty of time."

Henderson paused for a moment, then shook his head resolutely. "No, I've known this man for several years. He's an honored member of their government, a man who's fought on the front lines in the battle against Ebola. He's a doctor for Christ's sake!"

Red was kind of surprised by this at first, but it could explain a lot. If the man was a doctor, fighting Ebola, then he would have seen the carnage it caused, and as a senior politician, even before he became Vice President, he would have been on the front lines of fundraising as well.

And there was no greater source of relief funding than the United States, no matter how much the ill-informed in the world hated this country. The US was almost always the first to respond to natural disasters the world over, sending its military into harm's way when earthquakes, volcanoes, tsunamis and typhoons struck, sending hundreds of millions, even billions of dollars to help rebuild and care for the survivors, regardless of whether or not they were traditional allies.

America punched its weight, rarely receiving the credit it deserved and didn't seek.

America wasn't just the world's policeman, it was its fireman and paramedic as well, its search and rescue tech and doctor. It was everything to everyone, funded by the American taxpayer who realized that it was the responsibility of the greatest country on Earth to help those who were in need without any expectation of even a thank you.

It was the American way, it was the Western way.

He had always found it interesting how countries that hated us, who criticized our very way of life, who felt we should burn in hell for being infidels, contributed almost nothing when disaster struck. The Boxing Day Tsunami resulted in billions of aid from Western countries, and barely a trickle from oil rich countries like Saudi Arabia until they were heavily criticized, and even then their contribution was paltry.

Those who throw stones…

But when America did fail, as it had too many times in Africa, all the good it did around the world seemed conveniently forgotten.

Henderson had continued his spirited defense of Kargbo, but Red finally cut him off. "Nine of the perpetrators forced your daughter to inject them with the Ebola virus. A case was given to the Vice President that we believe may have contained the virus. We can't risk you or your wife getting infected."

Henderson paused for a moment at the mention of his daughter. "How could they possibly infect me? Besides, everyone who came off that flight was screened. No one had a fever."

Red opened his mouth to continue but Henderson raised a finger, cutting him off.

"Enough. The Vice President of Sierra Leone, my counterpart, was assassinated on our soil. The new Vice President was instrumental in the rescue of my daughter." *Huh?* "I can't just run out of here because I think someone in the room might be infected with Ebola."

"Red, he's coming right at you!"

Red spun, the warning from Spock through the comm heard only by him, the others wondering what was going on. Red's arm shot out, pushing Henderson into the corner as McKinnon and Savalas realized something was going down, putting themselves between the Vice President and the unknown threat, the crowd thick and loud leaving Red without eyes on the target.

"Your two o'clock!" Red spotted Spock pushing through the crowd, the start of a commotion resulting as Red adjusted his gaze to the right. Suddenly he recognized "Uncle" Bai Gondor from his immigration photo darting out from behind a large man not two feet from Red.

"For my people!" he shouted at the top of his lungs as he rushed forward, "For my people!"

His hand was raised high in the air, a knife gripped tightly. Red reached up, grabbing the man's wrist and stepping into the attack with his left foot, spun the man over his outstretched leg as he broke the grip, the knife clattering to the floor as screams filled the room. Gondor hit the marble floor as Red spun, his knee hammering into the man's midriff, taking the wind out of him. He glared at Red, his eyes filled with rage at his failure, when suddenly Red felt something jab into his thigh. He looked to see Gondor's free hand pushing the plunger of a syringe.

Red crushed the man's windpipe with a single jab to the throat then batted the hand away, the syringe skidding across the floor as he pushed his knee harder into Gondor's stomach.

Somebody bent over to pick it up.

"Don't touch it!" shouted Red. "It's got Ebola in it."

More screams were followed by panic as the crowd rushed for the exit at the far end. Spock shoved through to his side.

"No, stay back!" ordered Red, standing up, rubbing his thigh as Gondor gasped for air. He pointed at Henderson. "Get him out of here but keep him isolated. Nobody leaves here."

Savalas and McKinnon were already on their own comms barking orders as Red backed away from everyone, not sure what to do. His heart was racing with the adrenaline of the situation, but for the first time that he could remember since joining The Unit he felt fear.

Not the healthy, rational fear that you might feel in the field under fire. That just kept you sharp and alive.

But the fear of not being in control, the fear of the unknown.

The fear of never seeing his wife and son again.

Or worse, seeing them, but not being able to touch them before he died.

For he knew the numbers.

Up to ninety percent died.

And he had just been injected with an entire syringe full of the virus.

The room was almost silent now, empty save Spock and McKinnon, Savalas and his men having evacuated Henderson and his wife within seconds.

Footsteps echoed across the floor and Red turned to see Vice President Kargbo walking toward them. He stopped.

"It is unfortunate you interfered."

Red hid his shock, rage instead building inside. "So you admit to being involved."

"Of course. Your Vice President voted against increased funding for Ebola at the very time we needed it most. If that funding had been approved, thousands could have been saved. Instead he played politics, all over a pipeline. He and his family deserve to die."

"And I deserve to die?" asked Red, rage gripping him tightly. "What of my family? Do they deserve to see me die?"

"You are American, you are part of the problem."

"You'll go to prison for this," said Spock, stepping toward Kargbo, Red holding up a hand, warning him to keep his distance.

Kargbo laughed. "I have diplomatic immunity. I can't be touched." Spock charged toward Kargbo but the man wagged a finger, opening his jacket and withdrawing a gun from a shoulder holster.

The criminal was the only armed man in the room.

But Red had never let that stop him. He lashed out with both hands, hitting the inside of Kargbo's wrist hard while striking the top of his hand, the weapon clattering to the floor as the bastard cried out in agony. He kicked the gun to Spock who grabbed it, covering them.

Red yanked on the man's tie, pulling him toward the syringe that still lay on the floor nearby, Kargbo struggling as the tightening tie slowly cut off his oxygen supply. Red bent down and grabbed the syringe as McKinnon's jaw dropped.

"This is what I have to say to your diplomatic immunity."

He jabbed the syringe into Kargbo's neck and shoved the plunger the rest of the way, injecting what remained of the virus as Kargbo, brave and full of bravado a moment before when he couldn't be touched, gasped in shock, his eyes bulging with fear.

Red jerked the syringe free, shoving the man away from him, releasing the tie.

"Now you die too."

Samaia, Sierra Leone

"I'm afraid I can't allow that."

Sarah Henderson shook her head at Dawson. "I don't care what you *think* you can't allow, but I'm not abandoning these people. They're sick and they're dying! We just got the supplies we need to save them and I have no intention of leaving before relief arrives."

Dawson frowned, knowing there was no point in arguing with the woman. What she didn't know was that he could put her on a helicopter whether she liked it or not, there no chance of prosecuting him for violating her rights since he wasn't here.

But he didn't want to do that, because the woman was right. Abandoning these people would be compounding an already horrible crime. He turned to Captain Grimshaw. "When can we expect medical personnel?"

"It's being organized now. Several hours at least."

"Then we'll wait those hours."

Dawson's comm squawked. "Bravo Zero-One, Control Actual, I've got an update, over."

Dawson exchanged glances with the others, Colonel Clancy's voice sounding odd. He stepped away from the two doctors just in case it was bad news on Henderson's father. "Go ahead, Control."

"I'm afraid I've got bad news, guys." Dawson felt his stomach tighten. "There was an attempt on Vice President Henderson's life. He and his wife are safe, but in the process of saving the Vice President, Red was injected with what we think was Ebola." Niner kicked the dirt, spinning around as he clasped his hands behind his neck in shock, Atlas and Jimmy both putting hands on his shoulders as they all reeled from the words delivered from thousands of miles and an ocean away. Dawson's best friend was dying, out of reach, and there was nothing he could do about it, nothing any of them could do about it.

He had failed.

If they had arrived earlier, ignored the demands of the Sierra Leoneans in wanting to conduct the rescue themselves, they would have bought valuable hours that might have prevented the attack in the first place. But instead he had sat back and waited while the politicians figured things out.

"Does Shirley know?" The thought of Red's wife finding out on the news or through someone outside The Unit killed him inside. *I need to be there!*

"Not yet. I'm leaving now to take her to Howard University Hospital. Apparently they're set up for this type of thing."

"Was it Koroma?"

"Negative. It was someone on this end in cooperation with their new Vice President. He confirmed it was because of Henderson's tiebreaker vote against increased Ebola funding. We still don't have a location on him or the other eight."

Dawson looked at his men. "We're done here, but Doctor Henderson wants to stay to take care of the Ebola patients until the medical team arrives."

"Negative. She's a target and your job is to get her to safety. Do whatever it takes, I'll back you. Now I've got to go see Shirley. Out."

Dawson joined the huddle, his men grieving an impending death, a death that might take weeks, or never come. It was the uncertainty, the complete lack of control over the situation that Dawson found the most difficult.

And he wouldn't be able to even comfort his friend for at least half a day.

Or longer if Henderson continues to be a problem.

He looked over his shoulder at Henderson as she spoke to the other doctor, both beginning to gear up.

To hell with this.

"Dr. Henderson!" he called, walking swiftly over to her. "I have news about your parents."

Sarah froze and he could see the apprehension in her eyes. He felt a little bad about his delivery, but he was in pain and wanted to see the best friend he had ever known, and perhaps a little dose of reality might convince her to not make this situation more difficult. "Are they—?" She stopped, Tanya putting an arm around her.

"They're fine. There was an attempt on your father's life, but one of my men stopped it. Your parents are safe, but my man has been injected with Ebola."

"Oh thank God!" cried Sarah, collapsing to her knees as her friend supported her. Tears rolled down her cheeks when she suddenly stopped and looked up at Dawson. "Wait, what? What was that last thing you said? Did you say someone was injected with Ebola?"

Dawson nodded. "My second-in-command." His voice dropped. "And my best friend."

Sarah reached out and grabbed his hand, squeezing, Ebola protocols apparently forgotten. He ignored the gesture, instead pulling her to her feet. "Ma'am, you're a target. As long as you're here, the perpetrators could return to kill you in revenge for their attack on your father failing. We need to separate you from this location immediately."

Tanya squeezed her friend's arm with both hands, looking at her friend. "He's right. I'll stay, you go. It's only a few hours."

"No, you can't stay here! If it's not safe for me, then it's not safe for you either."

Tanya shook her head, putting her mouth to Sarah's ear, her whisper still audible. "I have to stay. After what I did, I just have to."

Sarah turned toward her friend, placing a hand on the Ukrainian's cheek, then suddenly hugged her tight.

Dawson stepped away, his job done. "Captain, we'll be leaving in two."

Grimshaw nodded, immediately radioing for one of the choppers to standby, both now in a field behind the repurposed community center. He could hear one of the choppers begin to power up as the two doctors finished their goodbyes.

He just hoped he wasn't returning home to say goodbye to his friend.

Outside the Republic of Sierra Leone Embassy, Washington, DC

"Is he contagious yet?"

"No," said the paramedic, shaking his head at Spock as Red lay on a gurney, something he felt was ridiculous. He had wanted to go under his own power in the back of the ambulance but apparently somebody somewhere had determined that wasn't a good idea. He agreed to bow to their presumed superior knowledge. "But he might be contaminated. Just a drop of this stuff can infect you. I can't allow it."

Red knew the man was right, and he knew Spock knew as well. They had both read the briefing notes on the virus. He also knew he'd be doing nothing different if he were in Spock's shoes. He'd want to travel with his fallen comrade.

It's just what you did.

Spock pointed at the man, dressed head to toe in a bunny suit with face mask, a special ambulance having been dispatched since it wasn't a life threatening emergency. "Then give me one of those suits you're wearing."

"I can't. Protocol dictates—"

"Spock, let it go," said Red, raising himself up on his elbows, looking over at his friend. "I'm okay. Just make sure my wife and kid get to the hospital safe, okay?"

The reference to his family nearly choked in his own throat, but it had the desired effect, Spock nodding and immediately rushing away as a plastic transparent bubble was pulled over his body.

He felt like ET.

Now I know why they wanted me on the stretcher.

It made sense. The biggest threat of spreading the virus was from sneezing or coughing up blood, or bleeding on someone through a leaking orifice. None of that applied in his case, but the protocol was the protocol, and what did apply was that there could be droplets of contaminated blood on his person.

It made perfect sense and he didn't begrudge these brave souls for doing their job in a way that would not only protect them, but anyone else from becoming infected.

As they had waited, McKinnon had kept them updated on what was happening outside. Apparently a large number of the party guests had managed to get outside the building before the lockdown could be put in place. The guest list was now being checked so everyone could be monitored for the next several weeks.

He didn't envy them.

At least he knew he had the damned disease.

There's no way I'm avoiding this one.

Now the question was whether or not he'd survive. He knew the numbers were grim, as bad as a 90% mortality rate, though with it being caught immediately, and being in a country with the most advanced medical system in the world, he was much more confident it would be closer to the 50% mark the literature said was possible.

Fifty-fifty.

He'd take those odds right now if he didn't have a wife and son depending on him, but as he was loaded into the back of the ambulance, isolated from the world around him, reporters gleefully snapping photos as gathered throngs held up their cellphones to get their fifteen minutes of YouTube fame, he felt dehumanized. With hundreds of eyes on him, he suddenly realized what his own father must have felt like after his heart attack a few years ago. Loaded onto a stretcher in full view of his neighbors, pushed into the back of an ambulance while strangers and friends watched on, all the while trying to put on a brave face, instead feeling completely humiliated inside.

And as the doors slammed closed, the prying eyes of those who should never see you in your most vulnerable state finally shut out, the cold, clinical interior of what might be your final ride in a vehicle, a mobile coffin if there ever was one, eliminated that last bit of humanity you were clinging to as people you'd never met until minutes before asked you about the intimate details of your life while hooking you up to monitors. And as a siren blared, the rear windows you faced provided a unique view of life in reverse as you pulled away from the cars behind you, as if pulling away from life, from existence, leaving you to wonder if you'd ever see your loved ones again, wondering what would happen to them if you were to die right here, right now, without ever getting to say goodbye.

Because you had put on that brave face and acted as if it were nothing, when deep down you were terrified you'd never see them again.

Today he knew how his father had felt, yet at least he knew he wasn't going to die soon, he at least knew he'd get to say goodbye.

But the thought didn't comfort him much.

For the first time in his life he felt fear. Genuine fear.

And it threatened to overwhelm him.

The very thought that his son might have to grow up without him, grow up to probably forget him, to never be able to remember the love his father had for him, was devastating.

A tear rolled down into his ear, surprising him.

There's no crying in baseball!

His drill sergeant's voice echoed in his head, the line delivered during basic training to the young recruits who had been broken down on their way to becoming men. It was a lifeline thrown at his sinking self, allowing him to refocus if only for a moment.

But it was all he needed.

He had never let the bastard see his pain.

And he wasn't going to start now.

He turned his head toward one of the bunnies.

"What do I need to do to beat this thing?"

The paramedic leaned over him so Red could see his eyes through the face coverings.

"Fight."

Belme Residence, West Luzon Drive, Fort Bragg

Shirley Belme closed the door of the dishwasher, hitting the button to start the cycle when she heard car doors slamming shut outside. Glancing through to the living room, she spotted Colonel Clancy walking up the driveway with Maggie.

Maggie!

She began to untie her apron, excited Maggie was back, when it suddenly hit her.

The Colonel!

Her heart slammed into her ribcage as she gripped the countertop, desperately trying to hold herself up as her world closed in around her. The doorbell rang, the sound distant, as if from another world, a world no longer hers, a world that no longer included her beloved husband, for there was only one reason the Colonel would be here.

Something's happened to Mike.

Her knees gave out and she collapsed to the kitchen floor, the linoleum cold and unforgiving as she slid along the cupboards, her shoulder coming to rest against the side of the fridge.

"I'll get it, Mommy!"

Bryson's voice was as far away as the doorbell, the pounding of heels as her son rushed down the hallway almost as fast as her heart. The door opened, voices faint then a cry followed by feet pounding on parquet flooring.

"Shirley! Are you okay?" cried Maggie, a hand gently lifting her face off the side of the refrigerator. "Can you hear me?"

A shadow crossed in front of her and she felt a strong hand grip her shoulder. "Mrs. Belme, I need you to listen to the sound of my voice. Try to take deep, slow breaths, okay? Deep… slow… breaths…"

The Colonel's voice was steady, strong, monotonous. His repeated words began to sink in and she suddenly took a long, deep breath in, then slowly exhaled, repeating the instructions as her world slowly came back into focus.

Suddenly everything snapped back and she reached out, grabbing Clancy by the arm. "What's happened to Mike?"

Clancy helped her to her feet then into a kitchen chair, Bryson, terrified, raced over to her, hugging her as hard as he could, burying his head into her side so he couldn't see the others. Maggie knelt on her other side as the Colonel took a knee in front of her, looking up at her tear streaked face. He took her hand in his.

"Mrs. Belme, Red is alive, but there's been an incident."

"Is he going to live?"

"He was injected with something we believe to be Ebola."

Shirley gasped, everything starting to spin again.

"Mommy!"

She squeezed Clancy's hand, hard, then looked down at Bryson.

Be strong for him!

"When will you know?" she finally managed.

"Testing will be done immediately. He's on his way to a hospital now that's equipped to handle this. They're the best, and if he does have it, it's been caught immediately. I give you my word that everything will be done to save your husband."

Shirley wiped the tears out of her eyes and stared up at Clancy for a minute.

"I'm going to hold you to that, Colonel."

She pushed herself to her feet, straightened her blouse then wiped her eyes dry with a tissue handed her by Maggie.

"Now take me to my husband."

Howard University Hospital, Washington, D.C.

Red held out his wrist as yet more blood was taken. He was hooked up to an IV drip and half a dozen monitors, constantly being checked by medical personnel he'd never be able to pick out of a lineup, their gear hiding them from him. He was in total isolation.

He felt like a lab rat, a specimen to be measured and examined.

In their defense, the staff were excellent, always talking to him, trying to be personable, but the down time was long and boring with entirely too much time to think.

He was scared.

Yes, scared for himself, but more for his family. The idea of his son growing up without him was crushing, of his wife grieving then moving on almost debilitating in his imagined transgressions.

But he would want her to move on, to be happy, to find a new husband who would take care of her, and she him.

To be a father to Bryson.

His chest heaved once, just once, the thought of Bryson calling another man Daddy killing him inside.

You're not dead yet.

He thought of what the paramedic had said.

Fight.

And that's what he was going to do. He was going to fight this disease, he was going to beat it, and he was going to kill the bastards responsible.

His blood pressure and heart rate triggered an alarm. He glanced over at the monitor and took a deep breath, slowing his heart rate back to normal within a few seconds as he set the thoughts of revenge aside for now.

"Are you okay?" asked one of the nurses, coming over to check the monitor.

"Yeah, just thinking too much."

She chuckled. "That's to be expected. But we need to keep your blood pressure and heart rate as normal as possible, okay?"

"Yeah, sometimes it's easier said than done." She began to walk away when he reached out and touched her arm. She jumped. "Sorry, I guess I shouldn't touch you guys."

"No, it's okay, what is it?" she asked, turning back toward him.

"Is it true that ninety-percent die from this thing?"

She shook her head. "That's worst case scenario in Africa. People don't die from the virus, they die from the effects of the virus, usually organ failure. We've got all the tools we need here to keep you alive, all the medicines to control the essentials. We'll keep everything in balance, give you the right meds, and you'll be right as rain before you know it."

Red allowed himself a slight smile. "You're a good liar."

She did a quick bow. "Community theatre!" She placed a gloved hand on his. "But I *was* being serious. This is the place to be if you have this disease, and this is the time to be here. You were exposed only a couple of hours ago. All we need from you is to tell us every little thing that doesn't feel right as soon as it doesn't feel right. Don't try to tough things out. You *tell* us, immediately, and we'll act on it. The only other thing we need from you is to never give up. No matter how bad things get, no matter how horrible you feel, or how hopeless things may seem, *never* lose your will to live, your will to fight this thing. If you're infected, things will get bad, they will get worse before they get better, but you need to remember that you *will* get better." She paused. "You said you've got a wife and son?"

Red nodded.

"What's his name?"

"Bryson."

"Well, every time you feel like giving up, you think of Bryson, and remember that twenty-four hours is a long time, and a lot can happen in that time. Ever had the flu?"

He nodded. "Of course."

"Well, just remember how horrible you felt with that, and how quickly you felt better once it had passed. This will be ten times worse than that, but you'll feel better ten times faster once you start to turn the corner."

"Ten times worse, eh? I think we need to discuss your bedside manner."

There was a knock on the glass and he turned to see Shirley pressed against the glass, holding Bryson, Colonel Clancy, Spock and Maggie behind them. He waved, the desperate urge to hold them both, to feel their touch, almost overwhelming.

But they were here.

And the mere sight of his son was enough to steel his resolve to survive.

The nurse flicked a switch on is bedside. "Use this to talk to them. They can hear you now."

"Hi guys, how are you?"

He could hear Shirley sobbing through the speaker, Bryson's eyes red but seemingly excited to see his father. Shirley looked about for a microphone, then just tried talking. "Are you okay?"

Red nodded. "I feel fine, just not happy about being cooped up. How are you guys doing?"

"We'll be fine, don't you worry about us."

"Where will you be staying?"

Clancy stepped forward. "We're arranging for a hotel nearby for both of them. Don't worry, we'll take care of everything."

"What's the latest, Colonel?"

"BD and the others rescued the doctors, no casualties. Henderson is on her way back now with the team."

"That's good. Koroma?"

"We don't know where he or his men are yet, but we'll find them."

Red paused then looked at Spock. "Hey, buddy, you been cleared?"

Spock stepped forward. "I've got to take my temperature every damned few hours for the next three weeks, but other than that, I'm good to go."

"That's good to hear. Doesn't look like I'm going to be that lucky."

"Hey, I've been talking to the doctors here. You're going to do just fine. Apparently one of the Ebola survivors here matches your blood type and they've already agreed to donate. You'll be just fine."

"Well, let's not waste any of that good stuff on that asshole."

"Mike!"

"Sorry, dear." Red grinned at his giggling son. "A-hole."

"That's not much better."

"Genuinely misunderstood individual?"

"Better," laughed Shirley, putting Bryson down on a chair that Spock had pushed up against the window.

"So, am I up sh—the creek for what I did?" he asked Clancy.

"What did you do? My understanding from Spock and Agent McKinnon is that you stopped the attacker, were injected in the process, then Vice President Kargbo confessed to his involvement and injected himself, committing a very slow suicide."

Spock leaned forward. "That's *exactly* how I remember it."

Red laughed, a smile breaking out on his face as Bryson pressed his lips against the glass and blew, his cheeks puffing out with a farting sound. "Sounds good to me. My report will be a little late though, Colonel."

Clancy chuckled. "You're excused." He jabbed a finger at him. "*This* time." He placed a hand on Bryson's shoulder. "Well, big man, why don't we go find something to eat and let your mom and dad have some private time."

Bryson's head bobbed up and down in excitement, the little guy knowing damned well he was about to get junk food.

"Bye, Daddy!" Bryson waved and jumped down from the chair, taking the Colonel's hand as they waved to Red then headed off, leaving Shirley alone at the window.

But it wasn't private time, there two nurses in the room with him.

"How are you doing, hon?"

Shirley burst into tears, pressing against the glass as his heart broke at the sight of the woman he loved falling apart.

"Not good."

"Listen, hon, everything's going to be okay. I need you to be strong for Bryson and for me. While I'm stuck in here, you need to take care of things out there, okay?"

"O-okay."

"I'm going to be in here for weeks probably, so you need to plan on that." He paused as a thought occurred to him. "Have you told my parents?"

She shook her head. "No, there was no time."

"Okay, then I need you to get yourself together and call Mom. Knowing them they'll be here before the day's out and they'll help you with Bryson. He can't stay here, he has to go to school. Let them take care of him and if you need anything, just ask one of the guys. They'll do whatever needs to be done, okay. Remember, The Unit will always take care of you guys."

She nodded. "I know," she murmured, holding a hand against the glass, the fingers splayed open. "I just wish I could hold you right now."

"Me too, hon, me too." He could feel his control loosening, the one thing he hated more than anything else in the world the sight of his wife in pain. "Now, why don't you go splash some water on your face and give them a call. The sooner you do, the sooner they'll be here to help you."

"Okay," she said, turning to leave.

"Oh, and hon?"

She turned back to face him.

"When Niner gets back, tell him you need him to do some dishes or laundry or something then tell me what he says."

She strangled out a sobbed-laugh as Red grinned at her, waving as she turned to leave. He pushed himself up on his elbows, not wanting to let her out of his sight for a single second, then when she finally turned a corner, he lay back down and turned his head away from the glass.

And silently prayed, a well of tears in his eyes finally running over the bridge of his nose and onto the pillow as self-pity threatened to overwhelm him.

He squeezed his hands tight, the fingernails digging into his palms.

Fight!

John F. Kennedy International Airport, New York City, New York

Koroma handed over his passport to the US Customs and Border Protection Officer. He was exhausted from the flight and wasn't exactly feeling himself. It had been two days since Sarah Henderson had injected him with the virus, and from what he understood, the method of infection and the amount of the injection being far more than a drop, meant he could very well be already showing symptoms. He had been relieved to pass the temperature check both in Senegal and upon arrival here, everyone from his part of the world being screened.

But as had been proven time and again, a normal temperature didn't mean you weren't infected, or infectious only hours later.

"The purpose of your visit?"

"Business with a little bit of pleasure," replied Koroma with a tired smile. "I'm attending a conference on Ebola then I hope to pay my respects at Ground Zero on behalf of my government."

His diplomatic passport was scanned and the officer looked at the screen. "Why did you come through Senegal and not Freetown?"

"I haven't been in Freetown for at least a month. It was the best way to guarantee to your government that I wasn't infected."

The man handed him his passport back. "Rough there?"

Koroma nodded. "You have no idea."

"No, I guess I wouldn't." He waved him through. "Enjoy your stay, Dr. Vandy."

"Thank you."

Koroma followed the throngs of passengers, his eyes scanning the crowds, slowly picking out his men as they headed for the exit. He glanced up at a television screen and paused as he read the headline.

UPDATE ON FAILED ASSASSINATION ATTEMPT

He frowned, continuing forward. He had heard the news in Senegal that the attempt on Henderson had failed. It was unfortunate it wasn't one of his men assigned to the task, instead a civilian volunteer used. It had been necessary to use an existing embassy employee since security would be incredibly tight and a new arrival would be a red flag to any security chief worth his salt. Kargbo had delivered the vial, the blood taken by himself before Sarah had even known of the plan. According to everything he had read in planning the operation, he knew injecting the blood would be enough, but getting vials of blood into the United States would be impossible outside of using a diplomatic pouch.

Enter Kargbo.

Kargbo's entire family had died from the virus at the outset months ago and had become one of the leading figures in his country in trying to raise awareness of the need to take drastic measures to stop the virus from spreading.

He had been accused of fear mongering.

Unfortunately, eventually, he had been proven right.

When Koroma's wife and son had died, Kargbo visited him to offer his condolences, Koroma's wife Kargbo's niece. Their deaths had come fresh on the heels of word that Vice President Henderson had voted against additional funding to help fight the outbreak, casting a rare tie-breaker vote in a split Senate.

It had enraged many in West Africa, including himself and Kargbo.

It was then that their plan had been hatched.

It began as casual conversation, wishful thinking, then as the night progressed, the ideas flowing, they realized that actual revenge could be possible, for they had the ultimate weapon at their disposal.

The virus itself.

It took months to finalize the plans and recruit the necessary people, almost two dozen volunteers recruited in the United States, all men he could trust, all men he had grown up with as a child, all men heartbroken by what their adopted country had done to their homeland through its inaction.

It wasn't enough to extract money and resources out of America; that had already begun. It was time to punish America for all that he and his country had lost, so that if it ever happened again, they might remember their own horror and act quickly so it never again reached their shores.

And Vice President Henderson would have been the symbol for America's politicians the next time a vote of this type came up. His infection with the virus, even if he didn't die, would be an event that would echo in every politician's memory for years and decades to come.

But the coup de grâce was to be Henderson's daughter.

When Kargbo had visited him with the exciting news that Henderson's daughter had just arrived in Freetown as a volunteer, they had quickly revised their plans to include her. Should their attempt on Vice President Henderson fail, his daughter's death because of his actions would punish the man for the rest of his life.

The plan had been triggered with Vice President Okeke's visit to the United States, his assassination necessary so Kargbo could take his place, his political maneuvers beforehand setting it up so he would be the clear choice.

It had worked.

And with the kidnapping of Henderson's daughter, Kargbo had immediately called for a face-to-face meeting with him to discuss the situation, which they knew couldn't be refused, the event too public.

But with the doctors' rescue, the discussion had been turned into a celebration.

It was the one piece of news he had learned in Senegal that had disappointed him. Apparently the doctors hadn't been killed by Mustapha as he had ordered, American and British Special Forces having freed them only hours after he had left.

Henderson wouldn't feel the pain he felt, but it didn't matter.

His village was now being looked after, his actions saving it from certain doom, and the Henderson family would be changed forever.

And now it was time to change America.

Forever.

Approaching US Airspace

"We were able to track two vehicles leaving Samaia, heading north. Satellites picked them up heading for the capital Conakry on the coast and eventually the port. We managed to find the ship they boarded, the Captain saying he was paid in advance to take on nine passengers, no questions asked. He dropped them off in Dakar, Senegal overnight. There's a direct flight from Dakar to JFK every day that leaves at one-fifteen in the morning local time. We think they boarded that flight."

Dawson frowned. "Anybody from Sierra Leone on that flight?"

"Lots, but no red flags. The government is using Dakar to shuttle their people back and forth. They've sort of set up a temporary headquarters for the privileged there so they aren't at risk of catching the disease and can easily travel throughout the world on diplomatic missions without terrifying their hosts."

"Makes sense," replied Dawson, already having experienced the delays the disease could cause. They had been delayed in Freetown a full day waiting for permission to leave, and with Sarah Henderson rescued, there hadn't been a lot of effort to grease the wheels from Washington, especially after Sarah had insisted on visiting her clinic in Freetown to see the body of Jacques Arnaut off.

It had been a wall-climbing delay, his friend potentially dying an ocean away. The Colonel assured him he was doing well and that Shirley was with him as much as possible and the boys were taking shifts during visiting hours to make sure he always had someone to talk to.

But everyone was taking it hard.

And everyone wanted Koroma's head on a platter.

"We're sending you photos of passengers from the flight from JFK. You should be receiving them now."

Dawson turned to Niner who nodded, handing him the tablet. "We're getting those now, stand by."

He pushed the tablet in front of Sarah and she began to flip through them. "Maybe this one…maybe him…I can't be sure, I only saw the eight other men for a few minutes, and I really didn't look at them much." She sighed. "I'm more going by build. They were all youngish and in good shape with military haircuts."

"Like mine?" asked Niner, winking as he ran his hair through his long locks.

Sarah smiled, shaking her head, then suddenly gasped. "Wait! That's him, that's Koroma!"

Dawson slid the tablet back over and glared at the image, his eyes trying to bore through space and time, to strangle the life out of the bastard responsible for so much death. "Langley, it's photo ID Charlie-one-seven-nine."

Leroux's voice replied, slightly surprised. "According to the diplomatic passport he used, he's Doctor Sahr Vandy, acting head of the Ebola Response Team, the previous head just died from Ebola."

"Yes, I've met Sahr. Very nice man, very committed to the cause, but that's not him," said Sarah.

Dawson frowned. "I'm assuming that this is a stolen or faked ID? Do we know what the real Vandy looks like?"

"Not yet"—fingers snapped in Langley—"but I've got someone looking into it as we speak."

Dawson looked up as the flight attendant began to walk toward them, the seatbelt light flashing. "We're about to land. Try and track Koroma's movements. We need to find him. Nine men are infected with the virus and they're roaming free in New York City."

"Yes, sir."

Leroux & White Residence, Fairfax Towers, Falls Church, Virginia

"You look exhausted!"

"I am." Leroux dropped onto the couch, laying his head back on the soft cushion, closing his eyes. He felt Sherrie pull his shoes off, but instead of a repeat of the other night, which he wasn't sure he was up to, she sat beside him, snaking her hands behind his back and beginning to massage his shoulders.

He groaned.

"That feels so good."

"I take care of my baby."

"You definitely do."

"So what's the latest? I saw on the news that Henderson's daughter is back but not much more."

Leroux let his chin drop onto his chest, exposing the tired neck muscles to Sherrie's strong fingers. "Once we knew who Koroma was we were able to trace back his ticket purchase and found the other eight, all made by the same agent around the same time. They all got in separate cabs and all were dropped off in the same area of New York City. But we hit the jackpot when one of the men actually put the real hotel he'd be staying at on his customs form. The others all put various other hotels, but none were anywhere near where they were dropped off. FBI raided the hotel room and get this, found eight hangers from a local tailor along with eight empty shoe boxes. And a lot of empty ammo boxes."

"Scoot."

Leroux shifted forward on the couch a bit, Sherrie wedging herself behind him, starting to massage all the way down his back as he leaned forward in bliss.

"We've got BOLO's out on all of them but there've been no sightings."

"Eight well-dressed men. Anything from the tailor?"

"Just that the measurements had been emailed to him several weeks ago for eight tuxedos, all the fixings."

"Why eight? I thought there were nine?"

Leroux moaned as Sherrie jammed her knuckles into the small of his back. "That's the sixty-four-thousand dollar question right now. About the only thing that's gone right so far is Ernest Buhari, the missing father of the little girl who led us to Bai Gondor, turned himself in. He's cooperating but knows nothing, unfortunately. Seems to have just been a patsy errand boy."

"So we've got nine men in New York City, all infected with the Ebola virus, and we have no clue where they are."

"That's right. They've only been here a few hours though, and judging by the Subway wrappers in their hotel room, they spent most of that time there. We're not far behind them, but I just had to come home and get a few hours zees, I'm dead and of no use. I've got the night shift in to continue the work."

The mention of them suddenly reminded him of a promise he had made to himself earlier, one that had been forgotten with all the stress and excitement of the investigation. He turned his head, leaning to the side so he could look the love of his life in the eyes.

"I've got something to tell you."

Sherrie looked at him with anticipation, her hands resting on his shoulders. "Yes?"

"I deserve you."

She smiled, one of the most genuine, thrilled smiles he could ever recall seeing as her eyes filled with tears. She jumped at him, hugging him hard, her chin on his shoulder as he held her tight, his self-confidence growing with each moment.

She let go and looked him in the eyes, holding his face in her hands.

"You have no idea how happy you've just made me."

Leroux wasn't sure what to say, self-confidence not erasing awkwardness and inexperience.

He just smiled.

"Speechless, huh? Well how about I show you?"

His few hours of sleep were delayed.

Significantly.

Howard University Hospital, Washington, D.C.

Dawson was numb, there was no other way to describe it. His mind simply couldn't focus. He felt a hand squeezing his shoulder and turned to see Spock beside him looking just as shocked as him. They all were. They had just received the news that the blood tests had come back positive leaving Shirley a wreck, sitting in a chair by the window to Red's room, hugging her son, both crying, the little guy though not sure why.

"Is Daddy going to die?"

Maybe he did know.

Shirley tried to get control of herself, to be strong for her son, but she was losing the battle. Dawson stepped over and knelt down beside them. "No, little man, your father is a fighter, and the doctors here are the smartest in the world. They're going to save your daddy, understood?"

Bryson nodded, reaching out and wrapping his hands around Dawson's neck. Dawson took him, giving Shirley a chance to wipe her tears away and blow her nose.

Dawson heard a bit of a commotion down the hall and several men in suits strode around the corner. His team immediately created a wall, blocking them from proceeding as Dawson handed Bryson back to Shirley.

"Step aside," said one of the men, flashing what looked like a Secret Service badge.

"Explain yourself," replied Dawson, stepping forward as his men parted to let him through.

"The cheery one is Savalas, Secret Service," said Spock. "He's the jackhole who wouldn't listen to our intel and got Red infected."

Savalas frowned, stepping toward Dawson. "Listen, I'm sorry about your friend," he said, looking past the Bravo Team wall and at the isolation chamber. "I tried to tell the boss but he wouldn't listen. You've provided security, you know how it is."

Dawson *did* know how it was, but it was hard not to blame this man. With a threat like Ebola, you *made* your charge listen. And because Savalas hadn't, Red was dying. "If he dies, you and I will have a discussion about how you deliver important intel to your boss."

Savalas seemed to pale a few shades, the muscles in his face slackening slightly.

Good, he knows I'm not joking.

"I-I understand. Let's hope it doesn't come to that." Savalas sucked in a quick breath. "Vice President Henderson is here with his wife and daughter. They'd like to see him, to say thanks."

"*If* he agrees."

"It's okay, BD."

Dawson looked over his shoulder to see Red awake, the button to raise the head of the bed in his hand. He stepped over to the glass. "Sorry to wake you, old buddy."

"Hey, don't be calling me old. I'm two years younger than you."

"Just a baby," said Niner, leaning against the glass as Savalas left, Dawson assumed to get the Hendersons.

"Christ, looks who's talking. You've still got pimples on your ass."

Laughter filled the room, little Bryson joining in, enjoying the fact someone had said 'ass'.

Jimmy smacked Niner on the butt. "What are you doing looking at his ass?"

"Hard to avoid. Every time he gets drunk he's dropping his pants asking people to kiss it."

"Not on zis side, not on zat side, but right in zee meedle!" shouted the team, the quote from the classically bad movie Hot Dog all too familiar to them, 80's Comedy Night at The Unit a favorite activity. Laughter filled the room and everyone could be forgiven for forgetting their troubles, even if just for a moment.

"I hope the joke wasn't at my expense."

Dawson turned to see Vice President Henderson round the corner, his wife and daughter just behind him. Sarah smiled at him, rushing forward, her hand extended. "Agent White! So good to see you again," she said, shaking his hand. "May I present my mother, Carla Henderson, and my father, Philip Henderson."

Dawson shook both their hands, bowing slightly. "Ma'am, sir."

"I understand we have you to thank for saving our daughter."

Dawson nodded toward his men. "It was a team effort, sir, and besides, we were never there."

Henderson laughed, tossing back his head, the move practiced so well Dawson almost believed he actually did appreciate the joke as much as his political training suggested. His face became serious as he stepped toward the glass, looking at Red.

"Can you hear me, son?"

Red nodded. "Yes, Mr. Vice President."

"I wanted to personally thank you for saving my life. What you did was the most incredible act of heroism and self-sacrifice I have ever seen. You are a credit to your family, your unit and your country."

"Just doing my job, sir."

Henderson smiled. "True, son, but your job, unlike most, demands the best from the best. I know your country asks much of you and your colleagues, and the very nature of what we ask of you necessitates little to no recognition. I've never served in the military myself, but I have tremendous respect for those who do. I know acts of bravery and selflessness happen every day in your line of work, but this was the first time I had ever seen it for myself." He paused, his voice more subdued. "Son, I've spoken to your doctor and I'm aware of your situation. Anything that can be done, will be done, of that I guarantee you. If you or your family need anything, you just let me know."

"Thank you, sir."

"My family will be praying for your speedy recovery." He looked at Shirley then back at Red with a slight grin. "Now I'll take my leave of you so you can spend time with people you'd actually enjoy talking to."

Red chuckled, giving a slight flick of his hand. "Thank you for coming to see me, Mr. Vice President. I'm happy your family is safe."

Henderson bowed slightly. "Thanks to you." He turned and started to leave the area when Sarah Henderson cried out.

"Oh my God, that's Dr. Vandy!"

Dawson spun toward her, his eyes scanning for Koroma or another hostile, when she pointed at a corner-mounted television silently showing CNN. He looked at the screen then motioned to Spock who grabbed a chair, kicking it over to the television. Niner stepped up on it and flicked down the front panel, cranking up the volume.

"*—hundreds of dignitaries and glitterati from Hollywood and around the world are gathered for the Ebola telecast. There will be several performances and addresses before the keynote speaker, Dr. Vandy, the current head of the effort to battle the outbreak in Sierra Leone will address those gathered. Dr. Vandy—*"

Dawson signaled for the volume to be cut as file footage of the doctor appeared. He turned to Sarah. "That's the *real* Dr. Vandy, isn't it?"

She nodded. "But didn't Koroma use Dr. Vandy's passport to get into the country?"

Dawson nodded. "That's too much of a coincidence. We need to find out if Dr. Vandy is actually in the country or not."

Sarah pulled out her cellphone, quickly dialing a number from her contacts list. "Hi, Terry, it's Sarah Henderson…I'm fine, thank you, listen, quick question. I need to know if Dr. Vandy is in Sierra Leone or the United States." Sarah listened for a moment then frowned. "Are you sure?" She looked at Dawson and he could tell he wasn't going to like the answer. "Okay, thanks Terry. We'll get together soon." She hung up, her head shaking slightly. "I don't understand."

"What?"

"He's here." She nodded toward the screen. "For that fundraiser. It's going to be broadcast all over the world. Some sort of telethon."

Dawson looked back at the screen then at Red. "Eight tuxedos and a black-tie gala fundraiser featuring the man whose identity was used to get into the country. I think we know where our missing terrorists are." He turned to Vice President Henderson. "Is Posse Comitatus still suspended?"

He nodded. "Go get the bastards."

Gotham Hall, New York City, New York

Doctor Sahr Vandy looked in the mirror, straightening his bowtie. He felt old. His hair was now a short curly gray, it once proudly black as night, luxurious to the touch. But now it just seemed dull, not the shiny healthy light gray his grandfather proudly sported until his death from the insidious disease a month ago.

It was draining them all.

Day in and day out he worked the phones, sent emails and faxes, attended meetings and even put hours in at the clinics when he could. It was a battle that they were slowly beginning to win, thanks in large part to the efforts of the new Vice President, Ibrahim Kargbo.

The news of his involvement in the kidnapping of Vice President Henderson's daughter and the attempt on the man's life was simply too impossible to believe. There had to be some misunderstanding, some mistake. He knew the man, worked with the man, *liked* the man. Both of them had been spearheading the battle against Ebola for a year now and they were finally starting to make some progress.

Why would he jeopardize that now?

No, it made no sense. There was no way Kargbo was involved. He ran a finger over his eyebrows. It wouldn't be the first time the news had got things wrong, it far too common in the Freetown papers—he would have expected more of American journalists, but then in watching their newscasts while visiting this great nation, he was often shocked at how the reporters were also too often the commentators.

Reporting and editorializing should be separate, like church and state.

Which made him take anything he heard with a grain of salt. Something as large as the conspiracy suggested would have taken months to plan and it was Kargbo himself who had organized a meeting between him and Vice President Okeke to coordinate a two-pronged attack on the wallets of America. Okeke would meet with government officials to try and pry open their budgets more, and he would attend this fundraiser to get into the deep pockets of celebrity America, the event to be televised across the nation and around the world, billed as a gala event to raise awareness and funds.

He was looking forward to the outcome, but not the event, his heart pounding as he glanced at the clock on the wall. The dinner before the televised portion had just finished and he was escorted to a private room backstage so he could prepare himself for his keynote address. He had spoken to gatherings of all types before, but never to something so large. He knew he could handle it, but he needed to deliver a message to the viewers that would compel them to pick up their phones and pledge.

If he failed, it would be a massive opportunity lost for all those battling the worst outbreak ever recorded.

Kargbo!

He shook his head. Never. It was impossible.

But the timing?

It was Kargbo who had helped organize this event, Kargbo who had helped organize Okeke's meeting that had resulted in his death, and according to all the news reports and his own briefings, he had been murdered by former citizens of his own country.

Could it be possible? He was now Vice President, a post everyone knew he coveted.

He frowned, looking at himself in the mirror.

Just the musings of a tired old fool.

Someone knocked at the door.

"Come in!"

Vandy looked in the mirror to see a man he recognized enter the room along with two others. He knew the man from somewhere, it taking him a moment to remember.

Kargbo's niece's husband!

"Major Koroma!" he said, smiling as he turned toward the man. "I haven't seen you in some time." He extended his hand then jumped back as a weapon was raised to his chest. "Wh-what are you doing? What's the meaning of this?"

"I'm afraid, Dr. Vandy, you won't be giving your speech tonight."

"I don't understand!"

Koroma motioned to the other men who quickly set upon him, forcing him into a chair and binding his arms and legs with zip ties.

"I have a message of my own to deliver tonight to the newly infected."

Vandy's eyes narrowed. *Newly infected?* "What do you mean?"

Koroma tapped his forearm. "I've been infected with the virus, all of my men have."

Vandy tried to push himself away but couldn't, his restraints constricting his movements completely. "You're infected?" He looked at the man, his forehead glistening slightly. "You have a fever, don't you?"

"Yes, it started a few hours ago."

"Why do you assume you're infected?"

"Because I had myself and my men injected with the virus."

"Why! Why would you do such a thing?"

"So we could transport the virus here, undetected."

Vandy's heart was pounding in his chest as he contemplated the implications. "Wait, you said 'newly infected'. What did you mean?"

"That dinner you all enjoyed? Two of my men worked the kitchen and infected the sauces after they were prepared. Every single person who ate their entrée has been exposed to the virus. Even as we speak the virus is working its way into their systems, through their mucus membranes and into their blood streams. Days and weeks from now they will begin to show symptoms, and the entire Western world will be glued to their televisions as they gleefully watch those they envy today suffer tomorrow, secretly enjoying their plights for it's in their very nature to hate what they love, to secretly thrill in the misery of others."

"But it's inhuman! It's murder!"

"And the death of over eight-thousand back home wasn't?"

"These people aren't responsible for that!"

"Yes they are. The media is filled with what they say and do every day, yet few if any ever said anything about our plight until it became fashionable to do so. Every single person out there tonight negotiated what table they would sit at in the hopes they would get on camera more than the others. This is publicity for them, not charity. And tonight they'll pay for their vanity."

Koroma nodded at him and a gag was stuffed in his mouth, a kerchief tied around his head to hold it in place. Koroma stepped in front of the mirror and checked his tie.

"Now if you'll excuse me, Doctor. I have a speech to give."

Dawson watched on a tablet the telethon broadcast's live stream. Langley and Control were also monitoring, computers across the intelligence community performing facial recognition on every face to hit the cameras, trying to find Koroma and the other eight men they had photographed at JFK. Security at the event had been notified to prepare for their arrival but to do nothing, it feared private security, untrained for these types of situations, could trigger a blood bath if they confronted Koroma's men. Instead they were to keep anyone else from entering.

He pointed at the screen. "Isn't that Koroma?"

"Facial recognition confirms it," replied Leroux over the comm. "Ninety-nine-percent match."

"Confirmed," replied Control.

Dawson watched as Koroma crossed the stage, the entire crowd of Hollywood celebs and other people too rich to fathom jumped to their feet, applauding, no one wanting to be caught in their seats by the copious amounts of cameras. "ETA?" he asked Spock who was driving their FBI supplied van and equipment, local NYPD clearing a path ahead of them.

"Two minutes."

"Control, any sightings of the other targets yet?"

"Negative."

Shit!

They needed to take down all nine here tonight to contain the terrorist threat.

And *only* the terrorist threat.

According to the doctors some of the men could already be contagious, which meant that anyone that had been exposed to them could now be infected, any surface they had sneezed or coughed on, bled on, intentionally contaminated, could be a source for the spread.

Even if we kill them all tonight, this might not be over.

And in the back of his mind he continued to wonder why there were only eight tuxedos, when there were clearly nine men.

Koroma held up his hands, urging the crowd to sit, the lights bright in his eyes, the speech Vandy had prepared displayed on teleprompter mirrors, the monitors with the actual text flat on the floor, out of sight of the cameras.

But he had no intention of giving that speech. He took a sip of water, his mouth suddenly dry as he watched his men fan out, taking positions near the exits to the large room.

Nobody leaves here until I deliver my speech to the world.

"Thank you everyone, thank you for that tremendous reception. I have to disappoint many of you, however. As those of you who know Dr. Vandy have already noticed, I'm not him. Dr. Vandy has fallen ill and I volunteered at the last minute to take his place." There were several concerned utterances from the audience. "Not to worry, I'm quite certain he hasn't been infected with the virus we are all here to battle tonight, Ebola."

He paused, letting the word sink in. "We've all heard of it, movies have been made about it, stories written about it, and we've battled it in the past. But never an outbreak of this size, never a death toll so high. And as I'm sure you'll all agree, a death toll that never should have been allowed to get so high." Applause erupted, a few jumping to their feet forcing the others to join in.

Little do you know this is the last time on camera for many of you.

He waved them down. "I see you get my point. This outbreak started on Boxing Day, 2013, when a little two year old boy from a small village in Guinea fell ill. He died two days later. And today, over eight thousand have died, with many more still facing death. For months we along with organizations like Doctors Without Borders begged and pleaded for assistance, but little was to come, leaving untold thousands to contract the disease and die unnecessarily, their suffering over, but the suffering of their families to continue for a lifetime. Our economies have been destroyed, our populations devastated, our entire way of life altered, perhaps forever.

"But thankfully, almost nobody has become ill here, and only one has died. For this is important, it is important that nobody in America, nobody in Europe, be inconvenienced in their lives. God forbid that someone here should genuinely fear for their lives, and God forbid that a single tax dollar go toward saving an unknown life."

He noticed glances being exchanged among the crowd, it clear they were beginning to question what was going on, question how he dare make them feel uncomfortable while cameras took close-ups of their faces, always more beautiful when they were smiling or looking on earnestly.

"America has a long, proud tradition of helping those in need around the world. When an earthquake happens, you are there. When a tsunami hits, you are there. Why? Because these events attract cameras and those cameras broadcast images for the world to see, for *you* to see, on your television sets. These disasters attract incredible attention, images of the dead and dying, the suffering survivors, the devastation wrought by man and nature make great television. And when you see these things, you demand your politicians act and they do, because they know it makes good policy and pleases the voters.

"But what of those who suffer in silence, who die behind closed doors? What about the story that builds slowly, with no single traumatic event to titillate the viewer? No large initial death toll to tug at the heartstrings of the voters? When no one is there to see our children die, to broadcast it to the world, what happens? I'll tell you what happens."

Koroma paused, then jabbed a finger at the audience. "Nothing!" There was a collective gasp. "That's right, *nothing* happens. As has happened time and time again in Africa, whether it is Ebola, the genocide in Rwanda or famine in Ethiopia or Somalia, nothing happens. Not until the cameras finally take an interest and the problem can be ignored no longer. And once again, the long list of humanitarian failures continues. My people are dying. My wife and son are already dead"—gasps—"and my daughter is battling the disease right now. She may yet survive, not because of anything the

American people did, but because of what *I* did, of what likeminded people in *my* country, who decided to take a stand, did."

Koroma took a drink of water, wiping the sweat off his forehead. He definitely wasn't feeling himself, there little doubt now he was infected and weakening fast, the amount of virus injected into him significant. He knew he didn't have long to live, but he only needed a few more minutes to deliver his message to the world.

"That's right," he continued. "It was I who kidnapped Vice President Henderson's daughter. It was I who forced America to act, to spend millions to rescue one person. And think about that. Millions to save *one* person. How many hundreds of my people could that money have saved?" Dozens of phones were out now, filming his speech, these celebrities so self-obsessed they had to post on their Twitter feeds and Instagram accounts exactly what was happening to *them* right now. He pointed at one A-list celeb in the front row. "You have your phone out now, recording what I'm saying, broadcasting it to your fans around the world. Why? Is it because you care about what I'm saying, about the people who have suffered, the people who have died? Or is it—and I believe this is closer to the truth—that you want to let your fans know what is happening to *you*, as if *you* are the victim, *you* were deceived out of the dinner and photo-op *you* were expecting." He paused, shaking his head. "You make me sick."

Dozens of phones dropped out of sight.

"Now let me let you in on a little secret." He pointed to his men along the walls. "These are my men, guarding every exit to this room. For the moment, none of you are allowed to leave." His men produced their weapons, a mix of Glocks and Berettas, several screams now erupting, momentary panic setting in as people jumped up from their seats, unsure of what to do. "I highly recommend you take your seats otherwise my men will open fire."

Some sobbing and much panicked muttering filled the room, but everyone sat back down, heads darting furtively, almost everyone on the edge of their seats, ready to bolt if they were given the chance.

"Let me assure you that none of you will die here. *Today*. When I have delivered my message, you will all be allowed to leave. But there will be one difference. There will be change to your lives that will affect you until the day you die."

He paused, leaning forward, both hands gripping the sides of the podium. "Did you enjoy your dinner?"

Nobody replied, instead the audience exchanging nervous glances as hands were held, shoulders hugged, genuine fear etched on the faces that those who survived would probably tap for future performances.

"Let me let you in on a little secret." He straightened himself, taking in a deep breath to make himself appear more imposing. "*I* have Ebola." Gasps, several cries, and someone in the third row of tables fainted. He pointed toward his men. "*They* all have Ebola. We are all prepared to die here today so America is made aware of our resolve, of the horrors we have been forced to endure, of the losses that haunt us every waking moment."

He wiped his forehead, suddenly growing weary.

"And today, thanks to the dinner you paid so much to eat, *you* now have Ebola."

Screams erupted, people jumped to their feet in shock and disbelief, curses shouted at him, wails of "why?" and the ever entertaining "why me?", "why us?", as if these people were a privileged class that should never have anything bad happen to him.

America will never forget your suffering.

"Jesus Christ, did he just say what I think he said?" asked Niner, crouched behind the main doors to the hall, the rest of Bravo Team, less Red, with him.

Dawson nodded. "Control, notify CDC. We might have a major problem here, over."

"Copy that, but I think they already know, over."

FBI Agent-in-Charge McKinnon's voice came in over the comm. "Perimeter secure, you're clear to go."

Dawson looked at his men. "Eight targets. One behind this door, three on the right wall, three on the left, one on the stage. It's a straight shot down the middle to the stage, take your shots as discussed, but I want Koroma alive. We need to know where that ninth man is, understood."

"Yes, Sergeant Major!"

"Okay, proceed in three, two, one, execute!"

Two SWAT officers pulled open the doors as Dawson burst through, Niner on his left, the rest behind him in twos, Dawson dropping the first hostile as he spun around in shock. Surging forward, Dawson trained his weapon on Koroma, his eyes scanning the audience for hidden hostiles as he heard his men behind him opening up on the remaining six men lining the walls.

Koroma raised his hands, stepping back slightly as screams erupted from the panicking audience, cameramen diving for cover, clearly none used to war reporting.

"Federal authorities! Everyone on the ground, now!" he shouted, the order being repeated by the others as they continued to rush the stage, Koroma doing nothing but stand there, watching them approach. Dawson stopped, his weapon trained at Koroma's chest. "Major Adofo Koroma, you are under arrest!"

Koroma shrugged his shoulders. "My work here is done." He reached into his jacket and pulled out a weapon, placing it against his temple.

Not this time.

Dawson squeezed the trigger, hitting Koroma in the hand, the gun skidding across the stage as the man dropped to his knees, gripping his hand. Dawson swung up onto the stage, Niner following, careful to keep his weapon trained on the bleeding Koroma.

The bleeding Koroma who was infected with Ebola.

Koroma, on his knees, glared at him, his face contorted with pain.

"You've stopped nothing here today."

Dawson looked at the man, then out at the audience, America's glamour class humiliated on live television.

"I stopped you." He stepped slightly closer, his bunny suit and face mask causing him to sweat from the heat. "Where's the ninth man?"

Koroma smiled. "Like I said, you've stopped nothing here today."

Uncle Ray's Burgers! Burgers! Burgers!, New York City, New York

Ahmed Gevao wiped his forehead, his clothes soaked, his entire body sweating.

It's the fever!

The thought was at once terrifying, at once exhilarating. He had already volunteered to die, but the way he was going to die would be horrible, painful. He knew firsthand what awaited him, having tended to his own pregnant wife's death from this horrible disease months before. He had no one left. It had been their first child, and she the love of his life. His parents had died years before, his sister of the virus only days ago.

All he had was his rage. His hatred.

When Koroma had approached him he had jumped at the opportunity to serve, especially when it was explained to him what they hoped to achieve.

"We want to prevent this from ever happening in the future. If we succeed, America will never forget, and will never allow an outbreak like this to happen again."

And with the non-stop coverage now playing on every channel, it appeared Koroma and the others had succeeded. Koroma was alive apparently, the others all dead, but the Hollywood stars and the other rich Americans at the banquet had been infected just like they had planned.

But he was the backup.

He ladled another order of burgers on buns, squeezing out a shot of ketchup onto each.

A special blend of ketchup.

He had arrived for work this afternoon with nine syringes full of blood, one from each of them, with many more sitting in his hotel room, a hotel room not connected to the others.

His orders: inject the blood into the ketchup, mixing it up, then serving it all day to the American public.

And continue doing this every day until he was captured or collapsed from the disease.

He had filled many dozens of orders so far, and before his shift was over, it would be many hundreds, this fast food restaurant extremely popular, owned by a cousin of a supporter, a cousin who was not in on the plan.

"Hey Ahmed, how's your first day going?" asked "Uncle Ray" Jambai. "You doing okay?"

Gevao squeezed another shot of ketchup onto a burger, wrapping it with the thin paper and shoving it down the slot for the cashiers to fill the constant orders. "Pretty good. Hot back here, but I'll get used to it."

Jambai laughed. "You're doing great, don't worry. Keep working hard and maybe one day you'll have my job."

Gevao laughed awkwardly, part of him feeling a little bad for the man, completely innocent in this. The outbreak started today would eventually be traced back here, destroying poor Jambai's business, probably destroying the man himself.

A small price to pay should it save thousands of lives in the future.

"Hey, boss, isn't that him?"

One of the pimply faced teenagers working with him was pointing at a television mounted to a wall out where the customers were. Gevao looked and his heart sank as he saw his picture from the airport displayed with a tag line under it, "FBI Most Wanted."

"Turn that up!" shouted Jambai as he stepped away from Gevao. The volume was suddenly cranked.

"—is considered armed and dangerous. He is wanted in connection with the terrorist attack earlier this evening at the Ebola telethon. If you see this man avoid contact as he may be infected with the Ebola virus—"

Screams erupted as the employees in the kitchen abandoned their posts, rushing out the rear entrance, some out the front, customers joining them as the confusion spread.

Which meant they were now out in the public, possibly spreading the virus, their ketchup covered fingers touching the doors of restaurants, offices, taxis, buses, subways.

And in the coming days and weeks, they'd become contagious and spread the disease further.

His work was done, even if he had been stopped far sooner than he had hoped.

Jambai reappeared, his eyes filled with rage, with hatred, a gun extended out in front of him.

Gevao raised his hands. "Please kill me."

Jambai froze, pondering the words. "How could you do this to me? What did I ever do to you?"

Gevao sneered at the words. "To you? Is that all you Americans think of? Yourselves? I just infected dozens of your customers with Ebola, yet your first thought is of yourself. You disgust me!"

Jambai lowered the weapon slightly. "You infected my customers? How?"

Gevao pointed at the large ketchup dispenser. "I'm infected with the virus"— Jambai took a step back—"and I put my blood in there. Every single hamburger I've sent out since I got here has been infected."

"Oh my God!" cried Jambai. "How could you do such a thing? What did these people ever do to you?"

Gevao laughed. "I think the question is, what did these people ever do *for* me?" Gevao looked at the gun, realizing he had an opportunity here that he couldn't pass up. If he were taken into custody, he'd suffer for days, possibly weeks, before either dying a horrible death, or surviving, only to face a lifetime in prison.

Neither sounded palatable.

He charged at Jambai.

"For my people!"

Jambai raised the weapon and fired.

Howard University Hospital, Washington, D.C.
Three weeks later

Sarah Henderson nodded, her personal protective equipment passing inspection. She stepped into the isolation chamber and walked over to the patient, word having reached her he was near death. She was of mixed emotions, which surprised her. As she looked down at Koroma, blood oozing from his eyes and nose, his skin pale, his breathing shallow, she felt at once pity and hatred. The chaos he had caused was still ongoing, at least one hundred people now confirmed infected with more showing up every day. It would take months to stop the outbreak, many would die, but it would be stopped.

For America had the benefit of a state-of-the-art health care system and deep pockets.

But if she thought of him not as the mass murderer he was, and instead as a grieving husband and father, fighting for a cause he believed in, avenging the deaths of thousands, part of her felt for this man who would have had her killed.

And there was one piece of information she felt any father should know before he died.

"Dr. Henderson," he whispered, his voice hoarse, weak. "You've come to see me die?"

Koroma had refused all treatment, yet had clung to life far longer than any of them had expected, his will to see the horror he had inflicted too great to let himself die. As a citizen of Sierra Leone, he was allowed regular Consular visits, those sympathetic to his cause feeding him the latest news reports which she knew he delighted in.

The bastard deserves to suffer for as long as possible.

The thought had her second guessing what she was here to tell him, but as she pictured the tiny, innocent five year old girl back in Sierra Leone, her hardened heart softened once again, just enough.

"I have news about your daughter."

The muscles in his face slackened. "Is she dead?"

Sarah shook her head. "No. She was never infected."

"Wh-what?"

"Tanya switched the samples so you'd think she was infected. I didn't know at first, and I'm sorry it happened. The medical staff in Samaia have confirmed that she has cleared the twenty-one day period and is free from infection. She's been given to her grandmother."

Koroma smiled slightly, his eyes closing.

"Thank you, Doctor." He opened his eyes and looked up at her. "Do you understand now why I did what I did?"

She shook her head. "Nothing could ever justify this."

"It's unfortunate. I thought you of all people would understand by now, you of all people would understand that suffering like my people have endured should never happen again, *can* never happen again. My actions will cause all wealthy nations in the future to think twice before ignoring the suffering of those less desirable than themselves." He coughed, blood spraying from his mouth. She reached forward to clean him off when he grabbed her arm, his grip weak. "I did it for my people."

His hand fell away, his eyes closing as a last gasp escaped his fluid filled lungs, the monitors all flat lining. She stepped back as the other personnel rushed over, one beginning CPR.

"Stop," she said, holding out her hand. "There's no point."

The doctor nodded, stepping back, Sarah turning away and leaving the room, a single tear rolling down her cheek, not in pity for the man or his actions, but for the people that he was trying to avenge.

Howard University Hospital, Washington, D.C.

Two weeks later

Red sat up in his bed, eating a bowl of oatmeal, feeling like a million bucks. The nurse had been right. He'd feel ten times worse than the flu, then feel ten times better when he started to recover. It had been hell, but he had to admit not as bad as he had imagined.

That's the benefit of having everything medical science has to offer available to you.

He thought of the footage he had seen on television and during the briefings, and couldn't help but feel blessed for being born into the greatest country on Earth. Because of a quirk of fate, he was here and not in some poor country in Africa where if he had been infected he most likely would have died.

His thoughts were of an image he had seen on NBC of a little four year old girl lying alone on the concrete floor of a clinic, dying, bodily fluids everywhere.

That could have been Bryson.

Yes, he was blessed.

And he was going to be okay.

He'd need to spend a couple of more weeks in isolation, but every indication was he was going to make a full recovery.

There was a knock on the window. He waved at Dawson and Niner. "Hey guys, slumming?"

Niner laughed then sniffed the glass, motioning toward Red's bowl. "Any good?"

Red cocked an eyebrow. "Are you kidding?"

"That's what I thought. My mom's promised you a feed of Korean food if you come down to Florida."

"That might have to wait."

"We'll have a helo fly it in," said Dawson with a grin. "I just saw Shirley on our way in. She's looking good."

"Damned good," winked Niner. "Pretty lonely too, I'm guessing."

Red pointed a finger at him. "You touch my wife, I barbecue your tiny balls."

"Hey, no locker room talk!"

Red laughed, nodding toward the television on mute. "What's the latest?"

"Not much has changed. About a hundred of the celebrities were infected, but most seem to be recovering, and because the banquet was isolated immediately, there was no spread from there. That burger joint was a different story, but once the news broke that they might have been exposed to Ebola, pretty much everyone showed up at ERs to be checked within a few hours. CDC says they're confident it's been contained since none of them would have been contagious that quickly."

"Well, let's hope the panic continues for a while so people don't forget, just in case."

"Amen to that." Dawson paused. "You heard about Kargbo?"

Red nodded. "Got the good news from Dr. Henderson earlier."

"Couldn't have happened to a nicer guy," said Niner. "Glad he hung on as long as he did, he deserved to suffer."

Red shook his head. "Nobody deserves to suffer like that."

Dawson nodded. "I suppose so. The President has declared all-out war on the virus so I guess in the end Koroma won."

Red put his oatmeal aside.

"I'm not sure that's a bad thing."

Aunt Luana's Aloha House, Honolulu, Hawaii

Tim wiped his forehead, already hating being home. His vacation in New York City had been cut short, his parents ordering him on the next plane when they heard about the Ebola outbreak. It had pissed him off, especially when his older brother Jeremy had backed them. Tim hated being treated like a little kid. He was nineteen, and just because he had dropped out of college didn't mean he was an idiot.

He was an adult, whether his family wanted to admit it or not.

And in his efforts to prove that he could take care of himself, he had found his own apartment with several friends, a job pushing slop to tourists, and even had a steady girlfriend.

Life actually wasn't that bad.

But when his vacation, paid for by his older, *far* more successful brother had been cut short because of some nutbars from Africa, he had been pissed.

But he'd get over it.

If only he could get over this flu.

His entire body ached and he felt horrendous. He was wheezing when he breathed, and if he could afford to take a day off, he would, but he had already nearly burnt the bridge by taking a few hangover recovery days recently.

He had no currency left with his boss.

But this was bad.

"You look like shit," said Kaholo, washing dishes next to him. "You should go home."

"I think I'm going to have to."

"Go ahead, I'll cover for you. Your shift's almost over anyway."

"Thanks."

Tim headed for the back, tossing his apron into the laundry bin before stepping into the bathroom to wash up. He splashed some water on his face then looked at himself in the mirror as his knees shook under him.

And gasped as rivulets of blood trickled from his eyes and down his face.

THE END

ACKNOWLEDGEMENTS

This was a difficult story to write. As those of you who have read my books know, there is a lot of research that goes into them, much of it to do with weapons, history, geography and politics, but this time there was a massive amount of research into a horrendous disease. Imagery in this book is taken from real-life accounts from the front lines, from the real Dr. Hendersons and Dankos fighting this deadly outbreak.

And some as heartbreaking as the NBC image described near the end.

Writing about this was difficult, and I hope reading it difficult as well.

This is a disease that needs to be stopped.

As is always the case with something as fluid as this outbreak, things changed as I wrote. One of the more horrifying statistics that did change was the medical personnel death toll. My initial draft had the number at 310, but by the time the book was finished, that had climbed to almost 500, and by the time you read this, it will certainly be higher.

These people are the heroes on the front lines of a war that has to be won.

Those of you who have read my previous books will have recognized many of the characters here. For those who haven't, if you enjoyed the Bravo Team, they got their start in The Protocol (James Acton #1) and have appeared in every adventure since. They also make appearances in several of the Special Agent Dylan Kane Thrillers, where the Chris Leroux character is introduced with most of the other CIA personnel. Please check these out to discover more about these characters.

As usual there are people to thank. Brent Richards for weapons, equipment and tactics info (how to take a handgun out of someone's hand is something I hope to never have to try!), Ian Kennedy for breaching and tactics info, Fred Newton for car mechanical info and one secret idea that I promised to never repeat (you know what it is, buddy!), Gregory "Chief" Michael for some military housing info as well as Anne and Alexa for catching a typo in The Riddle that had escaped the proof readers! As well I'd like to as always thank my dad for the extensive research and my wife, daughter, mother and friends for their continued support.

And to those who have not already done so, please visit my website at www.jrobertkennedy.com then sign up for the Insider's Club to be notified of new book releases. Your email address will never be shared or sold and you'll only receive an email or two a month as I don't have time to spam you!

Thank you once again for reading.

Available James Acton Thrillers

The Protocol (Book #1)

For two thousand years the Triarii have protected us, influencing history from the crusades to the discovery of America. Descendent from the Roman Empire, they pervade every level of society, and are now in a race with our own government to retrieve an ancient artifact thought to have been lost forever.

Brass Monkey (Book #2)

A nuclear missile, lost during the Cold War, is now in play--the most public spy swap in history, with a gorgeous agent the center of international attention, triggers the end-game of a corrupt Soviet Colonel's twenty five year plan. Pursued across the globe by the Russian authorities, including a brutal Spetsnaz unit, those involved will stop at nothing to deliver their weapon, and ensure their pay day, regardless of the terrifying consequences.

Broken Dove (Book #3)

With the Triarii in control of the Roman Catholic Church, an organization founded by Saint Peter himself takes action, murdering one of the new Pope's operatives. Detective Chaney, called in by the Pope to investigate, disappears, and, to the horror of the Papal staff sent to inform His Holiness, they find him missing too, the only clue a secret chest, presented to each new pope on the eve of their election, since the beginning of the Church.

The Templar's Relic (Book #4)

The Vault must be sealed, but a construction accident leads to a miraculous discovery--an ancient tomb containing four Templar Knights, long forgotten, on the grounds of the Vatican. Not knowing who they can trust, the Vatican requests Professors James Acton and Laura Palmer examine the find, but what they discover, a precious Islamic relic, lost during the Crusades, triggers a set of events that shake the entire world, pitting the two greatest religions against each other. At risk is nothing less than the Vatican itself, and the rock upon which it was built.

Flags of Sin (Book #5)

Archaeology Professor James Acton simply wants to get away from everything, and relax. A trip to China seems just the answer, and he and his fiancée, Professor Laura Palmer, are soon on a flight to Beijing. But while boarding, they bump into an old friend, Delta Force Command Sergeant Major Burt Dawson, who surreptitiously delivers a message that they must meet the next day, for Dawson knows something they don't. China is about to erupt into chaos.

The Arab Fall (Book #6)

An accidental find by a friend of Professor James Acton may lead to the greatest archaeological discovery since the tomb of King Tutankhamen, perhaps even greater. And when news of it spreads, it reaches the ears of a group hell-bent on the destruction of all idols and icons, their mere existence considered blasphemous to Islam.

The Circle of Eight (Book #7)

The Bravo Team is targeted by a madman after one of their own intervenes in a rape. Little do they know this internationally well-respected banker is also a senior member of an organization long thought extinct, whose stated goals for a reshaped world are not only terrifying, but with today's globalization, totally achievable.

The Venice Code (Book #8)

A former President's son is kidnapped in a brazen attack on the streets of Potomac by the very ancient organization that murdered his father, convinced he knows the location of an item stolen from them by the late president.

A close friend awakes from a coma with a message for archeology Professor James Acton from the same organization, sending him along with his fiancée Professor Laura Palmer on a quest to find an object only rumored to exist, while trying desperately to keep one step ahead of a foe hell-bent on possessing it.

Pompeii's Ghosts (Book #9)

Two thousand years ago Roman Emperor Vespasian tries to preserve an empire by hiding a massive treasure in the quiet town of Pompeii should someone challenge his throne. Unbeknownst to him nature is about to unleash its wrath upon the Empire during which the best and worst of Rome's citizens will be revealed during a time when duty and honor were more than words, they were ideals worth dying for.

Amazon Burning (Book #10)

Days from any form of modern civilization, archeology Professor James Acton awakes to gunshots. Finding his wife missing, taken by a member of one of the uncontacted tribes, he and his friend INTERPOL Special Agent Hugh Reading try desperately to find her in the dark of the jungle, but quickly realize there is no hope without help. And with help three days away, he knows the longer they wait, the farther away she'll be.

The Riddle (Book #11)

Russia accuses the United States of assassinating their Prime Minister in Hanoi, naming Delta Force member Sergeant Carl "Niner" Sung as the assassin. Professors James Acton and Laura Palmer, witnesses to the murder, know the truth, and as the Russians and Vietnamese attempt to use the situation to their advantage on the international stage, the husband and wife duo attempt to find proof that their friend is innocent.

Available Delta Force Unleashed Thrillers

Payback (Book #1)

The Vice President's daughter is kidnapped from an Ebola clinic, triggering an all-out effort to retrieve her by America's elite Delta Force just hours after a senior government official from Sierra Leone is assassinated in a horrific terrorist attack while visiting the United States. She battles impossible odds while the Delta Force tries to save her before her captors enact their horrific plan on an unsuspecting United States.

Available Special Agent Dylan Kane Thrillers

Rogue Operator (Book #1)

Three top secret research scientists are presumed dead in a boating accident, but the kidnapping of their families the same day raises questions the FBI and local police can't answer, leaving them waiting for a ransom demand that will never come. Central Intelligence Agency Analyst Chris Leroux stumbles upon the story, and finds a phone conversation that was never supposed to happen but is told to leave it to the FBI. But he can't let it go. For he knows something the FBI doesn't. One of the scientists is alive.

Containment Failure (Book #2)

New Orleans has been quarantined, an unknown virus sweeping the city, killing one hundred percent of those infected. The Centers for Disease Control, desperate to find a cure, is approached by BioDyne Pharma who reveal a former employee has turned a cutting edge medical treatment capable of targeting specific genetic sequences into a weapon, and released it.

The stakes have never been higher as Kane battles to save not only his friends and the country he loves, but all of mankind.

Cold Warriors (Book #3)

While in Chechnya CIA Special Agent Dylan Kane stumbles upon a meeting between a known Chechen drug lord and a retired General once responsible for the entire Soviet nuclear arsenal. Money is exchanged for a data stick and the resulting transmission begins a race across the globe to discover just what was sold, the only clue a reference to a top secret Soviet weapon called Crimson Rush.

Death to America (Book #4)

America is in crisis. Dozens of terrorist attacks have killed or injured thousands, and worse, every single attack appears to have been committed by an American citizen in the name of Islam.

A stolen experimental F-35 Lightning II is discovered by CIA Special Agent Dylan Kane in China, delivered by an American soldier reported dead years ago in exchange for a chilling promise.

And Chris Leroux is forced to watch as his girlfriend, Sherrie White, is tortured on camera, under orders to not interfere, her continued suffering providing intel too valuable to sacrifice.

Available Detective Shakespeare Mysteries

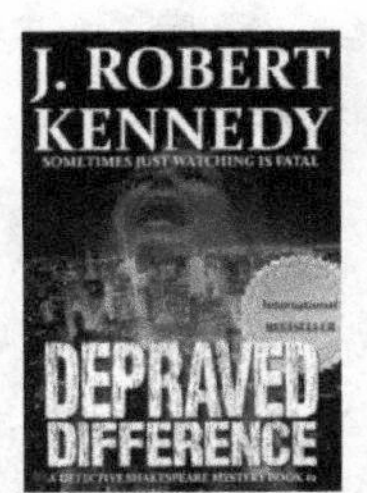

Depraved Difference (Book #1)

SOMETIMES JUST WATCHING IS FATAL

When a young woman is brutally assaulted by two men on the subway, her cries for help fall on the deaf ears of onlookers too terrified to get involved, her misery ended with the crushing stomp of a steel-toed boot. A cellphone video of her vicious murder, callously released on the Internet, its popularity a testament to today's depraved society, serves as a trigger, pulled a year later, for a killer.

Tick Tock (Book #2)

SOMETIMES HELL IS OTHER PEOPLE

Crime Scene tech Frank Brata digs deep and finds the courage to ask his colleague, Sarah, out for coffee after work. Their good time turns into a nightmare when Frank wakes up the next morning covered in blood, with no recollection of what happened, and Sarah's body floating in the tub.

The Redeemer (Book #3)

SOMETIMES LIFE GIVES MURDER A SECOND CHANCE

It was the case that destroyed Detective Justin Shakespeare's career, beginning a downward spiral of self-loathing and self-destruction lasting half a decade. And today things are only going to get worse. The Widow Rapist is free on a technicality, and it is up to Detective Shakespeare and his partner Amber Trace to find the evidence, five years cold, to put him back in prison before he strikes again.

The Turned: Zander Varga, Vampire Detective, Book #1

Zander has relived his wife's death at the hands of vampires every day for almost three hundred years, his perfect memory a curse of becoming one of The Turned—infecting him their final heinous act after her murder.

Nineteen year-old Sydney Winter knows Zander's secret, a secret preserved by the women in her family for four generations. But with her mother in a coma, she's thrust into the front lines, ahead of her time, to fight side-by-side with Zander.

Printed in the USA
CPSIA information can be obtained
at www.ICGtesting.com
LVHW041026251123
764902LV00047BA/882